FIRST ACTIVATION

OTHER TITLES BY THE AUTHORS

Fast Forward by Darren Wearmouth

Critical Dawn by Darren Wearmouth and Colin F. Barnes

Critical Path by Darren Wearmouth and Colin F. Barnes

Sixth Cycle by Darren Wearmouth and Carl Sinclair

Eximus by Marcus Wearmouth

Second Activation (April 2015) by Darren and Marcus Wearmouth

FIRST ACTIVATION

Darren and Marcus Wearmouth

Published by 47North, Seattle

www.apub.com

Amazon, the Amazon logo, and 47North are trademarks of Amazon.com, Inc., or its affiliates.

ISBN-13: 978-1477824849
ISBN-10: 1477824847

Cover design by Jason Gurley

Library of Congress Control Number: 2014951621

Printed in the United States of America

FIRST ACTIVATION

1

THE PLANE

Our Friday morning flight from Manchester to New York was making good progress over the Atlantic Ocean. I had looked forward to this trip with my brother, Jack, for months.

We were due to arrive at JFK at 2:30 p.m., and I could not wait to get through the airport and into New York. The cabin crew had just delivered my snack, which was some sort of fancy pizza pocket. I washed it down with a small plastic cup of lukewarm coffee and then stretched out. We had a free seat in between us, covered with iPads, magazines, and water bottles; Jack snored away in the aisle seat.

The seats on this British Airways A380 were pretty comfortable. Slightly larger than economy and near the front of the plane. I'd splurged and gotten us World Traveler Plus, even though Jack said we couldn't afford it. There was no way I was going to sit with my knees up under my chin for more than seven hours, so the money was well spent. And besides, there was far less of a chance we'd be next to a whiny brat or a screaming baby. Boardroom bullies I can handle; a drooling rug rat was another story.

I grabbed the free magazine from the pocket of the reclined seat in front of me. It had a fantastic photo of the Statue of Liberty on the front cover, but there was nothing inside that piqued my interest. Who buys the plastic plane, neck pillow, or branded teddy? There would be far better things for me to spend my hard-earned cash on in New York.

Nature called, so I edged past Jack and made my way up the aisle toward the vacant bathroom. Working as a landscape gardener had maintained my muscular build since leaving the army, and I had to squeeze my broad, six-foot frame sideways into the cubicle.

I decided on a childish plan and smiled at myself in the mirror. I'd make Jack jump by turning up the volume on his iPod. After two solitary hours, I wanted conversation and knew he would be eager to talk about the trip and which bar we would hit first.

I splashed my face with water, smoothed back my short dark-brown hair, and then opened the door right into the face of a lady who stumbled back as if I might assault her. She glared at me while clutching her purse in a white-knuckled grip and barely acknowledged my wry grin as I awkwardly nudged past her.

Nearing my seat, a sudden jolt of violent turbulence ran through the plane, triggering a ripple of curses from my fellow passengers. The plane dropped. I lost my balance and slammed into the closest headrest of the middle row of seats, and clutched it to maintain my footing.

The headrest belonged to a surly-looking, middle-aged man with a bald head and white mustache. I steadied myself and shrugged apologetically. He gave me a curt nod in reply before looking down at the coffee splashes on his shirt and his empty plastic cup.

"Sorry, mate," I said, and stepping across to my window row, I slid into the aisle seat.

A steward's calm voice transmitted through the loudspeaker, instructing passengers to return to their seats and fasten their seat belts.

". . . the fuck was that?" Jack had been jolted awake.

I smiled and passed him a bottle of water. "I'll give you two guesses."

He snatched the bottle and gave me a dismissive look as he continued to rearrange himself in his seat. With Jack back in the land of the living, we could talk about the delights that awaited us upon arrival in America. "So what are you looking forward to the most? A trip up to the top of the Empire State Building? A cruise on the Bay to get a few decent photos of the Statue of Liberty? Times Square?"

Jack hadn't accompanied me on my last trip to New York, but had looked at pictures online to get an idea. "What's in Times Square?"

"Massive electric billboards and . . . I'm not exactly sure . . . I went to McDonald's."

He shook his head, most probably at the thought of me stuffing my face with junk food. "Central Park. That's where I want to go. I've seen it in—"

Collective gasps and the general chatter of raised voices filled the cabin after a series of four more jolts hit the plane in rhythmic succession.

Jack tensed his legs and gripped his armrest. He wasn't a keen flyer, and any more turbulence would only add to his stress.

"We'll be there soon enough—just relax."

Closing his eyes, he laughed. "Relax? There's nothing natural about flying through the air at hundreds of miles an hour in a piece of metal."

Before I could reassure Jack any further, another safety announcement sounded through the cabin.

Time seemed to pass in super-slow motion as I sat in my seat, waiting to be tossed around again. Nothing happened. The seatbelt light flicked off after ten minutes, followed by a collective exhalation and the clicking sound of seatbelts unfastening. A couple of people made their way to the bathroom, and the stewards starting pushing a trolley down the aisle, crammed with duty-free items.

"Fancy some Chanel Number Five, Jack?"

He tried but failed to keep a straight face and snatched the magazine from me.

The middle-aged man whose headrest I had clutched earlier grunted as he hauled himself up by his armrest. He turned and glared at me with such directness, he could only be looking for an argument.

I elbowed Jack and motioned toward the man. "Keep your cool and let me do the talking."

The man maintained his icy stare and strode over. He was dressed in dark-blue jeans and a pink Ralph Lauren polo shirt stretched around his bulky torso, complete with coffee stains. Hoping to brush away any confrontation before it occurred, I tried to sound as friendly as possible and said, "Sorry about before, mate. Nothing I could do."

He shrugged halfheartedly. "Forget about it. My wife asked me to come and see you. Apparently, I was a bit grumpy when you apologized."

"I didn't notice," I lied, remembering his surly look.

A steward behind him said, "Excuse me, sir."

He awkwardly leaned into me, pushing his backside close to my face, as the trolley squeezed past. The stewards gave him a disapproving look. He crouched by my seat. "What's a couple of young guys like you doing in New York? Business or pleasure?"

I couldn't believe this man had actually started a conversation with us. Who did that? Still, I liked being described as young. It happened less often, now that we were in our mid-thirties, although Jack would deny it.

"Pleasure," Jack said, lowering the magazine from in front of his face. "It's our annual trip. Done it since leaving the army. See a few sights and drink beer. Our mates, Dave and Andy, arrived yesterday, so they'll probably have something sorted."

"You're gonna love it. We're just returning from vacation in England." He extended a hand. "Bernie."

I firmly shook it and smiled, mostly out of embarrassment. "Did you enjoy Blighty?"

He scrunched his thick gray eyebrows, leaned toward me, and said in a lower voice. "Is that a local beer?"

I tried to suppress a laugh. He probably had tons of words that I didn't understand. "It's old slang for Britain."

"Oh, right, Blighty. Linda loves researching her family tree. Visited the places her ancestors lived."

I looked across to his row. A woman with long brown hair peered over her seat. I smiled and waved. She appeared relieved, raising her hand before sinking down.

"Where did you go?" Jack asked.

Bernie glanced at the trolley, now returning from the front of the plane. "I'd better get out of the way."

With a chance to tap some local information, and him seeming like a friendly bloke, I crammed my gadgets and magazines into my backpack and took the middle seat.

I received a strong whiff of Old Spice as Bernie slumped down next to me. He continued, "We visited a couple of small villages in Yorkshire. Don't ask me to remember names, but the local pubs were great."

"Sounds cool," I said. "I'd love to cruise Route 66, stopping in motels, drinking coffee at a diner. You know, 'The classic American road trip.'"

"Visited Gotham before?"

Jack leaned forward. "Isn't that where Batman lives?"

Bernie shoved his shoulder into me. "It's slang for New York."

"Touché, sir," I said.

He continued to chat enthusiastically about some of the more obscure attractions of New York. Jack busily took notes. I glanced at the digital flight screen at the front of the cabin. We were less than an hour away.

The loudspeaker crackled. "This is your captain speaking. Unfortunately, we're currently experiencing communication problems with JFK and will be going into a holding pattern until the problem is resolved. I'll update you once we've confirmed our landing slot. Apologies for the delay, and enjoy the rest of your flight."

Bernie narrowed his eyes. "What does he mean, *communication problems*? Don't they have more than one way of speaking to the airport? I'm going to speak to that goddamn pilot."

He grunted, heaving himself up and out of his seat, surprising me at how quickly he turned from upbeat and chatty to stressed and irritated.

Jack said, "I wouldn't do that if I were you, Bernie. Air Traffic Control is probably asleep."

Bernie dismissively waved his hand and waddled down the aisle. One or two passengers leaned out of their seats, and he bumped his way to the cockpit.

Figuring this could provide some entertainment, I decided to follow. Jack groaned and threw his head back and stared at the air vents.

A steward confronted Bernie just before he reached the cockpit, and said, "Can I help you, sir?"

Bernie tried to ease him to one side. "I wanna talk to the pilot."

"You can't do that, sir." The steward put his arm up and calmly blocked Bernie's access. Bernie pushed forward, leaning his weight against the steward's arm.

"Sir, please go back to your seat," the steward said, raising his voice.

I could see this situation escalating, with the possibility of us getting arrested at JFK for causing a disturbance. A male passenger behind me said, "Get back to your seats."

The steward struggled to nudge Bernie away. "Sir, please . . ."

I grabbed Bernie's shoulder and hauled him back. "Come on, big fella. We'll find out soon enough."

Bernie turned and scowled. "They treat us like cattle."

"Don't you mean mushrooms?" I asked.

"Mushrooms?"

"We're kept in the dark and fed on shit."

He forced a smile, sighed, and returned to his own seat. I found Jack playing a game on his phone. He remained focused on the screen and said, "Are we spending our holiday in an airport cell?"

"I thought that was your specialty."

He shook his head and continued to fiddle. On our trip last year, Jack had gotten arrested when we landed in Majorca, for being drunk and taking photographs of random passengers.

I felt my ears pop. According to the flight screen, we had thirty minutes to go.

The loudspeaker crackled. "Ladies and gentlemen, this is your captain speaking. We are still experiencing communication problems with JFK and will remain in a holding pattern until contact is re-established. I apologize for the delay."

The last sentence drew a few nervous laughs.

My thoughts drifted to a conversation I'd had with Andy and Dave the previous day. They had chosen an earlier flight because of the price, and I took great pleasure in teasing them about being thrifty. With the extra hotel expenses, our trip costs worked out the same. I imagined smug grins plastered across their faces after checking out our flight's arrival time.

Jack flicked open the in-flight magazine. I took his constant change of activity as a sign of his nervousness. We swapped seats, and I stared out of the window for the next ten minutes, watching us sweep around our destination in a wide arc. Andy and Dave were probably already in a bar while we were wasting time in the air because of a technical fuck-up.

Jack tapped me on the shoulder. "How much fuel do these things have?"

"Enough. Don't worry about it." To distract Jack and chew up a bit of time I said, "Name your top ten movies."

He looked up and thought for a moment. *"Predator."*

"No way! That's just Arnie running around the jungle."

"What about *Gladiator*?" He faked a serious expression. "'What we do in life will echo—'"

"Ladies and gentlemen, this is your captain speaking. We are now starting our final descent and will be arriving in New York at 3:30 local time."

Jack placed the palm of his hand against his heart and let out a huge breath.

Ironic cheers rang around the cabin. I could almost taste the first beer of the day. The cabin crew came through the plane to check that we had our seatbelts on and tray tables up, before strapping themselves in for landing.

The engines whined as we made our descent. I held my nose and blew after feeling pain in my left ear. It did the trick and I relaxed back in my seat.

We touched down with a double bump and were pulled back into our seats as the plane quickly slowed. It taxied away from the runway and turned toward the terminal.

I found the lack of landing announcement slightly strange, but didn't care. We were here, and the last obstacle would be passport control, before we picked up our bags and dived into a taxi. Jack had a couple of police cautions in the UK for getting into bar fights. I checked the Internet, and apparently it wouldn't be a problem, but stories always circulated about people being turned away.

Jack grabbed his backpack from under his seat, ripped it open, and stashed his iPod and magazines. "I remember why I only do this once a year."

"I'll call Dave and Andy while we wait for our bags. Tell them we expect a foaming pint on arrival."

I checked my watch and brushed off the previous events. An hour delay was nothing, and our World Traveler Plus seats felt luxurious compared to traveling in a Hercules or Chinook. We really had nothing to complain about.

The plane juddered to an abrupt halt a hundred yards short of the terminal. I looked through my window toward the gates, each one numbered in black on large yellow signs, stretching along a dull, gray, military-looking building. I always found the front of airports far easier on the eye, probably because it's where the most effort goes into prying away cash.

Last time I'd visited JFK, white airport vehicles with chunky wheels had buzzed around docked planes, carrying luggage or fuel. Ground crew directed us in, jet engines whined and roared—the place was a hive of activity, and I was impressed by the whole slick operation. Today, all vehicles were stationary, some at odd angles around planes, as if parked in a hurry. I searched for members of the ground crew without success. I expected to hear the roar of distant engines but heard nothing. It reminded me of landing at Ascension Island, but that was a small military base on a remote Atlantic island, not a major international hub.

I frowned as I gazed at other gates, all seemingly lifeless, and wondered if we'd landed during a fire drill.

"Oh my God!" a lady screamed from two rows behind us.

Other shouts began to fill the cabin.

"What the . . . ?"

"Oh no. Oh Jesus Christ, look over there, at the gate on the corner!"

"Where?"

"The jet bridge."

I squeezed against the window to get a look at the gate.

A man wearing a day-glo yellow vest hung by his neck from the open end of a jet bridge. He looked like a member of the ground crew. There was little doubt that he was dead; his arms dangled limply by his sides, and he spun slowly in the breeze.

I elbowed Jack. "Swap seats and have a look at this."

We switched positions. I noticed Bernie trying to catch my attention. As soon as I made eye contact, he asked, "What did you see out there?"

"You don't want to know."

Jack spun to face me. "There's someone below the gate. Pool of blood around the body."

I tried to look over his shoulder. "What?"

He pushed me back and pressed his face against the window. "Two dead blokes in a luggage truck. What the fuck?"

A steward came over the loudspeaker, telling all passengers to remain seated. I could hardly hear his anxious instruction over the shouts of confusion around the cabin. Moments later, Bernie appeared by my seat.

He crushed my legs sideways as he staggered past, losing his balance and stopping his fall by thrusting a hand against Jack's back. "Let me see."

Jack rubbed his brow—a sign I recognized when he tried to calm himself. He shifted to the side, and Bernie wedged himself into the gap created. I turned away from his builder's backside.

Although most of the people around us were dumbfounded and could only splutter out short sentences of astonishment, Bernie had already developed his own theory. "Looks like a terrorist attack. They've taken the airport."

The steward repeated his plea for calm, but it fell on deaf ears. Turbulence was one thing; dead bodies around a deserted airport were another.

Jack said, "I can't see it. How would terrorists do it? Where are they?"

"Holed up inside with hostages? Homeland Security will be outside, figuring a way to manage the situation."

Jack nodded and looked at me for agreement. "Makes sense, right?"

I considered Bernie's premature theory against the evidence outside. It didn't make sense. I asked, "Wouldn't we at least hear a faint siren or see a chopper circling?"

Bernie rolled his eyes. "I'm speaking to the god-damned pilot, and no steward is stopping me."

He stormed toward the cockpit, barging past other passengers from the middle rows, who stood to get a view from various windows. I decided to follow. Others already had the same idea, and a small crowd, mostly businesspeople, gathered at the front of the plane, demanding answers from a red-faced stewardess. She pulled a phone receiver from the wall and spoke into it.

The cockpit door slowly opened, and the captain stepped into the cabin, quieting the crowd. I stood on a seat close to the front of the cabin, so I could get a good view of the captain. He was tall, with gray hair, and looked like a man of experience. A veteran of the air who would know the procedures for these types of situations. I felt confident that he would be our best source of information.

He looked around the passengers and cleared his throat. "I can only tell you what I know, but it's not much more than you've already seen. We're going against procedure by even landing here, but I had to make a decision before we ran out of fuel."

A chorus of questions all came at once. The captain raised his arms, appealing for quiet.

"Please, let me tell you what I know. I have no other information beyond that."

This brought silence. He continued in his odd British accent with an American twang. I guessed he had set up home in the States. "Just after the turbulence, we lost all communication with the ground and have heard nothing since. We also lost communication with the planes that landed shortly afterward, although contact is still possible with other planes in the air. All of this is understandable if the traffic control systems and communications are down. The procedure in these situations is to sit tight and try not to panic."

A man in a blue shirt shouted, "Are planes being diverted to other airports? Why did we land here?"

The captain wearily shook his head. "No other airports are responding. I honestly don't know what's happening."

Passengers continued to fire questions.

"Why did you stop?"

"How are we supposed to get off?"

"What do we do?"

"As I have already said, I've only seen what you've seen. Without ground crew, any docking procedure would be risky. We'll wait for one hour before using the emergency slide to disembark."

"Then what?" Bernie shouted. I'd expected him to get into the action at some point.

"I'll keep trying all channels of communication and update you all when I have further information. The last thing we should do is to make hasty decisions without establishing facts."

The passengers erupted with shouts and arguments. The captain threw his hands in the air and disappeared back into the cockpit. Feeling a mix of frustration and disappointment, I hopped back into the aisle and slowly followed the procession of passengers, heading back to my seat. A group stayed at the front of the cabin to talk about what had happened. Bernie stood among them and kept shouting about terrorism. Perhaps he was right. A mind-blowing amount of coordination would be required for such an attack. What else could it be?

Jack waited in his seat and gave me a quizzical look. "Any news?"

I shrugged. "Comms problems are widespread. No sign of help at the moment, so the suggestion is that we wait."

"The captain doesn't know shit, but we've got no other choice."

"We do, but I'm prepared to wait for a little while."

I started to think about how we could get off the plane. If it was a terrorist attack, then why wait for them to come and capture us? We could escape through the perimeter fence and win our freedom. The alternative might involve being on my knees reading out a forced statement to a video camera before being brutally beheaded by men in balaclavas. I had no intention of waiting around for that to happen. I racked my brains for other possibilities but kept returning to Bernie's theory. If the area had been cleared because of a dirty bomb, we were in the zone and needed to leave. This was more than the work of a serial killer.

"At last," Jack said, eventually looking up from his phone. "Got a network connection."

I leaned over and watched him thumb through Twitter. "Any updates about JFK?"

"Nothing obvious."

I fished out my phone and tried to get a signal without success.

"Have a look at this." Jack thrust his phone toward me. "Look at the responses from a tweet I sent in Manchester before take-off."

@cfieldhouse: Welcome to New York, Jack! Please come and help me, I am in a wheelchair and need assistance at the following address . . .

@atitlow: Jack, want to meet up so I can show you some of the best sights in the state? Come to my farm . . .

@saggyhr: Our friend said you were coming over; please visit me at the following hospital . . .

The tweets continued, but I had seen enough. Why did all of these strangers want to meet up with Jack? I decided to quickly update my location on Facebook to JFK Airport, in case Andy or Dave checked to see if we had arrived, and switched my phone off. If we were going to spend hours on the tarmac, at least one of us should conserve battery.

I watched other passengers using their phones. None managed to get an answer to their calls. One man thumbed his iPhone and looked in a state of total confusion. He dropped it on his seat and said, "What the hell . . . ?"

A lady's phone in the row behind chirped after receiving a text. I turned and watch her open it. She shook her head and said, "It's an invite to dinner from Billy in Stamford. I don't know a Billy in Stamford."

Jack leaned over his seat. "Reply, and ask him what's going down."

She tapped out the message and sent it, but didn't receive an immediate response.

We waited for another half an hour, debating our next moves with a few other passengers in the seats around us. Bernie and I wanted to mount an escape. Jack came around to our way of thinking.

We did not want to be sitting ducks for an enemy outside. Others viewed our plan as irresponsible behavior, saying it would only cause more trouble and confusion for Homeland Security when liberating us.

Liberating us from what? There wasn't a soul in sight.

A young man shouted at one of the stewards, demanding to leave the plane because he needed to catch a connecting flight. Others joined his chorus, and the steward left for the cockpit. Judging by the state of the airport, nobody would be departing any time soon.

The staff on the plane told us to stay in our seats and remain calm while they handed out the remaining food, small packets of peanuts, some chocolate, and cans of soda and juice. A reminder that we couldn't stay here forever, although the atmosphere seemed to be heading toward munity. I contemplated how long Jack and

I would wait before making our move. The answer came before I made my decision.

A male passenger a few rows ahead of us shouted, "Someone's coming . . . a security guard."

Passengers rushed to our side of the plane in a disorganized wave and watched as the figure approached, dressed in an official dark-blue uniform. He waved a gun above his head and appeared to be shouting. Of course, nobody could hear him. He slid his gun into his hip holster and spread his arms.

Bernie headed for the steward by the door. He bumped between two passengers, knocking them into opposite seats, like a bowling ball smashing between two skittles. "Open the door. Let's hear him out."

At last, we had contact with the ground, and the man wore official clothing. A sense of relief rolled through the cabin. Other passengers agreed with Bernie and pressured the steward. He rushed along the aisle toward the cockpit.

I glanced at the man outside. He placed his hand on his brow, protecting his eyes from the sun and mouthed something in my direction.

The captain appeared from the cockpit and held a hushed conversation with the steward for a couple of minutes, ignoring passengers' shouts of encouragement. They both approached the emergency exit at the plane's mid-section.

The steward struggled slightly with the door. He eventually managed to twist a large silver handle and open it. A cool draft rushed in, giving us our first taste of fresh air since England. The whole plane fell silent. All eyes were on the captain.

He leaned around the door. "What's the situation on the ground?"

The man moved closer. "You need to leave the plane and follow me."

"What's happening? Who are you with?"

The security guard gestured to a glinting badge on his chest. "I'll explain shortly, but please, we haven't got much time."

I wondered why he came on his own. Did he have any support? Not that it mattered. I think we were all prepared to follow his instruction, based on him being the first friendly face encountered since landing. Who cared if he wasn't part of a SWAT team?

The captain whispered into the steward's ear. He ushered a few passengers back from the door before cupping his hand over his mouth and shouting down, "Stand back. I am going to deploy the slide."

The security official gave a reassuring smile and stepped to one side. The yellow slide bulged away from the plane with a loud hiss. It quickly filled to a long rectangular shape and bounced against the ground.

The steward spun to address us, clicking back into official mode. "I will help you at the bottom. Leave all personal items stowed and remove any shoes with heels or sharp jewelry. Cross your arms over your chest and jump feet first."

The steward exchanged nods with the captain, crossed his arms over his chest, and jumped. He quickly slid to the bottom and skidded to a spinning stop on his backside.

I took a depth breath. The security guard drew his pistol from the holster, aimed it point-blank at the side of the steward's head, and pulled the trigger. Red spray covered the tarmac to the side of the steward. He rolled off the slide and slumped on the ground.

Screams and shouts filled the cabin. Passengers scrambled to get away from the open emergency exit.

The security guard crouched next to the steward and casually checked his pulse. Then, without even hesitating, he pointed the pistol under his own chin, pulled the trigger, and collapsed to the ground with a twist.

I jerked back from the window. "Jack, what the fuck was that?"

"No idea, but I'm not waiting for another one like him to show."

I scanned the terminal for other potential threats.

The captain ripped a mic from the wall. "Please, everybody get back in your seats and try to remain calm."

I could appreciate him following procedure and trying to stop his passengers from descending into a chaotic mob, but we were past listening after witnessing events outside. The plane filled with noise and confusion as passengers frantically checked their windows. I looked to the back of the plane. Someone had opened the rear emergency exit. A man leaned out, grabbed the handle, and heaved it shut.

Jack fastened his backpack and gave me a nervous look. "Let's make a break for it."

I nodded. "Agreed. Make a run for the perimeter fence."

Bernie had been listening to our conversation. He stood, pointed dramatically in our direction, and shouted, "These two are military! These two, sitting right here!"

Jack grabbed Bernie's shoulder and forced him back into a seat.

He struggled against Jack's grip. "Get your hand—"

"Shut the fuck up," Jack said through gritted teeth.

Unfortunately, Bernie's announcement attracted a lot of attention, including the captain's, who approached us.

"British army?" the captain asked Jack.

"No, I'm just here for a short break," Jack protested, his face reddening.

It felt like the whole plane was focused on us. Passengers whispered and stared at our row. I'd had enough of feeling useless in the increasingly claustrophobic cabin.

"Captain, we need to get off this plane," I said. "I suggest we form a small breakout team and scout the area. Jack and I will volunteer."

We both wanted to get clear of the plane and now had a potential opening. I couldn't decide on the safest place in the near vicinity, but no matter what was going on, a full plane provided a large, juicy target.

The captain looked dubious. "Official procedure is for everyone to stay on board."

"Do you really have an official procedure for what we have just seen?"

He opened and closed his mouth, but no words came out. I felt a pang of guilt as his shoulders visibly slumped.

Jack sprang from his seat. "We've done site clearance in the army and know what we're doing. If there's any help out there, we'll find it."

He closed his eyes and gave us a resigned nod. Our assertiveness had won the captain over.

Bernie bustled over. "I know my way around the airport—you need some local knowledge."

"Doesn't sound like a good idea," Jack said. "Three of us can draw a lot more attention."

"Come on, guys," Bernie protested. "I set this up for you, and four will be better than two. I know the airport layout, and Linda used to work here."

Linda looked a few years younger than Bernie, and quite glamorous with her wavy brown hair and expensive-looking clothing: the type of woman Jack would never approach on a night out, through fear of rejection, because he viewed them as out of his league.

Bernie's suggestion made sense. Having local knowledge would be a bonus. "You can come with us. But no more passengers. Four is more than enough."

Relief washed over Bernie's face. He linked hands with Linda and gently eased her from her seat. I saw through his brash exterior and knew he ran around like a wet hen, with Linda's safety at heart.

A middle-aged woman approached our small group. "Can I come with you? I don't want to stay on here, not after watching . . ."

Jack and I looked at each other. Neither wanting to hurt her feelings. Thankfully, Bernie stepped in. "Not on this mission. Sit tight and we'll bring help."

"Please," she begged, tears welling in her eyes.

Bernie rested a hand on her shoulder. "I'm sorry. It's not possible."

Nobody knew the possibilities. Nevertheless, we decided to go for it, so it would be by our rules.

Bernie stood up on his seat and announced our intentions to the passengers. He sold us as the breakout party who would find assistance. A few grumbled, but most seemed happy at the proactive step. Jack and I accepted a flashlight and two bottles of water, which we shoved into our backpacks.

A man in a light-brown blazer strutted down the aisle toward us. He stood in the junction between the two sections of the plane. "Right, guys, fill me in on what's happening."

Jack, who had just finished securing his backpack, glanced over his shoulder. "Who are you?"

"The name's Morgan. We've had a meeting in business class, and I'm going with you."

"No, you're not," I said and stepped toward him. "Take that back to your meeting."

He scowled while looking me up and down. "Like I'd put my life in your hands. We've got business leaders in our section. What you need is proper strategy and strong negotiation skills. It's sensible that I lead the group."

"Sorry, but the answer is no," I said, trying my hardest not to swear at this walking cliché. "Or perhaps you could have saved the steward with a flashy PowerPoint presentation?"

Morgan's eyes narrowed and his top lip curled into a snarl. He turned to the captain. "Are you going to allow this?"

"I'm sorry, but it's their call, sir," the captain said and swung in my direction. "I'll see if I can find anything useful from the cockpit."

The captain trudged away.

Morgan glared at the passengers around us. "Unbelievable, absolutely unbelievable."

He turned and followed the captain, shouting in his ear about people getting sued.

With the idiot put back in his box, I asked some passengers to check through the windows for signs of movement. We planned to head for the airport's barbed-wire–topped, chain-link fence, which ran around a less built-up section of the perimeter road. Away from the imposing main buildings where an unknown threat may be lurking. After climbing under or over, our destination was the temporary parking lot near the front of the terminal.

We figured that once outside the airport itself, we would be able to make contact with the agencies dealing with the situation, which were sure to be in the vicinity. Since everything looked deserted around the airport, we assumed the area must have been sealed off.

I had been part of an operation in the UK that had dealt with a bomb threat at Manchester Airport. I remembered every man and his dog turning up, and assumed it would be the same in America. After spending time chatting to US soldiers over a cold beer at the Volcano Club on Ascension Island, I knew, like us, they didn't leave things to chance in dangerous situations. I was also incredibly jealous of their equipment compared to British-issued weapons and clothing. They knew how to deal with threats.

Our team of four entered the cockpit to brief the captain and co-pilot. The captain rummaged around compartments, pulling out tools, electronic devices, and manuals. The co-pilot met me like an old friend and warmly shook my hand. I glanced out of the window and noticed the sun beginning to set.

After giving them an outline of our basic plan, I said, "If we're not back by nightfall, chances are we may not be coming back. But give us till the morning."

An increasing look of concern spread across the captain's face as he listened. He asked, "How can we tell it's you coming back?"

"I'll give three winks of the flashlight."

"We'll keep a lookout. Do you have everything you need? I think—"

Bernie shoved between us. "You can use a gun, right? Oh, but you're army or something—'course you can use a gun. Anyone got one?"

Jack sighed. "When we jump down the slide, I'll grab the gun from the security guard. Is there anything else we can use as a weapon?"

The captain reached for a box and popped it open, revealing a flare gun. "This is all I've got."

Bernie snorted. "What? So we can advertise our location to terrorists?"

Linda disapprovingly pinched his arm. I ignored his sarcasm. Who knew how useful a flare gun could actually be?

I took the box from the captain and held up the gun. "If we can't make it back, but we're still around, I'll fire into the sky. Keep a lookout."

The co-pilot handed me another box containing six cartridges. The gun had a familiar mechanism, so I didn't require instructions. Load, pull back the hammer, and bang.

We couldn't delay any longer if we wanted to make use of the natural light. The captain shook our hands and walked to the open exit in the mid-section of the plane.

Most of the passengers avoided eye contact, although we did receive some nods of encouragement, and a few people wished us luck.

One by one, we jumped down the slide. Jack first; he picked up the security guard's gun and familiarized himself with it. I followed next, peering at the two corpses and wondering about the guard's motivation. If he'd wanted to shoot himself, why not just go ahead and do it before? Bernie and Linda slid down together. They immediately spun away from the corpses, once at the bottom of the slide. He put his arm around her and led her toward the front of the plane.

Having my feet on solid ground gave me the sense of regaining at least some control. I thought we could now face whatever was happening instead of simply awaiting rescue or death on a stationary plane.

2
THE AIRPORT

Jack released the magazine from the gun and visually checked it before sliding it back into the grip. He thrust it forward and headed for Bernie and Linda, who waited for us at the front of the plane. I scented an unrecognizable bittersweet odor in the air, unlike the usual pungent stench of plane fuel on this side of the airport.

"What have you got?" I asked.

"Sig P229. Nice bit of kit," he said, inspecting it from different angles.

I approached Bernie and Linda, who stood at the front of the plane, gazing into the distance. "Bernie, you're the local. Lead the way."

"Okay. It's pretty simple. Over there." He pointed to the left of the terminal, toward a parking lot behind a fence.

He set off with Linda by his side. Jack and I followed closely, looking around at the terminal building and empty runways. I turned to see our stationary plane parked just off the main runway, casting a long shadow across the tarmac from the setting sun.

I checked my watch. Seven in the evening. Perhaps less than an hour of light. I took the lead and increased my pace, scanning for any signs of movement or threats.

Sunlight reflected off the terminal windows. The building appeared to be empty. On the road outside the perimeter, abandoned cars were strung along it, as far as I could see.

We arrived at the chain-link fence and surveyed it for signs of weakness. Jack identified a potential spot at the bottom where rust had set in. It rattled as he tried to rip it from its fastenings.

Linda sharply inhaled and clamped a hand over her mouth. She looked beyond the fence and took a couple of steps back.

Everyone froze. I quickly surveyed the road. About two hundred yards away, where the road curved around toward the front entrance of the terminal, a body slumped against a green Chrysler.

Bernie crouched by the fence and squinted through the links. "I can see two."

The car stretched across both lanes at an angle that suggested it had come to an emergency stop. A pair of legs wearing orange shorts and leather sandals protruded from beneath the front of the vehicle.

"Both dead," I said. It seemed unlikely that JFK had come under a sleeping gas attack.

"Told you it was terrorists," Bernie said.

Jack paused from trying to rip the fence free and shot Bernie a disapproving glance. He swept the Sig around the area surrounding the car.

"Who killed them?" Bernie asked.

"We'll find out soon enough. Leave the guessing for now," I said.

Bernie's patience appeared to be similar to Jack's, and I didn't want either mind racing when we had more important things to think about. We needed to stay focused on getting around to the front of the terminal. Finding a member of the security services, a TV with a newscast to shed some light on events, or even a computer terminal, remained priority number one.

I wanted to be completely fair with Bernie, but speculating on events would only provide a distraction. If an exclusion zone had been created, a sealed-off area to protect the public from a localized threat, it must be huge, stretching well beyond the airport. The only apparent signs of life were unrecognizable, distant, sporadic noises, nothing to even remotely suggest the airport remained functional.

Jack continued to work the fence with Bernie's assistance. I gave Linda an arc to observe, and we both searched for signs of movement. I scanned from the terminal to the plane for around five minutes. The man hanging off the jet bridge took up much of my attention at first, but as I continued my sweeps, I spent less time staring at his gruesome silhouette.

I stretched up the bottom of my polo shirt and wiped sweat from my brow. The late spring sunshine felt much warmer in New York compared to Manchester. Jack and I had turned up at the airport in similar clothes, a complete accident but slightly embarrassing that we both wore navy polo shirts, light blue jeans, and walking boots.

All selfish thoughts of a ruined holiday had melted away, replaced with a desire for immediate survival and avoidance of the threat that had caused JFK to become a ghost airport, apart from the steward-killing nut case. In the army, I'd been taught to tackle threats and not let them dictate destiny. To be proactive, not reactive.

Jack let out a big grunt, and I heard three metal pops. "We're in business. Let's go."

I turned to see Bernie pulling up on a freed section to maintain a gap. Jack quickly wriggled free and stood on the other side. Linda went next, moving awkwardly on her hands and knees. The back of her cream blouse caught on the fence. I knelt and freed her, and she crawled through. I slid through on my back and thrust my boot against the chain-link, taking the strain from Bernie. He scraped along on his belly, like an elephant seal, and puffed his way to the other side.

I stood and dusted myself down. "First hurdle out of the way. Crack on, Bernie."

"You mean head for the terminal?"

"Yeah, the terminal."

Jack walked alongside Bernie, with his gun extended to the front. Linda and I followed. We walked between two small buildings with dark tinted windows and crossed a sparsely populated parking lot. The main terminal building loomed up to our left. I remembered leaving through the bottom entrance after arriving two years ago. A busy place, filled with people, taxis, and official vehicles.

Bernie quickened his pace, probably out of excitement, and forged ahead. He hopped over a small barrier and disappeared down a road leading to the front entrance. Jack glanced over his shoulder, and I shrugged. "He'll be back."

Thirty seconds later, as the three of us approached the barrier, he zipped around the corner, looking flustered. "Get back—*now*!"

We retreated ten yards and ducked behind a black SUV. Bernie joined us and hunched over, hands on knees, struggling to catch his breath.

"W-what did you see, Bernie?" Linda asked, her voice trembling.

He swallowed hard and looked up. "People . . . at the front of the terminal . . . over cars, on the ground, everywhere!"

"All dead?" Jack asked.

Bernie rested his back against the SUV and slid to the ground with his head in his hands. "It's a fucking nightmare."

Linda wrapped her arm around his shoulder and gave it a squeeze. "Wanna go back to the plane?"

We'd come too far now to turn back. The possibility of a large group of armed men, lying in wait to spring an ambush, seemed remote. We were on a commercial flight and posed no real threat to whoever had taken out a whole airport. However, the worrying thought that we might be breathing in some kind of germ occurred to me. Had a biological weapon been used?

Jack peered over the hood and spun back. "We take it slow and find some help. A working phone line—anything."

"Agreed," I said and turned to face Bernie. "You can always go back."

My words seemed to stiffen his resolve. He shook free of Linda's embrace and stepped toward me with a look of intent. "We're staying right here and completing the mission. Both of us."

Behind him, Linda fidgeted with her necklace. She already looked like she hadn't slept for a week.

With natural light beginning to fade, I didn't want to delay any longer. "Let's get this out of the way. No turning back."

I loaded a cartridge into the flare gun and circled around the SUV. Jack joined me, Sig thrust out in front of him in a two-handed grip. We moved with conviction. Bernie and Linda's footsteps pattered behind.

My foot crunched against a piece of broken glass. I looked to my right and noticed a shattered passenger window of a Ford, with a red stain on the inside. I resisted the temptation to investigate and continued.

I could understand why Bernie wanted Linda by his side. I doubt either Jack or I would have been part of this endeavor individually.

Jack and I hopped over the barrier and joined a sweeping road that led directly to the main entrance. After proceeding thirty yards, I froze, open-mouthed, after getting a view along the terminal's front edge.

Bernie's comment about a nightmare proved reasonably accurate; it looked like a medieval battlefield, apart from the cars and buses spread around the road.

Over three hundred bodies lay among the vehicles, but most were spread around the glass doors of the front entrance. I moved closer for a better look. Many of the butchered corpses had improvised weapons close to their hands: a wrench, a broken bottle, or a rock. Others seemed to have turned their weapons on themselves.

One young man splayed over a luggage trolley. His stiff hands clasped a knife's handle around his mouth. A woman in a purple business suit had gouges in the side of her neck. A pair of nail scissors dangled from her bloodied thumb.

I crept past a police cruiser and stared inside. It appeared the officers had taken part in a quick draw contest. One of them leaned against a shattered window, with a bullet hole in his eye. The winner had decorated the interior ceiling with his own brains. I reached in the passenger side of the car and shook free the Glock service pistol from the limp hand of the loser.

I slipped off the magazine and checked that it still contained rounds. After a successful inspection, I slammed it back into the pistol grip, stowed the flare gun in my backpack, and turned to look at the rest of the group. Jack stepped closer to me. I could see Linda's lips quivering, and Bernie silently shook his head, his hand on her shoulder.

"What the hell happened here?" Jack asked.

Keeping my voice low, I replied, "No idea. It's like they turned on each other."

Jack lowered the Sig and slumped against the cruiser's hood. "None of it makes any sense."

"They obviously knew something we didn't," I said.

In nearly every visible area I observed, a violent act had taken place.

A metallic noise rang out from the opposite end of the terminal. Jack and I quickly ducked behind a car. Bernie and Linda did the same.

Bernie glanced across. "Did you see anything?"

Jack shook his head. "No, just heard it."

We peered around the sides of the cars and waited. An elderly woman in a green tracksuit appeared, picking her way through the carnage toward us, around a hundred yards away.

She wandered slowly among the bodies, leaning down and touching each one around the neck area. Probably checking for signs of life.

"There's no way she caused all of this," Jack said.

I maintained my focus on her. She seemed unmoved by the corpses that surrounded her and eagerly moved from one to another. "She's checking for a pulse like that mad security guard."

"When she gets close, we get her to talk."

"Okay, you give the signal."

I looked over to Bernie and Linda and gestured for them to stay where they were.

A bead of sweat ran down my temple. I squeezed the Glock's grip and contemplated the fact that I might have to shoot. Her footsteps approached, slapping along the road, very close to our location.

Jack sprang from his position and aimed. "Freeze. Hands in the air."

She continued toward us.

I reclined over the hood and trained my gun at her chest. "Take one more step, and I'll shoot."

"Thank God . . ." the woman said, her voice flat, her posture drooping with exhaustion. She focused on the gun and slowly raised her hands, but she didn't smile like the crazy guard. Even if she suffered from whatever had affected the whole airport, she looked close to her mid-80s and unarmed. We could easily handle her if she tried to attack us.

Bernie and Linda stepped out from behind their car, and he began an immediate cross-examination. "Where did you come from? What's your name?"

Good questions, I thought. *Let's see how normal she is.*

She sighed. "Maureen. I've come over from Hook Creek. I'm so glad to find people alive."

She appeared to be scared, which I took as a strangely positive sign. The security guard had showed no fear.

"Why come to the airport?" Bernie snapped.

"I heard shots fired and wanted to find help."

I thought her explanation sounded genuine. If I were a nice old lady and suddenly found myself among such gruesome surroundings, the sound of shooting might have been a potential source of rescue, or at least life.

"Any idea about what caused this?" Bernie asked, sweeping his arm to indicate a group of bodies.

"I'd like to know too. All this senseless killing . . ." She broke off momentarily and looked down at an empty coke can, rolling past her cheap sneakers, the type bought at a market stall or supermarket. "You probably know more than me. I've only just arrived here."

Bernie's voice grew in confidence as he stepped toward her. "What do you remember from the last few hours?"

"I went for a walk on my own. When I came back to my car, somebody had smashed into it. I heard the gunshots over here and decided to come looking for help. Can you lower your guns, please? You're frightening me."

Jack looked at me, and I shrugged. "Okay, but stay where you are."

"Thank you."

She rummaged in her large brown leather bag, no doubt for a mint or maybe even a cigarette, and simultaneously shuffled toward me.

I raised the Glock and curled my finger around the trigger. "Stay where you are. Get your hands out of the bag."

"Please, don't be worried. I have a cell in here. It appears we all need help."

She took a few steps toward me and angled her bag, showing me the contents while she hummed in a friendly way.

I turned to Bernie and Linda. "Should we take her back to the plane?"

30

Linda's eyes widened and she screamed. *"Look out!"*

I instinctively ducked to my left and felt a slash across my right arm just below the shoulder. Maureen hunched to attack again with a carving knife in her right hand. I gave her a split-second opportunity, and she took it. Jack reacted immediately, slamming his boot into her chest. She toppled backward and skidded along the ground.

I wouldn't make the same mistake again. "You'd better start talking. What the fuck's going on?"

Maureen panted like a feral animal and winced as she rubbed her ribcage. She scrambled to all fours and spat on the ground. Bernie and Linda retreated behind us. The old woman sprang up and lunged at Jack with a speed that belied her age. He jumped to his left and smashed his fist into the side of Maureen's temple. She staggered and tripped over a dead body.

Bernie shoved me in the back. "Shoot her. She'll get one of us eventually."

"Not yet—unless you want to do the honors?" Jack said, keeping his eyes fixed firmly on our assailant. "I want information."

I agreed with Jack. We needed to know why she attacked us. Shooting her would get us no answers. Besides, I also couldn't bring myself to kill an octogenarian, regardless of her attack. I had no intentions of spending my time in an orange jumpsuit if the authorities arrived and figured out that I had a small part in the death around us.

Bernie cracked his knuckles and took a step back.

Maureen regained her footing and started circling us. Her light-blue eyes narrowed and she scrunched her wrinkled face. A string of saliva hung from her bottom lip. Jack and I kept pace with her, shielding Bernie and Linda behind us, but I felt Maureen sensed that we might not use our weapons.

"I only want to kill one of you. The other three can leave," she said in a surprisingly rational tone.

"What's wrong with you? What will it take to make you stop?" Bernie pleaded over my shoulder.

Maureen ignored Bernie's question and carried on circling. She appeared to be looking for a momentary lapse in concentration. She also seemed unafraid of our guns and openly admitted to wanting to kill one of us. She had clearly lost her marbles, and I needed to put a stop to it.

"Bernie, take this," I said and passed him my gun while keeping my eyes fixed on Maureen for any sign of sudden movement.

He snatched it from my hand and took my place alongside Jack. I ducked behind them, slung off my pack, retrieved the flare gun, and clicked back its hammer.

"How's your arm?" Linda asked.

A thin stream of blood ran down it and dripped off my little finger. "Just a flesh wound. Don't worry about it."

She pointed a trembling finger at the flare gun. "What are you going to do with that?"

"Put a stop to this stupidity."

I stepped to the side of Jack and aimed at Maureen's face. I intended to knock some sense back into her and show we meant business. She might get some slight burns, but it would be worth it, if it worked.

The gun made a loud popping noise after I pulled the trigger. A glowing projectile shot through the air and slammed into the right side of Maureen's forehead. She dropped like a stone. The flare brightly sizzled on the ground a few feet away.

Jack approached Maureen, kicked the knife away from her hand, and reached down to check for signs of life. "She's out cold. Her head's a mess."

Bernie kicked the flare underneath a vehicle, trying to quell the sulfurous red smoke that began to envelop us.

Both living people we had encountered since landing were total maniacs. Whatever gripped them must also have taken hold of everyone outside the terminal.

I motioned for us all to get down. "We don't know who might have heard that. Keep your eyes out."

"What about her?" Bernie asked, pointing the Glock at Maureen. "She won't stay like that forever."

"We question her. I want to know her motivation," I said.

"Did you see any cuffs in that cruiser?" Jack asked.

"I'll go and have another look."

Restraining and interrogating Maureen might be our quickest way of finding out the truth. The others waited while I darted thirty yards to the cruiser. I opened the left door and purposefully tried to avoid looking at the faces of the two officers inside while rifling through the driver's belt. I found some handcuffs, extra ammunition, and a can of pepper spray, and crammed them into the top of my pack.

Jack waved me over. "She's coming round."

I sprinted back and took out the cuffs. They were already in the loaded position. Jack and Bernie twisted her onto her front. She groaned as I slipped the cuffs on and crunched them tightly around her wrists. We propped her up against the car wheel.

Linda flinched after hearing a distant spray of gunfire. "We need to find cover. I know a police building not far from here."

Dusk had firmly set in, and I liked Linda's suggestion. It would give us a chance to regroup and probe Maureen for information. "Lead the way, Linda. I don't want to be wandering around here at night."

"Any cells in there?" Jack asked.

"No idea . . . I mean, probably," Linda stuttered. Bernie massaged her neck and attempted, not very successfully, to give a reassuring smile.

"Jack, you take Maureen. I'll bring up the rear," I said.

Maureen mumbled and rolled her head around groggily. Jack lifted her up by her tracksuit collar, and we started walking in procession toward the police station. He held her out at arm's length. She occasionally swung a clumsy kick at him, but her legs were too short to make any kind of meaningful contact.

I followed the others, snaking through bodies and stepping over suitcases. I had an irrational thought that all the dead might just rise up at any moment and attack, such was the weirdness of our situation.

"It's a good thing she's not a two-hundred-fifty-pound guy," Jack said, as he momentarily paused to adjust his grip. Maureen put up a good fight for a small old lady; a strong man with the same mentality would have been a lot more of a handful.

We needed to reassess our tactics when we had time.

Linda rounded the corner of the main terminal and led us to the police building. A drab concrete, single-story structure with a solid dark-blue front door over which a crest was displayed.

"Linda, try to remember—do you know what's inside?" I asked.

Bernie gave me a disapproving look. "She's already told—"

"Holding cells for people arrested at the airport, I think . . ."

It sounded like exactly what we needed, if empty. We could secure the building, lock up Maureen, and plan our next move. I gestured for everyone to continue. We broke cover and headed for the entrance. I scampered to the front and crouched with my back to the door.

"Bernie, we're going in. You two wait outside."

Jack handed me his Sig and took the flare gun. He pressed its barrel against Maureen's head. "No monkey business. You got it?"

She sneered and turned away.

I turned the handle slowly, and the door clicked open.

Bernie raised his eyebrows, booted the door. It swung open and banged against a rubber stopper on the floor. He aimed forward and ducked inside. I quickly followed into a seemingly deserted room. Through the gloom, I surveyed the area. Metal lockers ran along one wall, and two workstations sat on a long wooden reception desk, an internal steel door behind it, probably leading to the cells.

I vaulted over the desk and skidded to a stop by the steel door. Bernie covered me and I twisted the handle. Locked. I moved to the lockers and tried to open each one. Four were locked, two opened. One contained clothing on hangers, the other a jumble of snacks, paper towels, and plates.

I relaxed slightly after we fully cleared the room. "Bernie, what was that at the door? I wanted to sneak in."

He rested his hand on the locker next to me, revealing a large damp patch around his armpit. "Why give someone time to prepare by coming in slow?"

I didn't agree with him—Bernie could have rushed right into a group of crazies like the old lady. Or gotten shot by someone holed up in there. Arguing with him now wasn't going to change anything. We had gained access, and the place looked empty. But if we didn't start communicating and working together, someone was going to get hurt.

We sifted through the desk drawers, trying to locate any keys that might open the steel door.

After unsuccessfully searching, Bernie said, "Maybe the cop rushed outside and joined the battle?"

I noticed a few uniforms among the bodies and nodded in agreement.

We headed back outside after hearing raised voices.

Maureen struggled against Jack's grip. "Let me go, you bully. I don't want to hurt anyone."

She started to look and act her age, slumping in Jack's grip and wheezing like Muttley the dog.

Jack dragged her toward the door. "You're going nowhere."

She jumped up and spat in his face. Jack flinched away as spittle rolled slowly down his cheek.

I recognized his furious look as the one that usually preceded a right hook. Jack had reacted to less in previous situations. His intentions were always better than his solutions. A night on the beer often meant me firefighting tense situations as a peacemaker, keeping him out of barroom dust-ups.

The constant horrors of our current situation left me numb to the dead all around. Linda looked drained and shaken. Bernie also noticed and had his arm around her waist, pulling her toward him protectively.

"We still need to find the keys to the steel door," I said.

Bernie eased Linda gently toward Jack. "You go inside, get some rest."

Bernie and I scanned the bodies in the near vicinity and picked out two potential candidates by looking for shoulder epaulettes on the uniforms. Each body had a set of keys. I got a faint whiff of death when I leaned down and unhooked a bunch from the corpse's belt. We returned inside to join the others.

I tried keys in the steel door. The locked snapped open after my third attempt. "Thought that might be harder."

"How could things *be* any harder?" Bernie asked.

We could have faced an army of Maureens, but I kept the idea to myself. If somebody had suggested to me on the plane, while I was drinking my lukewarm coffee, that I'd soon be thieving from corpses to break into secure areas of police buildings, I'd have spat the bitter drink over the seat in front of me.

I twisted the handle and dragged open the heavy door.

A male voice shouted, "Who's there? Who is it?"

Bernie shoved his weight against the door, and I twisted the key.

We still hadn't discussed how we were going to deal with other people, since meeting Maureen. I said, "Let's secure the place, quick."

36

I locked the front door, Linda closed the blinds, and Jack pushed Maureen into a corner while we figured out what to do.

Maureen scrambled to her feet and shouted, "*Help!* I'm being kept prisoner. There're four here."

Jack and Bernie ran over and pinned her to the dark red vinyl floor. I remembered a roll of masking tape in the desk drawer and used it to tape her legs together. She gnashed her teeth and spat as I wrapped her mouth shut. By the time I finished, she lay wriggling in the fetal position, masking tape muffling her screams. Good enough for the moment.

Jack nodded his head toward the locked steel door. "How are we going to handle this?"

"We only heard a single voice," I said. "We open the door and let him know we're armed to the teeth and will shoot immediately if he tries anything."

"He might be in a cell," Linda said.

"She's right. It's not like he tried to burst through the door," Bernie said.

Conscious of the increasing gloom, I flicked a switch next to the steel door. Light flickered before steadily seeping through a thin crack at the bottom of it.

I turned to the group. "Linda, you watch Maureen. Jack, you take the Glock off Bernie and stand with me. Bernie, you open the door and tell him to stay back."

Bernie exchanged weapons without protest. I felt comfortable with my more experienced brother standing by my side. Bernie stood by the door and prepared to twist the key. "What if he attacks?"

"We shoot him," I said.

All murmured in approval except Maureen, whose muffled protests were ignored.

"Go for it, Bernie," Jack said.

We braced ourselves for action. I dropped to one knee and aimed.

Bernie pushed the door ajar.

A male voice shouted, "Help me. I've been stuck in here for hours."

"If you try to come through the door, we will shoot you. Do you understand?" Bernie shouted through the gap.

"I'm in a cell. The police arrested me in the airport this morning for being drunk," his voice trailed off.

"Open the door, Bernie," I said.

It swung open to reveal a prison cage at the end of the room. The cage split into three individual sections, and the cell on the left contained a single adult male. He looked about thirty, had a greasy brown mullet, and wore a bright blue Hawaiian shirt.

He held the bars with both hands and squinted. "Who are you? You're not the police."

I advanced forward, aiming directly at him. "Get to the back of your cage."

He scrambled back and sat on a wooden bench. I quickly moved forward, keeping him in my sights and rattled the cage's door. The stench of stale body odor invaded my nostrils.

"Where are the cops? Can you let me out?"

I refused to believe anything we heard from anyone outside our own group. After nearly paying a heavy price for trusting Maureen, nobody received a pass until we established their motivation.

"Why? So you can kill us?" Bernie said with the subtleness of a brick.

The man raised his eyebrows and stood. "What do you mean, 'kill you'? What the fuck are you talking about?"

"Get the keys, Jack," I said. "We'll throw Maureen in the right-hand cell, have a coffee in the other room, and decide what we're going to do."

I stepped back after the man poked his hand between the bars and tried to touch me. He gave me a tired smile. "Can I at least have some water?"

His request fell on deaf ears. He may have been genuine, but we were taking no chances.

After securing Maureen in the opposite cell, Jack shut the steel door and we finally sat down in relative safety. Linda made use of the reception area coffee maker and brewed a fresh pot. I blew on my steaming mug and took a sip, appreciating a hot drink and the chance to think.

I stripped off my shirt and looked down at my arm. The cut probably needed stitches but had stopped bleeding. Linda, proving resourceful in our confined area, found a first-aid kit. She washed my arm with a stinging antiseptic and taped a large, padded bandage over the wound. I inspected her handiwork and slipped my shirt back on.

Linda packed away the box and placed it back in a locker. She said to Bernie, "We should leave the door locked till the police show up. It's not worth the risk, is it?"

Bernie, who had jealously watched her tending to my arm, nodded. "Right. We can't trust these people. He can't hurt us in there."

Jack created a gap in the blinds and peered outside. "Would you bet against someone playing dead out there? It's nearly dark. I vote we sit tight."

The plastic clock on the wall clicked around to two minutes past eight.

"Why don't we test him?" I asked.

"Test him?" Bernie questioned.

"We can drag Maureen right up to the edge of his cage and see if he tries anything. If he's anything like her, he'll probably try to attack."

"You want to experiment with humans?" Linda replied with a look of slight disgust.

"Don't look at it as experimenting; look at it as humane. If the man doesn't want to kill her, then we'll find out and save an innocent life."

She sighed. "I can't be part of this. No way."

Jack grabbed his gun from the desk and stood. "Let's get it out of the way."

I unlocked the steel door and approached the man's cell. He stood to greet me. "Guys, let me out. This isn't funny."

Jack and I ignored him and dragged Maureen from her cell and placed her wriggling body in front of him.

"What the hell are you doing?" he asked.

I looked between the bars and into his eyes, trying to get a sense of his intent. "We've got something for you."

"What? You got some water? Food?"

"I've brought you a victim. Can you get your hands through the gaps?"

Maureen began wildly struggling against her taped restraints. A trail of snot flew from her nose as her breathing became heavier. I rolled her closer to the bars.

The man crouched and swept back his sweat-drenched hair. "The poor old thing. Let me check her pulse."

Check her pulse? She flipped around like a salmon. Clearly alive and kicking.

He slyly smiled, licked his lips, and reached forward. In the blink of an eye his face transformed to a grimace. He thrust his hands through the cage. Saliva sprayed through his gritted yellow teeth as he tried to crush each side of Maureen's windpipe.

I smashed the grip of the Sig across his fingers. He gasped and retreated away from the bars, sat back on the bench, and glared at me with a look of pure hatred while he rubbed his fingers.

Jack dragged Maureen back into the other caged section by her legs.

"So we were right all along," Bernie said. I hadn't realized he had followed us in. "Leave these crazy bastards to rot."

Linda looked over his shoulder at the man in the cell. "Come on, Harry."

I hadn't finished yet and dropped to one knee in front of the bars. Surely, somewhere inside these crazy people, they still had a scrap of decency. I wanted to try to appeal to that part. "Why did you try to kill her?"

"I tried to check her pulse. You attacked me. I'm not the one who tapes up old ladies."

I rolled my eyes at his tedious response. "Stop bullshitting. You tried to kill her. Why are you doing it?"

Jack grabbed my arm. "You're wasting your time. Bernie's right. Leave the bugger to rot."

They were right, but I had one more card to play. "I've got a deal for you, if you listen and speak honestly."

He sat forward. "A deal? What deal?"

"I'll give you Maureen if you tell us the truth about why you want to kill her—"

"No way, Harry," Bernie said. "Attacking us, fine. But using her as bait?"

"Give her to me and I'll tell you after," the man said.

We stood in silence for a moment. I think Bernie felt disgusted, but I knew Jack would be as curious as me about his answer.

Jack pulled me to one side and whispered, "Think about the security guard at the bottom of the slide. I'm not saying these people will all act in the same way, but if we give him Maureen first, he might try and kill himself straight after."

"No deal," I said to the man. "You take the offer or we go."

I thought this would put him at his breaking point. Instead, he disappointingly returned inside his shell. "I'm not a killer. Let me out, please."

"This is a waste of time. He's not going to tell us anything," Linda said, hugging herself. Bernie followed her out, trying to soothe and comfort her with empty promises.

Jack put his hand on my shoulder. "Can't say we didn't try."

He had been an inch from cracking, and I felt a sudden surge of anger at this man's death wish.

"Fuck you," I said and headed for the door.

An anguished cry came from the cell. I spun around.

He gripped two bars and pressed his sweaty face between them. "Wait. You've got yourself a deal."

I approached to just outside of his reach. "You'll tell us everything?"

"If you promise to give me the old woman," he said, innocence finally replaced by desperation. He reminded me of my alcoholic friend, when he went a day without a drink, although his poison was vodka, not murder.

"Scout's honor," I said.

I glanced over my shoulder. Bernie and Linda watched by the door.

"Harry, you can't," Linda said.

"Linda, if you or Bernie don't want to be part of it, leave the room. This is happening whether you like it or not."

They both stayed by the door. I surprised myself, but the game of life had changed. I knew that even one sign of weakness could make him clam up.

"You're not lying? She's mine, right?" the man asked.

"We're not repeating ourselves," Jack said. "You've got ten seconds."

The man dropped his head, ran his fingers through his mullet, and then gazed into my eyes. "I've got to kill myself."

"Go on," I said.

"I've got to kill myself as soon as possible."

He paused, bit his lip, and glanced up at me in expectation. It didn't make sense. If the simple goal was suicide, nothing stopped him from doing it.

I shook my head. "Not good enough. You've got one last chance."

"Oh, what have I got to lose?" The man threw his arms in the air and continued in a slow, cold voice. "I want to kill myself.

The final unstoppable goal is to kill myself. But I can't kill myself until I kill another person . . . kill one, kill yourself, kill one, kill yourself . . . I must use whatever means necessary, and I have to do it as soon as possible."

A stunned silence followed. His chilling words reminded me of the stomach-turning video clips I had seen on the news, where extremists made twisted statements before carrying out a suicide attack. They believed what they were saying, and nothing indicated that this man told us lies.

"You don't have any other option?" Jack said incredulously.

"There is no other option. This is the only way. Now, let me carry out my mission."

"Oh Jeezus. That's exactly what the security guard did to the flight attendant, right? Isn't that what the old lady was trying to do?" Bernie asked.

"Can you tell us anything else? How long have you wanted to do this?" I asked.

He grunted as if I had just asked a stupid question. "My objective is simple."

I turned and walked past Jack, Bernie, and Linda, into the office area and flopped into a swivel chair behind the reception desk. The man shouted for us to come back and honor our promises, but Jack slammed the door and twisted the key. As I slowly spun in the chair, I tried to rationalize the man's odd behavior but couldn't think of why he would act in such a way. Hopefully, one of the others had more of a clue.

Muffled sounds of screaming and rattling came from behind the door for a couple of minutes and then abruptly stopped.

Bernie wrapped his arm around Linda. She rubbed his hand and looked at me. "You could have told us you had no intention of sacrificing Maureen."

"The whole act with him had to look genuine, or he would have sniffed my bluff. These people may be focused on killing, but they're not completely stupid. Both of them have tried to manipulate us in order to kill."

"You still should have told us. We would have been convincing. Next time, don't scare us like that," Bernie said.

"There won't be a next time. We know Maureen and that guy in the cell wanted to kill someone, anyone. The security guard killed the steward, then himself. There's a pattern."

"What's that supposed to mean?"

"You've seen it yourself, Bernie. Since we landed, everyone we have met has tried to kill. No matter how convincing they sounded, they can't be trusted. So yes, I would sacrifice one of them if it meant our safety."

"We need to plan how to handle situations in the future," Jack said, backing me up. "People could be armed, strong, or sneak up on us, giving us only seconds to respond. We need a zero tolerance approach."

Linda bowed her head. "We can't just start shooting people on sight."

Jack gave her a sympathetic look. "The people with a pulse that we have come across so far have appeared completely normal until they managed to find an opportunity to kill. We can't afford to let them get close enough."

"I know a way," Bernie said. "We don't have to shoot if we see two or more people together."

"You're gonna have to explain that one to me." I said.

"Think about it. If they're anything like those fruitcakes,"—he gestured to the steel door—"they'll be trying to kill each other, not travel together."

Jack stood and started pacing the room. "Do we need to split up so we are not seen in a group?"

"Wouldn't make a difference, would it?" I said. "Together or apart, they'll try the same thing."

Bernie slumped against the desk, his small burst of enthusiasm gone. "Why are they doing it? What kind of crazy brainwashing . . . ?"

I stretched over the desk and gave him a friendly pat. "It isn't that much of a stretch to think that the loss of communications might have something to do with it. We'll be all right, mate."

"But how could something like this happen? Russia? China?"

I certainly didn't have the answer. I'd read on the Internet last month about radio waves being developed for mind control, and particle-sized computers being released into the atmosphere, but that all seemed like crazy conspiracy talk. A serious organization had to be behind this. But who and why, I couldn't even start to imagine.

"We're all working on the same information as you," Jack said.

Jack had a strange way of sounding sarcastic because of the way he often emphasized the last word of each sentence. He didn't mean to come across this way—it was just a personal tick. A short period of awkward silence followed.

"Ninety-nine percent of the people around here are already dead. Just how far has this thing spread?" Linda asked plaintively.

I imagined the scenes in front of the terminal when this deathly impulse took hold of its victims. There must have been stabbings, shootings, suicides, blood, and screaming everywhere—everyone with the same purpose.

A thought struck me. "Jack, those tweets you received . . ."

He shrugged. "What about 'em?"

"They were probably from people trying to draw you in after finding your tweet."

"Why me, though?"

"I doubt it was you specifically. I imagine they would have tried anyone they could find after searching Twitter for New York."

Jack looked at me blankly. "Not following you."

"Think about it. The profile picture of a man in a wheelchair, a guy in a hospital, and a farm owner. All in a similar situation to the man in the cell—unable to get their hands on another human. They were in remote locations or unable to move without putting themselves at risk."

"Remote locations? Let me have a look," Bernie said as he quickly shuffled to Jack's side.

Jack slipped his phone out of his back pocket and thumbed the screen. "I'm not picking up any signal, and Wi-Fi needs a password."

He opened up the Twitter app and passed it to Bernie. He pulled a case from his pocket and put on a pair of silver-rimmed glasses. After reading a few tweets, he took a sharp intake of breath.

"What is it, dear?" Linda asked.

"The addresses in the tweets . . . the farm's upstate."

She tried to grab the phone. "It can't be, Bernie. Our family, friends . . ."

He held the phone away from her. Jack reached over and took it back. "Don't think about that. We'll get out of here and find them."

Bernie and Linda had lived in New York for years and probably had a whole network of friends and family nearby. Linda seemed the most concerned about events outside our immediate area, but I wanted us to remain focused on the here and now.

"The captain said other airports had the same issue. Which do you think he meant?" Jack asked.

I wanted to avoid this conversation as Linda appeared close to cracking up. I pushed thoughts of my own family and friends to the back of my mind. We had to remain switched on. I hoped that whatever we were witnessing was confined to the state of New York, but my head told me otherwise. Although we didn't know which airports the captain had tried to contact, the lack of communication made it seem like not just a local phenomenon.

The plane. I ran over to the blinds and pushed two slats apart. Darkness had fallen and we'd missed our agreed cutoff point.

Bernie cuddled Linda, who buried her face in the crook of his arm. Her stifled whimpers stabbed at my heart.

Jack joined me at the blinds. "Should we fire a flare? Let them know we're here?"

We had to let them know we were still in the local area and give them at least a little bit of hope through the night. The people on board were bound to be hungry and scared. At first light, we could grab some supplies and head back.

"No," Bernie said. "Anyone on the lookout for a kill will immediately come here."

I could see his point but still wanted to do it. "Think about the passengers and crew. If one killer sees it, hopefully another will, and they'll both wind up dead."

He turned away from me. "Don't say I didn't tell you."

I ignored his comment. Our survival was paramount, but people were relying on us. I knew the strategy had a big element of risk attached, and hoped the captain wouldn't let any strangers on board—but why would he after the incident when we'd landed?

"On my head be it," I said and snatched the flare gun from the desk. "Jack, open the door. I'll run out, fire over the plane. No hanging around."

"Got it," Jack said, and he unlocked the door and held the handle. "Ready?"

I loaded a cartridge and pulled back the hammer. "Ready."

He swung open the door. I ran out a few yards and thrust the gun in the air, aimed toward the star-studded sky, and fired in the direction of the runway, hoping I wasn't making a mistake. The flare shot up with a hiss and curled in a high, bright red arc before settling in the distance and slowly starting to drop. People on the plane would see, as it must have lit up the whole area

47

DARREN AND MARCUS WEARMOUTH

around it before slowly floating to the ground on the other side of the terminal.

Jack poked his head out of the door. "Get back in here. It's not a bloody fireworks display."

Once I was back inside, Jack locked the door.

"Let's kill the lights in case of any unwanted attention," I said.

All agreed, and I flicked the switch.

We shared snacks that we found in the locker and carried on our discussion by the thin light that seeped through the blinds from the streetlights outside.

"Imagine if the airport is just a small snapshot of the rest of the globe," Jack said.

"It's not worth thinking about," I said. "We've all got people we love out there. Let's keep it positive until we know more."

"What makes us so different?" Linda asked.

"I dunno. We were on a plane?"

"So only people that were on the ground have been brainwashed?"

"I didn't quite say that, but it stands to reason—"

The front door rattled violently.

I instinctively ducked and reached for my gun. "Get down, under the windows."

All three slid across the floor to my side of the room, and we sat under the window. The front door rattled again, followed by three blows, possibly kicks.

Footsteps echoed outside, moving around the side of our building. Something smudged against the window. I imagined hands being pressed against it, to shield eyes for a better view.

The glass shuddered after a loud bang.

Bernie cupped his hand around Linda's mouth and whispered in her ear. Tears rolled down her cheeks. Her trembling hands clamped around Bernie's waist. The footsteps went back to the front door. It shook violently again, followed by four loud thuds.

A calm voice said, "Come out. I heard voices. I'm here to help you."

Bernie squinted at me through the gloom. We both shook our heads. I gripped the Sig and glanced across to Jack. He pointed his Glock at the door.

"If you don't come out now, I'll burn the fucking building down," the voice said, switching from calm to aggressive. We remained silent. "Last chance, motherfuckers."

The footsteps echoed around the side of the building again, followed by two loud bangs on the window.

I tensed, ready to jump up and fight if necessary, but prayed the person outside would lose interest. It seemed unlikely.

The window banged three times. A heavy object smashed into it. The glass splintered. Maybe he'd found a rock. The glass must have been the protective sort; it held after another three heavy thuds.

A minute later, the footsteps faded away from the building.

3
DEPARTURE

I watched the hands on the plastic wall clock tick around as we lay in silence for hours. The man never returned. At three in the morning, I leaned up and slipped open the blinds. Circular shatter marks peppered the window.

"That was you and that fucking flare. I told you not to do it," Bernie said.

I resisted the urge to punch him. We were all tired and under severe stress. "Drop it, Bernie. There's probably more where he came from."

Linda scrambled to her feet and ran over to the desk. She picked up the phone. "I'm sick of this. I'm calling 911."

Had she lost her mind?

"Bernie, sort her out, will you?" Jack snapped.

He let out a weary sigh. "Just let her do it."

Linda punched in the numbers, put the call on speakerphone, and waited. The ring tone echoed in the silence of the room. Nobody would answer, surely . . .

After four rings, somebody did pick up at the other end. "Er . . . hello?"

She ducked down and frantically said, "Please come and help. It's awful out here."

"What is your current location, madam?"

"We're at JFK. Inside the—"

Jack jumped up, slammed the receiver down, cutting off the call. "Linda, are you stupid?"

Bernie rushed over to where Jack stood and grabbed his arm. "Don't talk to my wife like that!" he snarled.

Jack threw off his grip and squared up to him. "Who answers 911 by saying, 'Er . . . hello?' Well done—we've just fired out another flare."

They glared into each other's eyes. I moved quickly between the two of them. "Everyone calm down. Try to get some rest before sunrise. We've all been through a lot."

"How do you expect us to sleep?" Linda asked petulantly.

"You need rest, Linda. Jack and I'll keep watch."

Bernie shouldered Jack to one side and guided Linda to the far corner of the room. They settled down in silence.

Despite my plan, nobody slept before sunrise. We were all way out of our depth. I resolved to make more allowances for Bernie and to remember that the pressures we were dealing with would affect us all differently.

At first light, just before six, we decided on a plan to rush into the terminal, grab some food from the closest outlet, and make our way back to the plane. That was about as elaborate as it got. In our current state, we didn't need complicated.

Jack and I checked our guns, and Bernie loaded a cartridge into the flare gun. For some reason, neither Jack nor I could convince Bernie to take a gun from one of the corpses outside.

I cautiously led us out of the police building and crept toward Departures, our best chance of finding a shop near the entrance. The faces on surrounding advertising boards seemed to be laughing at me. The friendly welcoming design now felt creepy.

A female corpse with a rag stuffed into her mouth wedged open the entrance door to the front of the Departures. Her eyes were fixed open with a look of terror. The gunshot wounds, stabbings, and beatings were awful to look at, but there was something horribly forced about this particular death. I couldn't quite put my finger on why it stood out so much, but out of all the scenes at the airport, I found this one the hardest to forget.

Inside the terminal, the scenes of horror were no less gruesome. Whatever happened must have started around a busy lunchtime period. Bodies lay thick in all directions. I found the sight almost as unbearable as the smell.

Strange formations of corpses lay where passengers lined up to check in for their flights, only to turn on one another. Some appeared to have ripped the extendable handles off their suitcases to use as weapons. I noticed a metal rod plunged into the eye socket of one unfortunate victim. The improvised weapon had proven a popular choice around the check-in desks. The check-in assistant lay dead, draped across the scale for weighing suitcases. The electronic display registered her at one hundred and twenty pounds.

A group of three people surrounded an ATM. One man looked like he'd been beaten severely before slicing his own wrists with a broken shaving mirror from his suitcase. A woman lay strangled by the shoulder strap of a handbag. Next to her was a large man dressed in a white linen suit; he appeared to have no visible injuries. One moment, they were obediently waiting their turn; the next, they were in deadly combat.

Many around the security gate had gunshot wounds. Armed officials must have acted first, and then others took advantage of the weapons until the magazines ran dry.

I nudged Jack and pointed to a mousy-haired corpse. "Does he look familiar?"

"Should he?"

Bernie and Linda stepped across a couple of bodies. He asked, "What are you staring at?"

"Is that the guy from *Ocean's Twelve*?"

Bernie squatted for a better look. "Sure is. Poor guy."

We walked further into the madness of the terminal and headed for the shopping area. I glanced to my left over Linda's shoulder and felt an electric shock of horror. The large man in the white linen suit rose silently like a ghost and ran straight at us, his face contorted in fury, a machete raised above his head.

"Look out!" I shouted, ducking to one side and bringing up my gun.

Bernie, Linda, and Jack spun to face me. The man leaped over bodies and approached at high speed, only yards away from reaching them.

Jack must have heard the approaching footsteps; he quickly dropped to one knee and twisted around. Bernie and Linda froze. I tried to aim the Sig but couldn't get a clear shot past them.

I dived to the left and fired twice. Rounds thumped into the man's shoulder and neck, only slightly checking his momentum as his weight carried him forward.

The man let out a gurgled scream and buried his machete into the top of Linda's head, splitting it down to eye level.

He kicked her in the back to free the blade. Linda dropped to her knees and slumped face first to the ground. Her legs violently twitched three times, and a pool of blood started to surround her head.

"Linda!" Bernie shouted.

I fired twice. The rounds zipped into the attacker's hip and arm. He screamed and fell into a check-in desk. With his uninjured arm, he raised the machete against his own throat. Stepping forward, I gritted my teeth and kicked his arm, knocking the blade free, and followed up by driving my knee into his face.

Jack dived on top of him, forcing the man down, and pinned him to the ground.

Looking around, I realized that he might not be the only one who played dead. The vast terminal building suddenly felt claustrophobic. I scanned the bodies, looking for any signs of slight movement, a twitch, chest movement from breathing—anything.

Bernie sank to his knees next to Linda. At first, he shook her shoulders and shouted her name, but even he could see that the chances of reviving her were nonexistent. Finally, he hugged her close to his chest and sobbed. Linda's blood caked his hands, shirt, and right cheek. I felt my heart wrench and spun away, turning my attention back to the killer.

"Jack, we need to sort this out quick. There could be others like him."

The killer struggled weakly under Jack's hold. Large expanding red patches soaked his linen suit.

"Leave me alone. I'm going to kill myself," he said in a raspy voice.

"You don't get to choose, fuck-face," Jack said and shoved a forearm against his neck.

I looked across at Bernie. He held Linda's hand and stooped to kiss it. "Bernie, we need to get the hell out of here."

He slowly raised his head, his devastated expression changing into one of hatred. "Hold him there."

Seeing Bernie approach, the man's wriggles became more desperate. Bernie picked up the machete; he looked at the blood gleaming on the blade and wiped tears from his eyes.

Coming back to us, he swung the machete over his head and brought it down straight across the attacker's head with a sickly crunching noise. Jack and I rolled away quickly to avoid being covered in blood or hit by a rogue thrust from Bernie. He continued smashing the blade downward several more times before dropping to his knees. The machete dropped from his shaking hand and clanked on the floor. He covered his face and started to sob.

I placed my hand on Bernie's shoulder to offer some comfort. "I'm sorry, Bernie."

He glared up at me with a loathing in his eyes. "Get the fuck away from me, you. It's your fault."

I backed away and glanced around the terminal, paranoid about another surprise attack. Jack tried to put his arm around Bernie, but he shoved him away. "And you. You're the same."

"He took us all by surprise," Jack said and attempted to crouch next to him. "What do you want me to do?"

"I want you both to fuck off," Bernie said before looking directly at me. "If you hadn't fired that flare and brought him here, Linda might still be . . ."

He put his fist in his mouth and squeezed his eyes tightly shut. I didn't want to point out that it could just have easily been Linda's call to 911. I knelt next to him, "We don't know that. No matter what, we can't stay here."

Bernie pushed both Jack and me away and pointed the flare gun, switching aim between us. "I'm staying with my wife. Got a problem with that?"

Jack held out both of his palms toward Bernie. "No problem. Do what you have to do. We'll grab some supplies."

We both retreated to a safe distance. I could see the strain showing on Jack's face.

I spotted a newsstand by the information desk. "Let's empty a couple of suitcases and fill them with food and water for the passengers. Give Bernie a few minutes with Linda."

"I'm not hanging around all day waiting for him. There're hundreds lying here, and any could be waiting for a moment of weakness."

It sounded callous, but I had to agree. After gathering supplies, we'd have to manage the difficult task of getting Bernie back to safety.

We gathered supplies in a pair of suitcases on wheels and hung around the newsstand for another ten minutes. I flicked through a newspaper from yesterday morning to see if I could find a hint of what might have caused the mayhem, while Jack maintained watch. I couldn't find anything specific, but a few stories stood out that would get a conspiracy theorist's juices flowing. Iran sent a chimp into space. Had they secretly developed a chemical weapon that they then released over the US? A large explosion had been reported in the Middle East. Nothing new there. A meteor shower had lit up the sky. I discounted the idea of aliens as ridiculous. My stomach growled, so I put the paper down and decided to have a bar of chocolate.

Jack peered over to Bernie, still on his knees, next to his wife. "Should we go and see how he is?"

Any time we gave him to mourn would be inappropriately short, but we didn't have a choice. "Why don't you call him over? Keep our distance till he calms down."

"Bernie, are you okay? Can we come over?" Jack shouted.

"Fuck you," Bernie replied and pointed the flare gun directly at us.

A bright projectile shot from the barrel and fizzed straight between Jack and me, slamming into the newsstand.

"Jesus Christ, Bernie, what the fuck are you doing?" I shouted as we both scrambled behind a check-in desk.

Within a matter of seconds, a healthy blaze licked around the newsstand. Piles of papers and magazines smoldered, sending smoke billowing into the air. A fire alarm burst into life, which seemed to bring Bernie back to his senses.

He wedged the gun in his belt and stood. "I'm sorry, I just didn't . . . I don't . . ."

The tears streaming down his face were quickly joined by the water from the sprinkler system, which petered out after a few seconds.

"Let's grab him, Jack."

With our free hands, we gripped Bernie by the arms and started pulling him toward the exit, dragging the suitcases in our other hands.

He resisted and tried to shake free. "I'm not leaving Linda. Get the fuck off me!"

"We'll come back," Jack said, angry now. "If you don't want to die, get moving."

Bernie's resistance weakened, and he staggered along between us. He probably knew deep down that this was our only sensible option.

Once outside, Bernie looked back into the terminal, increasingly filling with thick smoke.

"Linda," he said with quiet emotion.

I grabbed his arm and eased him away, focusing on getting back to the gap in the fence. Once away, Bernie ran freely as we both followed Jack.

Ten yards along the path, a wiry old man sprang out from behind a car holding a golf club behind his head. Jack immediately raised the Glock and shot him in the forehead. A cloud of red mist appeared as the old man collapsed with a grunt.

Yesterday, both of us would have hesitated or tried to tackle the man without killing him. But running past the body, I knew that I would've done the same thing. A single person showing danger signs required an immediate response.

Once we reached the gap in the fence, Jack wriggled through and held up the loose section. I slid the cases through and followed Bernie to the other side.

Bernie knelt and stared at the terminal. Smoke drifted from it into the clear blue morning sky. The fire alarm rang in the distance.

He shifted around to face me and said in a stern voice, "Zero tolerance."

I knew what Bernie meant. Who could blame him? "I'm truly sorry about Linda."

I didn't say it just to comfort Bernie. The poor woman had gone through sixteen hours of hell before her death.

He sniffed and turned away. For a moment, I thought of ripping the flare gun from his belt, but decided to give him the benefit of the doubt, for now.

Jack stood and picked up a suitcase. "They'll be wanting these bad boys. Come on."

We made our way over the tarmac toward the plane, still parked in the same position, just off the runway. I noticed a 777 behind it, slide deployed. As we approached within fifty yards of our plane, I could see more bodies around the bottom of the slide. In addition to the steward and the security guard, perhaps another four or five.

The captain's head appeared from the emergency exit door, and he waved. I felt immense relief that people were still alive, but we had no good news, so I resisted the urge to wave back.

When we reached the plane, I looked up at the captain, who stood at the open entrance.

He looked down and frowned. "There're only three of you. What happened?"

Bernie shook his head.

"Do you have any rope?" Jack asked.

"Why?"

"We've some drinks and chocolate for the passengers. Once we get this stuff up, I'll give you a full debriefing," I said.

The captain appeared distracted by something behind us. I turned to see thick black smoke belching into the air from the terminal. So much for remaining inconspicuous.

He glanced down and shook his head before disappearing into the cabin. A minute later, a single piece of rope slithered down the slide. I tied it around both suitcases, and the captain and a passenger dragged them up. Jack, Bernie, and I climbed the slide on all fours and stood in the entrance.

Four people appeared behind the captain. I looked along both sides of plane. All overhead compartments were open, a few oxygen masks hung down, but no other passengers.

The captain looked knackered. He leaned against a seat. "We had a terrible time last night. After your flare, we had a stream of visitors. The first one said he had a bus waiting for us at the front of the terminal. We told him to stay at the bottom of the slide. Another man sneaked up on him from nowhere and stabbed him in the chest before slicing his own throat."

"Sorry about that," I said. "We wanted to let you know we were still around."

The captain shrugged. "Glad you did. Shortly after, another man turned up. He said he thought he had heard voices coming from the police building and wanted us to help him investigate. When we refused, he went crazy, tried to climb the slide. When a passenger kicked him down, he threatened to set fire to the plane."

"What happened to him?" Jack asked.

"A woman knocked him to the ground with a pipe and strangled him. She took the knife from the other body and sliced her own throat."

I slapped my hand against my forehead and ran it down my face, feeling a mixture of disgust, disbelief, and despair.

"What about the other passengers?" Bernie asked.

"There're only four others left on board. Most fled at first light after the experiences of last night. That guy, Morgan, led them through the gap you created in the fence. They headed toward the safety cordon."

Bernie walked away and flopped in a seat.

"What safety cordon?" I asked.

"The general consensus was that a terrorist attack had taken place. Morgan stirred up the rest of the passengers, claiming your flare was a signal that you'd reached safety. He led them out despite my protests, and they disappeared along the road toward the city. I wouldn't leave because four passengers decided to stay. Lieutenant Marsden accompanied the group."

The captain's words chilled me. Bernie had planted the terrorist seed, but I'd fired the flare that Morgan had used to talk most passengers into leaving. Who knew what they were going to find or how many would survive? I knew we weren't completely to blame for the passengers making a break for it, but I couldn't help feeling partly responsible.

The four passengers behind the captain were made up of an elderly couple from Long Island, who couldn't travel very far on foot even if they wanted to, and their adult children.

While Jack and I recounted our story, the small audience looked visibly horrified. We told them about the front of the terminal, our encounter with Maureen, finding the man in the police building. I lowered my voice when moving on to what had happened in the terminal.

The family offered their condolences to Bernie. He brushed them away, but I didn't blame him; his mental wounds were raw.

The man's confession in the police building created the most astonishment. It connected with what they'd witnessed during the night.

Once we finished our debriefing, I had a few questions of my own for the captain. "You said you were communicating with other planes in the air. What happened to those?"

"I landed first. When I saw the deserted runways and the scene by the gate, I advised all the other planes in the vicinity to try another airport."

"Have you heard from any of them since we left yesterday?"

"A couple of planes landed at Newark. They encountered the same thing."

The captain seemed to be holding back. I had no idea why. We were all in the shit, and his official capacity no longer held any sway. "Then what?"

"Most passengers left the planes on foot and tried to find the authorities. They came to the same end."

If the rest of our plane had waited to hear what we'd managed to discover, we could have at least alerted them to the dangers they might face. Morgan annoyed me, for leading them away before our return, but I could understand their need to search for safety.

"How far do you think this has spread?" I asked.

The captain looked nervous and straightened his tie. "Honestly?"

"What do you mean, 'honestly'?" Jack said. I shared his irritation, but he openly showed it.

"I don't know, but I would say it goes a lot further than New York. One of the pilots who landed in Newark managed to connect on the emergency frequency with a plane trying to land at Heathrow. He said they were having similar problems."

Jack put his head in his hands and said what I was thinking. "Fuck."

"So it's global?" the old man said.

"Why not?" Bernie said, finally joining in. "I don't believe in coincidence. We're all screwed."

"We can't stay here any longer," I said. "If the flare last night attracted quite a few killers, imagine what the tower of smoke from the terminal will do. We know there're a few hundred people from the plane wandering around the New York area. I say we make our way into the city."

"And take out any killers on the way," Jack said.

"Killers? Is that what you call them?" the old man asked.

"I can't think of a better description. Can you?"

The old man folded his arms and took a step back, clearly not a fan of Jack's confrontational style.

The family talked quietly among themselves for a moment while we unloaded the suitcases and spread the contents on the floor.

"We don't want to go into the city," the younger man said. "We're taking our parents home."

The old couple wouldn't be suited to ducking around the streets, avoiding maniacs, and scavenging for supplies. They probably just wanted to get back to a familiar environment. Who could blame them?

"Can you drive?" I asked, thinking about the abandoned cars on the road to the terminal.

"I'll drive them to Long Island," the captain said. "I need to get home and find my family."

As much as I feared for their safety, I also felt a sense of relief. Smaller groups would be much more mobile and easier to manage. I hoped that Bernie would volunteer to drive them to Long Island. Jack and I needed a conversation about him if he wanted to remain as part of our group.

Jack stuffed some water and chocolate into his pack and slung it over his shoulder. "Let's get out of here. The longer we hang around discussing our options, the more likely a killer will show."

Bernie pulled himself from his seat and groaned. "So, it's just the three of us then?"

"We'll be all right, Bernie. Zero tolerance, remember?" Jack said.

The eight of us jumped down the slide and made our way to the gap in the fence. My cheek warmed from the heat of the terminal building as we passed it.

A shot split the air.

The captain crumpled to the ground. I dove for cover and pushed the old man down. Jack kicked my boot and pointed to a silver car on the other side of the fence. Behind it, a bearded man in a lumberjack shirt reloaded a bolt-action rifle.

I looked across at the captain. "Are you hit?"

He shook his head. "I don't think so, although I'm missing an epaulette."

"Pretend you're dead."

"What?"

"Pretend you're dead, now," I said.

He closed his eyes and let his head loll sideways.

I didn't want this killer taking any more pot shots. I crawled over to the captain and pretended to take his pulse, tensing my shoulders, expecting a round to thud into my back at any moment.

A few of the group gave me confused looks. I said, "Stay down."

I sprang up, ran over to the fence and shouted, "You've fucking killed him. You've killed him. You murdering bastard."

The man behind the car watched my antics for a few seconds before placing the rifle muzzle in his mouth. He strained to reach the trigger with his fingertips and gagged as he forced the barrel further down his throat. Once able to reach the trigger, he instantly pulled it and fired down his own throat. He wobbled for a couple of seconds with his arms outstretched before collapsing to the ground.

I grabbed a fence post to keep myself steady, and let out a deep breath.

Jack stood and ripped up the loose section of fence. "Get moving."

One by one, we all crawled through and made for the cars on the road.

Bernie jogged alongside me. "How did you know?"

"I didn't. They seem to need confirmation—remember the pulse checks? I tried to give him that."

Jack went over to our assailant and took his rifle. He found a box of ammunition resting by the wheel. Bernie opened the car door, climbed in, and started the engine. He powered down the electric window and said to the captain, "You take this one."

The family didn't need a second invitation and quickly got into the car and shut the doors. The captain took the wheel. I approached the window and held out my hand.

He gripped it tightly and shook. "Good luck. Hopefully, we'll meet again."

I couldn't let them leave without some form of defense, and passed him the Sig. "Take this. You might need it."

"Thanks," the captain said.

I gave him a quick lesson on how to use it and said my farewells. Jack and Bernie did the same.

The family waved as the car headed off, weaving through a jumble of stationary vehicles, away from the airport. I felt glad the captain had some protection, but as they disappeared into the distance, I thought it might not be enough.

Jack passed me the Glock and loaded his newly acquired rifle.

"Okay, guys, I have an apartment in Elmhurst. I want to collect some of Linda's things. It's not far, and I'd appreciate the company . . ." Bernie said.

I could think of better options but kept my face neutral as I looked to Jack, who stared toward the raging inferno engulfing the terminal.

"How many entrances does the apartment have? Can we be seen through the windows?" I asked.

"It's a basement apartment in a quiet neighborhood, with a solid front door. I'll close the blinds. We'll be safe."

"Do you have any alcohol or smokes in your apartment?" Jack asked.

Bernie frowned. "Why?"

"Because we've all been through a lot, and I am sure we could all use some stress relief," Jack said.

"You want to get drunk? This is hardly the situation—"

"Bernie, he means rest and recuperation. If we don't have some downtime soon, we're going to make stupid mistakes. We need a secure place where we can work out what the hell is going on and what to do next."

"Okay, I get what you mean. That could be my place. I've a couple of bottles of vodka and some cigarettes, Marlboros, that have been in the kitchen drawer for about a year."

Jack took a deep breath and gave Bernie a friendly pat on the arm. Alcohol was last thing on my mind, but I supported Jack's general point.

It took us ten minutes to find a car with keys in the ignition and an interior relatively clean of blood. We pulled out the corpses and placed them respectfully a short distance away.

"You're the local here; you drive," I said.

Bernie nodded, and we climbed into the Lincoln. I took the back seat and gazed at the airport as we jerked away.

4

ELMHURST, QUEENS

I thought driving away from the confines of the airport would bring some relief. The state of the Van Wyck expressway kept me firmly anchored in the same reality. Smashed and stationary vehicles littered the lanes as far as the eye could see. Bernie diligently picked his way through the carnage.

"What about Andy and Dave?" Jack asked.

"We'll worry about them once we're safe," I said, keeping my attention outside in case a psycho darted from a gap. "We need to get ourselves into a state where we can help."

Our car passed a burning SUV. A short intense wave of heat radiated through our windows as Bernie edged past. He said, "In a weird way, I'm glad Linda never got to see this."

I guessed he said it to make himself feel better. From what we had seen at the airport, I thought that very few people had survived. Even if a handful somehow avoided getting affected, they would still struggle in a city full of killers. The chances of Andy or Dave being alive were next to nothing. If they weren't dead, they'd probably want to kill, so I half-hoped they'd met a swift end.

Bernie continued to bump, scrape, and pick his way toward his neighborhood, a short distance from the expressway. On more than on occasion, there seemed to be no way through the chaos, but inch by inch we advanced.

My gut wrenched as Bernie squeezed between two cars and our wheels bounced over a body. He nosed the Ford through a group of smashed and charred cars spread around a fallen tanker. Smoke drifted from the blackened frames into the clear morning sky as our tires crunched through the mess.

The digital clock on the Ford read 9:47.

After clearing the tanker mayhem, we came to a relatively clear section. Bernie slowed to a stop. "Good place to take a look."

I glanced around and detected no movement. As we had no reason to rush, I didn't argue, and I popped open my door, took a deep breath, and stood on the highway.

I scanned the road and surrounding area. On the opposite side of the expressway, a station wagon headed a pile-up that completely blocked it, like a demented demolition derby. The driver hung from her window with a fist-sized chunk of skull missing from her head. Behind her vehicle, bodies lay around the cars in a scene similar to the airport terminal. Sporadic noises echoed in the distance, but there was nothing in the immediate vicinity apart from the noise of Bernie's feet scraping against the road surface.

In the distance, several towers of smoke rose from the city, an indication that this was more than just a local event. Bernie's shoulders slumped as he wearily returned to our car. Jack rubbed his eyes, clearly exhausted after being awake for over thirty-six hours. He smoothed his greasy dark-brown hair against his head. We looked at each other without speaking before trooping back to join Bernie.

Jack tried the radio but couldn't pick up a station.

I sat back and stared at the light fixture in the roof above me. Twenty hours ago, these people were in hell. Had an evil force managed to trigger off some hidden primal instinct? The man in the cell had told us what he needed to do, which was a general demand rather than specific instructions. People carried out this need to kill in any way possible to reach their goal of suicide. I found it hard to wrap my head around the concept.

Survival remained our goal. Perhaps we were beginning to change too. Jack had already shot a man in the head, and I'd tricked another into killing himself. The only small comfort was that we hadn't been on the ground when things went south.

I snapped back into the real world when Bernie slammed on the brakes, bringing the car to a skidding stop. I put my head between the two front seats. "Problem?"

"No way through," Bernie said. "It's an easy walk from here."

A thick tangle of cars blocked our path in scruffy rows. It actually looked similar to the junkyard I used to visit as a young teenager. I would slip through a gap in the fence every night to check through the new arrivals for coins down the side of seats or items left in a glove box. We didn't have a lot of money growing up, and my efforts would occasionally be rewarded with some loose change or a packet of half-eaten breath mints.

Jack grabbed his backpack from the footwell. "How far we talking, Bernie?"

Bernie's fingers scraped across his white stubbly chin. "Fifteen minutes, I guess."

I would have preferred to travel by car, but it was easy to imagine that driving on any two-lane road would be difficult once we managed to exit the expressway. We could handle the fifteen-minute walk as a patrol, like the ones Jack and I had both carried out around the streets of Belfast.

I slung my pack on my back and twisted my head in all directions, looking for movement. Dogs barked and multiple alarms rang in the distance. "Bernie. You lead the way and I'll cover you. Jack, bring up the rear."

Bernie grunted over the median strip, crossed the opposite lanes, and led us through a small industrial area. He twitched at every sound and kept looking over his shoulder. I encouraged him forward, and he proceeded with flare gun in hand.

Jack had his rifle shouldered and swept it from side to side.

We entered a street that took us toward residential housing. Our first taste of a neighborhood since the shit hit the fan.

I heard a sudden noise of rapid soft pattering against concrete and, dropping to one knee, twisted in the direction of the noise and aimed.

"Oh, my God," Bernie exclaimed, pointing his gun toward a golden retriever that bounded at him from the other side of the road.

I let out a deep breath and lowered the Glock.

"Put your gun down, Bernie," Jack said and stepped forward to offer the dog the back of his hand to smell. The dog disregarded his hand and excitedly jumped at him with its front paws outstretched. "What's your name, boy? Hey? What the hell have you seen?"

The dog seemed in good spirits as it licked Jack's face and bounded around, loudly barking. Seeing it react to us so normally made me feel safer. I had no idea why.

Jack read the dog's collar and stroked its back. "He's called Bouncer."

Bouncer appeared to hear something in the distance that only a dog could recognize, and scampered away. I watched him race between two buildings and disappear.

Bernie continued along a couple of tree-lined streets with smart detached houses on either side. It looked like a leafy English neighborhood rather than what I expected to see in New York.

"Where are we?" I asked.

Bernie stopped and gazed at one of the splendid 1930s red brick homes. "Cutting through Forest Hills. Don't worry, Harry, you can't afford it."

I probably could in the current climate of the housing market.

We continued along for another ten minutes, moving through an area that matched my imagination of Queens. The properties were more tightly clustered together, apartment blocks mixed with smaller houses with wooden frontage. Overhead wires crisscrossed the street.

Bernie stopped in his tracks, lowered his gun, and clamped his other hand over his mouth. I jogged to his side and followed his line of vision.

Two bodies lay by the entrance of a small, scruffy house, its gray paint peeled away from the wooden exterior and weeds dominating the small garden. The first was an old lady who must have had her head repeatedly smashed against the step. Blood stained the concrete around her barely recognizable face. The second, a man, hung by his neck from the door handle. He must have used his own brown leather belt.

"Guys, keep moving," Jack ordered as he approached, but I noticed something flicker behind a curtain in the house.

I pointed my gun at the window. "I think there's somebody in there."

"Which is why we should go."

Bernie moved away from the house and ducked behind a van. "I agree with Jack. Let's get the hell out of here."

I held my position and watched the window, wondering if the old couple owned the place. Houses in that kind of state in Manchester usually belonged to students. The elderly had more pride in appearance.

"We're only a couple of minutes away from Bernie's place. Why bother?" Jack said.

I still had some hope that we would find sane people who hadn't transformed into living nightmares. A sprinkling of survivors or other plane passengers might be around, although the chances were pretty slim.

"We're not here to hurt you," I called out. "It's safe to come out."

I received no reply. Maybe I'd imagined it, or the curtain had just fluttered in the breeze. I sighed and followed Bernie away.

"Please, come and help me," a young girl's voice cried out.

Jack trained his rifle on the house. "Well done, brother. How do we deal with this one?"

"Come out with your hands in the air," I said.

"I'm scared. Please help me," the high-pitched voice replied.

We looked at each other, waiting for somebody to speak. I knelt in the middle of the road and focused on the house. A small figure flicked past a window.

"We're all armed, right? Why should we be scared of a little girl?" Bernie said.

I waved Bernie forward. He staggered across the road and crouched next to me. "You open the door, Jack, and I will cover. Let's be quick about it."

"Why me? Why don't *you* open the door?"

I waved the Glock. "Jump right out of the way once you do it. We'll take it from there."

Bernie rose with a groan and crept up to the front entrance. He untied the man from the handle and hauled him to one side before looking back at us. "You guys ready?"

Jack and I had advanced and stood in the weeds, aiming at the entrance.

"Go for it," I said.

Bernie screwed up his face and put a finger to his lips as he slowly twisted the handle down. It looked like bad acting, but adrenaline and nerves can do strange things to people. The door opened a couple of inches. Bernie kicked it wide open.

I peered at the empty entrance hall. A Persian rug covered most of the varnished floorboards. Bernie pressed himself against the wall by the side of the door and looked back at me. I shook my head. He stooped down and slowly craned his head around the doorframe.

A little girl in a red-and-white-checked dress sprang out and smashed a plate on the top of Bernie's head. The kind of thing I laughed at on YouTube a couple of days ago, today it had no funny side. She retreated a couple of yards, skidded to her knees, and picked up a cheese knife.

Jack ran forward and kicked her in the arm. She buckled against the staircase, dropped the knife, and attempted to escape on all fours. Bernie picked her up. She screamed and squirmed under his arm. Blood trickled from the top of his head and rolled down his cheek.

Bernie turned and glared at me. "I'm leaving you to fix this shit."

I frantically tried to think of a less obvious solution. "Give me a minute."

The girl sank her teeth into Bernie's forearm. He gasped and forcefully readjusted his grip. "So much for zero tolerance."

None of us had had this in mind when we'd agreed on our approach.

"I'll search the house. Find a place we can secure her."

Jack guarded the entrance and scanned the street through his sights. I scrambled up the stairs and flung doors open to every mildew-smelling room, hoping to find a lockable door. The bathroom had one, but internal—no use.

I clambered down the stairs. The girl pleaded with Bernie and Jack. "Please, let me go. Please? I promise to run away—you'll never see me again."

Nobody proposed the obvious way to deal with her. Jack offered an alternative. "Let's put her in the recycling bin at the side of the house."

"You want to put her in a garbage can?" Bernie said.

"We can't take her with us, can we? If we put her in the bin and she cries out, she might attract another killer." Jack positioned himself in front of her face. "If I were her, I'd keep quiet to stay alive. She'll be able to escape soon enough by rocking about. By then, we'll be long gone."

The inventive idea saved us from making a potentially terrible decision. By normal standards it seemed cruel. But children didn't usually go around smashing plates over heads or trying to gut people with a cheese knife.

"No, no, you can't do this to me!" she cried and desperately kicked her legs.

Bernie carried her around to the side of the house. Jack opened the bin, and Bernie dropped her into the large plastic container, slammed the lid, and rested his elbows on it. I found two concrete blocks among the weeds and placed them on top to slow down her escape time, and we walked cautiously back to the road. The bin rattled a couple of times, but nobody turned back.

"Straight to your apartment, Bernie. No more messing around," I said.

———

Bernie gave us an accurate description of his apartment. Solidly built, at the bottom of a block, with blind-covered windows, below street level. His thick, hardwood door had a five-point locking system and would be impenetrable to anything other than heavy force. It provided the right kind of protection for us to finally relax.

Linda had designed the apartment to be neat and simple—although that was only my assumption. The kitchen and living area were both part of one long room, with a separate bathroom and bedroom toward the back. For some reason, I'd imaged Bernie to be wealthy. I had no basis for my belief, apart from the fact that he and Linda wore expensive clothes. The two black leather couches in the living room looked inviting compared to the cold vinyl floor of the police building. I resisted the temptation to flop down on one and close my eyes.

I checked my watch. Nearly midday on Saturday morning. So much for a short trip from the airport. I felt like I'd been in New York for three days rather than twenty hours.

Bernie stared at a picture on the wall, of Linda and him on a beach. I stood by his shoulder. "Where was that taken?"

"Fort Lauderdale in 2008. Best holiday we ever had." He sighed. "Are you married?"

"Only to my job. I seem to naturally repel women."

He shrugged. "There's someone for everyone out there."

"You both look happy. At least you can cherish those memories. That's what we all have to do," I said, immediately regretting my horribly clichéd remark.

He let out a heavy sigh and trudged to the kitchen area. "I suppose you want something to eat and a drink?"

"Now you're talking," Jack said. He stretched out on a couch and took off his boots. The sickly sweet smell of his walking socks started to challenge the clean wooden odor of Bernie's apartment for supremacy.

I shifted Jack's legs to one side and flopped down next to him. Bernie went through his cupboards. He stopped and turned. "Guys, I'm beat. What say we get a few hours' sleep and eat later?"

Feeling safe and hearing Bernie talk of sleep, I felt a small release and yawned. "Good idea."

He closed the cupboards and went to his bedroom. I moved to the opposite couch; its leather creaked as I sank into it. Jack plumped a cushion and used it as a pillow. He quickly began to snore. I tossed and turned for a couple of hours, playing events through my head, before eventually dropping off.

———

Footsteps passed me. My eyes slammed open. Outside, natural light had already started to fade, meaning I must have slept for six hours. Bernie reflexively flicked on a light, illuminating the kitchen area.

"Have you tried the TV?" I asked.

"You're awake. No, didn't want to disturb you."

Jack yawned and stretched his arms over his head. "Time is it?"

I walked over and picked up the remote. "Quarter to eight. Had a good kip?"

"Grand. Slept like a log. Got anything to drink, Bernie?"

"Sure. Coffee?"

Jack held up his thumb and pulled himself into a sitting position.

I switched on the TV and flicked through the channels. Nothing. I tried the digital radio but again received no transmission.

"You got Internet access?" I said.

"Yeah, but isn't the network down?"

"The mobile network. We can try to access the Internet if you've got a cable connection."

Bernie stiffly waddled to a desk behind the couches and switched on a computer. On his way back to the kitchen, he dropped a bottle of vodka in Jack's lap and said, "Enjoy."

"Thanks, Bernie," Jack said. "I'll get a couple of glasses. Harry, fire up the 'net. I'll join you in a minute."

I opened up a browser while Jack opened the vodka. All of the major news sites loaded, but none had updated since lunchtime yesterday. A dead end.

Jack dropped a shot glass next to me and pulled the keyboard toward him.

He logged into Twitter and found more tweets from strangers. They had a sinister feel, now that we knew the intention behind them.

@claretmills: Jack, I'm a sexy lady who is dying to show you a good time in New York. Let's hook up. Direct message me.

@pizzalover23: Hope you have a good time in the Big Apple. Interested in some free Yankees tickets? Meet me at Port Jervis train station.

@bcat1975: You have been invited to a surprise party. Details will be provided at 4 pm on the corner of 27th and 8th.

Jack searched for "New York," and we read through the tweets. Quite a few recent ones were from people who claimed to be at JFK, asking for information and assistance. With no mobile coverage at the airport, I wondered if it had become a killing ground. A mutual place for crazies to meet up and have a final duel.

"How can we spot a genuine message?" I asked.

"I'll type in 'Newark' and check for recent tweets. We can look at the profiles of the ones that sound like they know the shit's hit the fan," Jack said.

We knew from the pilot that two planes had landed at Newark, and those passengers made it off on foot. It would just be a case of hoping some of them had the same Twitter addiction as Jack and had found a computer to tweet.

We found a number of updates from just after landing, but nothing since. Only one user stood out from the generically sly crowd.

@LeaAsh: Landed at Newark. What's happening? Help us, we are stuck at Newark.

Jack clicked on the profile. I expected it to be like all the rest and that I'd see no further updates, but there were three more tweets, two posted today.

@LeaAsh: Managed to make it into NY City. Please, please, get in contact with the army or whoever. New York's under attack, there's no one left.

@LeaAsh: There's 3 of us in a Manhattan apartment. I am not giving our location away, but we need help.

@LeaAsh: Is there anybody out there who isn't trying to kill me? #GA

"Send her one of those direct messages, Jack, quickly."

"I can't. She has to be following me to be able to do that."

I thought for a few seconds. "Tell her that three of us are coming to Manhattan tomorrow, we're currently in an outer borough, and arrived on a flight into JFK yesterday afternoon."

Jack raised his eyebrows. "Are we going to Manhattan tomorrow?"

"Depends if we get a reply."

"Why risk traveling in the open? I'll ask her to follow me so we can get more info."

Jack @Swankey1974 to @LeaAsh: Also a group of three but arrived on a JFK flight. We are in Queens at the moment.

Jack @Swankey1974 to @LeaAsh: Please follow me so we can direct message. What have you got to lose? What have any of us?

We watched for the next ten minutes, naïvely expecting an immediate response, more in hope than expectation. The best we could really wish for was a response before tomorrow morning, unless Lea Ash had herself glued to a screen, which seemed improbable.

"Ready to eat," Bernie called from the kitchen.

"What about those Marlboros you've hidden in a drawer somewhere?" Jack asked.

"I've never allowed smoking in my apartment . . ." He ran his finger along the kitchen counter before bumping his fist against it. "To hell with it. Just let me eat first."

Jack and I sat on the same couch. Bernie handed us each a bowl of lukewarm baked beans. "Bernie, you really know how to roll out the red carpet," Jack said.

Bernie withdrew Jack's bowl from his outstretched hand. "You don't have to eat it, you ungrateful prick."

"I'm sorry, Bernie. I didn't mean . . ." Jack stammered and trailed off.

I believed Bernie's anger for a moment, until I caught the older man's sly smile as he turned to grab his own serving. He had pulled Jack's leg in return and had done it quite well.

After our dinner, Jack slid three cigarettes out of the packet. It turned out that all of us had smoked at some point in the past. Jack and I had smoked in the army. As an impressionable young man, I'd wanted to fit in. A stupid thing to do. I'd had to force myself to like it during the first couple of days of inhaling, while coughing my guts up. Forcing myself into an unpleasant addiction seemed baffling with the benefit of hindsight.

Bernie said he sometimes had an occasional sneaky one, but not for a year because Linda hated it. We sat smoking in companionable silence, apparently lost in our own thoughts.

Jack used a bean can as an ashtray and poured us all a large vodka. The last one for me; if we were to visit Manhattan tomorrow, I wanted a clear head.

"If we receive a reply, are we going?" I said.

Bernie reached over and crushed his cigarette against the side of the can. "We're safe here. Why put ourselves at risk? They could be dead by sunrise."

"If we can find three more people and get everyone armed, we'll have a strong group," I said. "Maybe we can secure a building with plenty of supplies? As we are, the three of us would struggle to hold a place with more than one door."

"Imagine the state of Manhattan? Full of danger, corpses, and killers. There're a few local stores a couple of blocks away."

"Let's at least consider the option if we get a response. If we get no reply, we stay here."

I collected the bean juice–stained white bowls and took them to the sink.

"Come on, Bernie," Jack said. "If it's too dangerous, we come straight back. At least give us a chance to meet another survivor and check for our mates."

Bernie massaged his temples, which made his mustache bob up and down. "Think one moment about how many killers we could be exposing ourselves to. Thousands of windows look down on those streets. All anyone would need is a gun and a bit of patience."

"If we don't get a reply, none of this matters," I said.

Bernie and Jack continued to debate the issue. I logged in to my gmail account and sent a couple emails home, in hope of a reply, rather than letting them know I survived. I used Bernie's landline but got voicemail for Andy and Dave. I returned to the couch with a glass of water.

A few hours' sleep, food, and a feeling of safety had a loosening effect on my concerns, and I started speculating on the motivation behind the attack.

"Maybe this is the result of a secretly developed weapon. If you wanted to destroy your enemies, would there be a better way to do it? Divide and conquer. You get to keep your hands clean while they wipe themselves out. An invasion afterward would simply be a case of rounding up stragglers."

"Why not just get people to kill themselves? Why bother making them kill somebody else first?" Jack asked.

"Maybe to ensure those who avoid the effects get taken too? Or to bump off anyone incapable of finding a way to complete their own mission?"

The more I thought about it, the more it seemed like a chillingly effective idea to spread. Who were the architects of doom?

Bernie sat forward, his gut hanging below his belt. "How would the terrorists keep themselves immune?"

I shrugged. "Maybe they all got into planes or had an antidote? Perhaps they didn't expose their own geographic area. Wherever that might be."

"The Middle-East."

Jack slammed down his vodka and poured another glass. I hoped he didn't intend to get blottoed. He exhaled in satisfaction and said, "I hadn't thought about an invasion before. Maybe it's the Chinese."

We chatted for hours, going around in circles. We all agreed that events like this couldn't be an accident. Who did it, how they did it, and what they planned to do next remained a mystery. Around one in the morning, Jack suggested that we all get some sleep, and Bernie and I agreed. I stretched out on one of the couches and closed my eyes.

———

Jack nudged me awake.

"Get up. We've got a reply!"

I felt disoriented for a few seconds but quickly recognized Bernie's apartment and heard Jack behind me, tapping on a keyboard. Sunlight shone through the cracks in the blinds.

I pulled on my boots and joined him at the computer. "What does it say?"

He turned the monitor toward me. I knelt down and gazed at the screen.

Bernie yawned after appearing at his bedroom in a white tank top and briefs. He plodded over and peered at the monitor.

Direct messages from @LeaAsh: Where did you fly from? How can we trust you? There are only 2 of us now.

Bernie snorted. "How do we know we can trust her? She could be anyone."

"We don't know," I said. "Maybe whoever it is will know where the other passengers from Newark are heading. An organized group would have a far better chance of fighting off the killers' attacks."

He narrowed his eyes and leaned toward me. "A larger group provides a bigger target."

If he intended to intimidate me, he failed. I put it down to Bernie still being tired, stressed, and cut up over Linda.

"True, but let's try one more message." I sat at the computer and hit the reply button. "Bernie, where can we see each other from a reasonably safe distance?"

"The Queensboro Bridge, I suppose. It's close to here and heads into Manhattan. If they don't show, we come back here. Deal?"

Jack smiled. "So you're in?"

He let out an exaggerated groan and headed back to his bedroom. "Whatever."

Direct messages to @LeaAsh: We left Manchester, England. You'll have to trust us as much as we will you. Come to Queensboro Bridge at 11. We'll be on the other side.

We had three hours to eat, wash, prepare, and get to the bridge. I usually showered every day as part of my routine picked up in the army, although I didn't shave as regularly, now that I didn't risk a fine or extra duties.

I waited impatiently outside the bathroom door for Bernie to finish. He appeared after five minutes with a towel around his neck, thin slivers of shaving foam around his ears, and stinking of Old Spice, clearly his favorite brand. I didn't have the heart to tell him it had become a bit of a joke in England. Grandad's aftershave.

Splashing fragrant, soapy water over my body and face had a positive effect. The same type I got while taking a shower after a mountain climb or game of football. I toweled myself down, carried my clothes in bundle to the bedroom, and checked Bernie's wardrobe for a clean shirt. Unfortunately, Bernie was a few sizes smaller, and no matter how hard it got, I refused to wear his underpants. I reluctantly climbed back into my old clothes and returned to the living area.

Jack had already commandeered the bathroom. Noises of splashing and banging about echoed through the door.

Bernie warmed up beans in a pan and brewed coffee. I sat on the couch and flicked through a baseball magazine. As a massive sports fan, I had planned to watch the Mets on our trip.

Bernie brought me a cup of coffee and a steaming bowl of beans. "Enjoy."

"Cheers." I scooped a spoonful and swallowed. The bean juice tasted far sweeter in the States, and I liked it. "I didn't realize you had these for breakfast."

"We don't. They've been in the cupboard for months. Got them for a barbeque that didn't happen. That's a long story."

"You'll have to tell me one day."

Bean juice dripped down his yellow Nike polo shirt after he shoveled a large spoonful into his mouth. I nodded at his chest. He looked down and held out the shirt. "Ah, shit."

He disappeared to the bedroom, cursing under his breath.

I began to think that Bernie might have been right after all. What if we could sit the whole thing out in his apartment? The symptoms people were suffering might not last forever. At least here, we had warm food, relative safety, and no need to risk our safety unless we were getting supplies.

Jack came out from the bathroom with damp hair; he swiped his beans and coffee from the kitchen counter and took them to the computer.

Bernie sat back down in a brown Ping polo shirt with a section of paper towels stuffed down his neck, a makeshift napkin. I wondered if he played golf, but avoided bringing up the subject. Golfers usually bored me to tears. I liked my action fast and furious.

Jack spun in the swivel chair. "We've got a reply. Says they'll try to get there."

Bernie and I bumped into each other as we quickly got up and headed for the computer. I stared over Jack's shoulder at the on-screen message.

Direct messages from @LeaAsh: Try to make it. See you @11.

"I'm still not sure about this, guys," Bernie said.

"It's a risk, but I think we need to find other people," I said.

Jack kicked himself around to face Bernie. "We have two potentially important people here. They may know more than we do."

I grabbed his shoulder and rocked it. "Come on, Bernie, we've gotta go for it."

He rolled his shoulder away. "Do I have a choice?"

———

Just before ten in the morning, we stood in the hallway of Bernie's apartment block. After readying our weapons and carrying out an equipment check inside, we were ready to move out. I prepared myself mentally for the next few hours, knowing that we could encounter a hostile force or individual.

Bernie led us down a long residential street toward Queens Boulevard. A row of symmetrical three-story houses ran along one side. I loved the design of the roof wrapped around the upper story—very efficient. Queens Boulevard led straight to the bridge that Bernie had identified for our meeting place.

I spun after hearing a noise. A red curtain flapped out of a broken window.

"Don't even think about it," Jack said.

A mass pile-up had taken place at the stop where we arrived at the boulevard. We turned left along the sidewalk and followed it for three hundred yards, until the road appeared to open up again. At the head of the pile-up, the cars were too mangled to drive, but fifty yards further up the road, I identified a pickup. We approached cautiously and found it empty, with the keys in the ignition.

Bernie scratched his head while looking inside the cabin. "Isn't it slightly suspicious?"

"What do you mean?" Jack asked.

The smashed cars, debris, and bodies all around us were a contrast to the clean interior. Although I thought *suspicious* was a wrong choice of word. I would have said *different*. "Come on, Bernie. You drive—let's keep moving."

Bernie heaved himself behind the wheel, twisted the key, and the engine roared into life. He crunched into gear and smoothly pulled away, weaving through cars and over bodies. Jack and I aimed from the back and side windows.

After rumbling along for twenty minutes and nudging two cars out of way, we arrived within sight of the bridge.

Vehicles were packed together tightly leading up to the bridge, but we made enough progress and had time on our side. We'd left Bernie's with enough time to briskly walk to the bridge, if required, so we still had thirty minutes to wait until our meeting at eleven.

I suggested that we stay in the car for the next twenty-five minutes instead of drawing attention to ourselves by walking around. Bernie turned off the engine, and we ducked.

Bernie nudged me in the back. "Ten minutes. That's all we wait."

I sighed. "Okay, Bernie, chill out."

"I'm not happy with this," Jack said. "We can't see anyone coming."

He sat up and lolled his head to one side, keeping his eyes open, playing dead.

None of us spoke as we waited to move. I watched the second hand of my watch make sixteen revolutions.

A shadow passed in front of the pickup. I glanced up. A sheet of newspaper floated over the hood and drifted harmlessly away.

Bernie drummed his fingers against the wheel.

"Stop it," Jack said.

This felt almost as bad as the police building at JFK.

Gunfire rattled in the distance. Miles away.

Bernie sat up. "Let's move out."

I jumped out, and my boots thudded against ground. Bernie and Jack joined me at the front of the pickup, and we crept between vehicles toward the bridge.

From this point, I had a stunning view of the Manhattan skyline set against a clear blue sky. An unnatural number of birds seemed to be swooping around the buildings, possibly scavenging a new food source.

As we approached the point of the bridge where it began to cross the East River, we stopped and took cover behind a yellow taxi.

Bernie peered over the hood to get a view of the bridge. I joined him while Jack sat with his back to the taxi, covering the rear. In the distance across the bridge, an engine revved.

Jack switched his attention to the bridge and aimed his rifle over the top of the vehicle. "Reckon it's a signal?"

"A signal? It's a pretty dumb one if it is," Bernie said.

I wasn't ready to give up hope just yet. I looked through the maze of cars but couldn't see anything approaching. "Let's play it out, Bernie."

The engine noise grew louder.

"It's there," Jack shuffled to one side and pointed along the left lane. "Coming right this way."

"How many in the car?" Bernie asked.

"I can't see. It's about one hundred yards away, coming in slow," Jack said, and he ducked between us. "What's the plan?"

Bernie kept his gaze fixed on the trunk. "Jump out, weapons pointed at the windshield?"

"No," I said, conscious that we had to make a quick decision and kicking myself for not thinking about it sooner. "They might shoot first and ask questions later. Let's give them a chance to see us first, but keep our weapons ready."

"And if it's a killer?" Bernie asked.

Jack tapped the stock of his rifle. "Then I put an early end to his mission with this."

We stood up and moved into a gap between two cars in the middle of the road. I caught a few brief glimpses of a silver car weaving toward us.

It stopped around fifty yards from our position and flashed its headlights three times, acknowledging our presence. Then it continued forward, sun glaring off its windshield.

Within thirty yards, I saw two people in the car. It disappeared again to make its way around a van. I ran toward the car and reached the driver's window, keeping my gun behind my back. A red-haired man with a goatee beard, wearing a pink T-shirt, sat in the driver's seat. Beside him was a female passenger who rested her elbow on the window frame and looked in the opposite direction. The driver's window wound down about four inches.

I leaned forward. "Lea Ash?"

A hunting knife shot through the gap and stopped an inch from my eye.

The driver's clenched hand wedged in the gap, just too small to fit through. I skidded back, dropped to one knee, and aimed. "What the fuck are you doing?"

The car reversed back. Smoke drifted from its wheels as they screeched against the surface and spun forward. It hurtled toward me at lightning speed. I dived out of the way, and the car slammed into another vehicle.

I rolled and aimed, ready to fire.

A shot split the air. The driver's window splintered after a round punctured it.

The driver collapsed forward, his head landing on the horn. It let off a continuous blast of noise. Jack jogged up to the car, put his hand through the window, and pushed the driver's head away from the wheel.

Footsteps slapped behind me. Bernie appeared by my side. "What the fuck just happened?"

I twisted around and looked at the silver car.

"He tried to kill Harry," Jack said as he reloaded the rifle.

"What about the woman?" I asked.

"You mean the dead woman? I followed you and went to the other side of the car. By the time I worked it out, he'd already made his move."

Feeling confused, I approached the passenger window. Inside, the woman looked blankly out of the car with her elbow on the window frame. I nudged her. Stiff as a board, probably dead for hours.

This killer used cunning and knowledge of the situation in his attempt to attack us, which meant these people were conscious of their instructions and could plan how to achieve them. Bernie had little doubt about what had happened after looking through the car.

"Meet Lea Ash. Just like the others. Back to my place, guys."

This time I had no complaints. The shot and horn could have been heard for miles around. After our incident, the safety of Bernie's apartment seemed like our own little paradise in this horrible world.

"Back to your place, Bernie, no stopping," Jack said.

We ran back to the pickup, and Bernie started to weave his way back toward Elmhurst. I watched for signs of movement out of the window but inwardly cursed the failure of our mission. It didn't take long to arrive back at the vehicle blockade. We checked our weapons again and headed onto the street, Bernie in the lead, Jack bringing up the rear.

We took an alternative route to Bernie's in case anyone had followed and now lay in wait for our return. I'd learned in the Army that routine killed. If you followed the same patrol route every day, it wouldn't take long for a watching enemy to work it out and set up a trap.

A shot split the air. A puff of dust spat from the road about two yards in front of me.

Something moved in my peripheral vision. "Quick! Behind the car."

I dashed in the opposite direction and dropped behind a BMW. Jack joined me and looked through its windows to the opposite side of the road. "Did you see anything?"

"Other side of the road, didn't get a good look," I said and peered over the hood at a quiet row of two-story houses.

Bernie rushed around the trunk and flopped to the ground. He looked at me and said through gritted teeth, "I've fucking had enough of this."

I glanced around the side of the BMW. The girl we'd trapped in the recycling bin jumped out from behind a mailbox. She pointed a pistol toward us with both hands and fired again. The round smacked into the BMW's front tire. It quickly deflated with a loud hiss.

"It's the girl from before," I said.

Bernie peeped through the windows and quickly ducked. "She's coming over. We need to do something."

Jack's hands trembled as he shouldered his rifle. "I can't, I can't . . . fuck. Fuck!"

Another shot thudded into the car's body. Bernie grabbed my arm. "Shoot her. Do it."

Jack and I exchanged looks. He slowly nodded. "I'm going to hell for this."

He stood up and fired. I heard a faint squeal. His right knee buckled, and he fell back against the BMW's back wheel.

"Did you get her?" Bernie asked.

"Why don't you see for yourself?" Jack said in a low voice.

Both Bernie and I stood. Her body lay about ten yards away. I looked back down at Jack, who stared into space.

Bernie extended his hand to Jack and hauled him up. "Back to my place, before anyone else shows."

We jogged straight for the apartment with a desperate need for safety. Within minutes, we crashed through the main entrance and stood outside the door.

Bernie opened it, and we piled through before slamming it shut. Jack slumped on the couch, and Bernie started making coffee. I couldn't relax and paced around. Nobody spoke for two minutes.

I eventually sat next to Jack. "You did the right thing back there."

"It's done. I want to forget it."

He looked away and started thumbing his phone. I'd noticed earlier in the morning that his battery had died.

5
TEMPTATIONS

We had landed at JFK forty-eight hours ago, but it felt like weeks. I'd witnessed and experienced enough horror in two days to last several lifetimes. If we didn't get some control back, I knew we wouldn't make it another two days, with killers ready to hide, deceive, and attack us.

Jack hadn't said a word for the last hour. He seemed troubled after the shooting this morning, and I could understand why. I had to take my share of tough jobs, and Bernie needed to get armed with more than a flare gun.

"I usually have a full Sunday dinner," I half-joked when he handed me another bowl of baked beans. I wondered what kind of barbeque he'd planned with the amount of cans he had.

"We usually went to the movies on Sunday afternoon," Bernie said. His shoulders drooped and he returned to the kitchen.

I decided to change the subject. Not for the sake of cheering Jack or Bernie up, but to get them talking, to distract them from their grief. "Did you have a job before?"

Bernie sat opposite me with a bowl of pineapple chunks balanced on his knee. "Been a plumber for the last thirty years and built up a pretty strong business locally. I had twelve employees on the books and was starting to take things easy.

"Less hours and more social?"

"Got a place in Orange County, and for the last few years we'd started to travel overseas. I can't see the phone ringing anytime soon, so that's me, retired. What about you two?"

"We both spent time in the army. Jack in the infantry, I worked in comms. For the last five years we've run a landscaping business, but as you say, we're retired. Any hobbies?"

He swallowed a large spoonful of chunks without chewing. Juice ran down his chin. "Spending time with Linda. We would eat out, go to the movies, and watch the Yankees. Nothing special, but we were happy."

"Used a gun before?"

He shook his head. "Don't need one in New York."

I smiled at his response. If we came across anyone expecting to be rescued and led to a safety zone by three members of Delta Force, they were going to be sorely disappointed. All we could offer at the moment was a bowl of baked beans in a basement apartment and some speculative arguments.

I looked beyond him at a sparsely populated open kitchen cupboard. "How much food you got left?"

"A couple more meals. Who stocks up before going on holiday?"

"Let's get stocked up so we don't have to move. We can also find you a gun." I paused and waited for Bernie's reaction.

"I haven't seen you kill anyone yet," he replied, maintaining eye contact.

"It's not a competition, Bernie; we all need to be armed if we're going to stay alive," I said.

Jack sat quietly at the computer and fiddled with the mouse.

"Are you up for a trip to get some food and drink, Jack?" I asked.

"Yeah, whatever," he said without a hint of enthusiasm.

I stepped over and put my arm around him. "Found any new updates?"

"Same old shit from a couple of days ago."

"You checked Twitter?"

He sighed, sluggishly typed in the address, and logged in.

Jack bolted upright after seeing a direct message.

Direct messages from @LeaAsh: We were on our way there and saw a man on the bridge get into a car. We hung around for a few minutes and heard a shot. Are you ok? We want to get out of the city. What's your location?

I gestured Bernie over. "What do you make of this?"

He squinted at the screen. "Could be a killer. They just didn't get to us first."

"Why didn't she try to take out the other killer on the bridge?" I snapped.

"Fine," Bernie said. He moved to within an inch of my face and glared into my eyes. "One more chance, but I'm not going near Manhattan. Your friends are dead, just like Linda."

I hadn't even been thinking about Andy and Dave. I'd already given them up. Bernie maintained his position, daring me to make a move. Without wanting the argument to escalate, I backed away and turned to Jack. "What do you think?"

"We could give them a general location and keep an eye out."

"Send them for supplies, then give our address." Bernie said.

"That's not a great way to meet," I said. "I prefer Jack's plan."

Jack typed out:

Direct messages from @Jack: That was us on the bridge. A car came over to our side, and the driver had a corpse in the passenger seat, so be careful.

Come to Elmhurst and make contact. We have a safe place and are just going to get some supplies.

"We can't all fit in here," Bernie said.

Jack screwed his face and swung to face Bernie. "They won't be expecting the fucking Ritz-Carlton, Bernie. Besides, I'm not sure if it serves bowls of baked beans for lunch."

I bit my tongue. We needed to be a cohesive unit.

Bernie sat down on the couch. "I'm not taking shit from you about my food. You're choosing when we get to the store."

"I choose and cook, no worries," I said.

"Any gun shops around here?" Jack asked.

"I wouldn't even know where the nearest is. We could go to the Shoprite. It's only three blocks away, and we can get there without attracting any attention."

Jack tilted his head. "The Shoprite?"

Bernie smiled. "The local supermarket."

———

Just after four o'clock, on Sunday afternoon, I stepped outside Bernie's block and swept my gun around the area. I knew we were taking a risk, but staying inside after this morning would be giving up, and we needed supplies. We had to tackle the situation head on and get control.

Jack and Bernie followed. I knelt by a lamppost until they caught up. "Keep quiet, hug the shadows of buildings, and stay alert."

Bernie pointed forward. "This way."

He crossed the street and kept in the shadows of apartment blocks. The sun continued to beat down, which would only speed up the decay. The stench increased by the hour and would only get worse in the next few days.

Within minutes, he stopped and nodded across the street. "That's the place."

"How many entry points?" I asked.

"Not a hundred percent sure. One front entrance. I've never planned to raid it."

I imagined Bernie holding the place up with a plunger and suppressed a smile.

Outside the store entrance, a dog licked a woman's head. A bloodied hammer lay by her side.

I patted the sidewalk a couple of times to attract the dog's attention. "Here boy, here . . ."

The dog looked up and ran away; at least it didn't have a murderous obsession.

I put a finger to my lips and crossed the street in a low run, to the front of the store. Listened for any sound, looked down the street in either direction. After twenty seconds, I waved the other two over.

Bernie bowled straight through the store's entrance and almost immediately sprang back out. "Somebody's in there."

I aimed at the window and took a couple of paces back.

"Did you see them?" Jack asked.

"No, I heard them. Sounded in poor shape."

Whatever their condition, they knew we were outside. I had to make a snap decision. "Bernie, cover us with the flare gun. We'll clear the store."

"I know the layout, so I'll go first. Harry, you cover us from behind."

I begrudgingly swapped weapons with Bernie and planned to retrieve the girl's pistol as soon as we finished our shopping expedition. Nobody had wanted to approach the body earlier, but holding a flare gun suddenly amped up the priority.

"Now," Jack said, as he pulled open the door. Both Jack and Bernie vanished inside.

I tensed, waiting to hear gunshots, and readied myself to follow into a fight.

With my back to the store, glancing in both directions at hundreds of apartment windows, I shivered at the thought of watching eyes.

"Clear," Jack eventually called.

An electronic tone beeped above the door as I entered. Somebody had trashed the place. Shelves of food spilled in every direction. I found Jack and Bernie standing over a man, surrounded by canned vegetables and packet mixes. His hands were clasped around a broken bottle that protruded from his eye.

He raised a knee and groaned. "Is she? Is she? Help me, the bottle . . . Finish it."

"What do you want?" Bernie asked.

I looked down at the man and swallowed hard. The difference between us was a plane ticket. "He wants us to help him complete his mission."

"Grab my hands . . . push the bottle."

"There's nothing we can do for him," Jack said.

"Perhaps we should help him?" Bernie looked at me.

"Fill our bags and reconvene here, okay?"

I hoped the man died while we filled bags with food. I packed cans of soup, chili, fruit, and some bottles of cola into two plastic bags. Bernie and Jack stood over the man when I returned, each with a full bag of groceries.

The man moaned and twisted on his side. "Please, end it."

Bernie pointed the Glock at the man's head and closed his eyes.

"Don't do it, Bernie," I said.

He didn't need this kind of kill on his conscience. I wondered if he knew the man.

Tears welled in Bernie's eyes. "I can't leave him to die like this. I can't."

I moved toward him, placed my hand on the outstretched Glock, and eased it down. "Don't do something you might regret."

"Fuck this," Jack said.

He stamped on the bottle, forcing it deeper into the eye socket. A thick purple stream of blood ran down the side of the man's face. He let out a long breath, and his head flopped to the left.

Bernie looked over at Jack with fear in his eyes. Jack picked up his shopping bags and headed for the entrance. His action concerned me, and I decided to keep a closer eye on him.

Jack looked over his shoulder. "We need to stop debating and start making decisions."

Jack ended the man's suffering and gave him what he wanted, but it still didn't sit easily with me. Realistically, the man had carried no kind of threat, so we should have left him alone. All lines of morality were blurred because of the situation we found ourselves in. In the store, Jack had firmly crossed one, and I worried about his mental state.

As we made our way back to the apartment, Bernie kept his distance from Jack. I walked with the older man to try and quell any doubts he might have about my brother. This was like one of his pub fights, but on a nuclear scale. We needed to stick together.

As we neared his apartment, I had an idea. "What's the view like from the roof?"

"Pretty good. Why?"

"It's time to get a handle on our situation."

Jack heard us and closed in. "What are you thinking?"

"We need a diversion, some way of attracting attention. If killers turn up and take each other out, away from us, all the better."

"What's that gotta do with the roof?" Bernie said.

"We choose a distant location," I said. "Find a car and turn on some loud music. We can watch what happens from relative safety, observe patterns of behavior and keep them away from here."

"You want to draw killers to Queens?" Bernie asked.

"Will anyone hear the music outside of a few blocks away?" Jack said.

I stopped them both to explain further. "We observe an area a reasonable distance away for a couple of hours. Run down, create the signal, come back, and watch what happens from the safety of the roof."

"Why bother?" Bernie said. "We can lay low in the apartment."

We reached the hallway, and Jack gazed at the stairs. "We create a loud enough noise for the local area. I'm going up to take a look."

"Steady on, Jack," I said. "Dump this first and take our time."

We dropped our supplies in Bernie's apartment and reconvened to the elevator. Bernie pressed a circular silver button; nothing happened.

He fingered the button repeatedly, as if playing a retro athletics computer game.

"I thought this might happen," I said.

Jack ran back to Bernie's apartment. Moments later he appeared at the door. "Just tried the computer. Same thing."

I had wondered how long we'd have electricity with an unmaintained system.

With communications to the outside world gone, we were on our own, and it also probably meant an end to our hopes of meeting Lea Ash. I just hoped the rest of our family was safe and didn't face the same problems. I needed to remain focused, but thoughts of my father among this kind of carnage gnawed at me.

"Probably need to grab as much fresh supplies as possible," Jack said. "Stuff's going to ruin pretty quickly."

"You got any camping gear, Bernie?" I asked.

"Got some candles. I know a place where we might get a stove," Bernie replied.

We trudged up the stairs, discussing what the possible effects of no electricity would be. I remembered hearing that the Hoover

Dam would continue to provide electricity for one hundred years without any human contact, but that obviously didn't extend to New York City.

At the top of eight flights of stairs, Bernie leaned against a blue metal door, peppered with spots of rust, and slid open its heavy latch. It protested against its hinges as it swung open to reveal the roof, about the size of half a football field, with a couple of large air-conditioning units in one corner. We had a great view of the surrounding area. Jack and I sat against the small protective wall running around the perimeter and scanned the immediate vicinity, looking for a potential ambush location.

Jack pointed down to a space between two buildings. "Bernie, what's that?"

"A parking lot for those two stores. Might work, I suppose."

Very workable for what I had in mind. Around half a mile away, and we could see the approach from both sides. "We watch for an hour. If it's all clear, I'll nip down and ramp up the volume in one of the cars."

"Take one of my CDs," Bernie said. "Just in case . . ."

"I had my eye on your Celine Dion already, Bernie—although we might scare people away."

Bernie stared into the distance. "That was Linda's."

"Sorry, Bernie, I didn't know."

"Forget about it."

————

After observing the parking lot and surrounding area for an hour without detecting any signs of life, I decided to hatch the plan. "Jack, you stay on the roof and cover us."

"Might not be accurate from this range, but at least it gives you a warning."

"Good enough. Bernie, you all right with covering my ass?"

"Sure," he said. He rose to his feet and cursed under his breath after seeing a small blob of tar on his cream chinos. "I'll grab the gun too, if it's still here."

We descended the staircase, grabbed the CD, and headed out.

"What made you change your mind about the gun?" I asked.

He gave me a dismissive look. "I need one. Simple as that."

We walked briskly to the scene of the shoot-out. Neither of us said a word as I retrieved the girl's weapon, another Glock. I carried out a make-safe procedure, and checked the magazine. It still contained rounds, so I slid it back into the pistol grip and handed it to Bernie. He rocked it in his hand, feeling the weight, and pulled back the slide. He didn't look inexperienced to me, but I'd question him later on that.

"Follow me," he said.

Seemingly empowered by the Glock, Bernie marched back through the neighborhood to the parking lot. The quiet streets started to take on a familiar feel, but I kept my guard up.

Once there, I shielded my eyes from the sun and looked at the top of our apartment block. Jack waved and I returned the gesture.

"Got one here," Bernie called over from a Honda.

Two corpses lay a few yards away. One strangled, judging by the marks on her neck; the other face down in a pool of her own congealed blood.

Bernie clicked into neutral, twisted the key, and pumped the accelerator. The engine rumbled and smoothly ticked over.

I passed him the CD. "Full blast."

Bernie used the volume control on the steering wheel and clicked to maximum. He fed the CD into the slot, and the stereo smoothly ate the disc.

"My Heart Will Go On," by Celine Dion, belted out of the speakers at an ear-splitting level, taking both of us by surprise.

"Let's get out of here," I said.

As we left the car park, a single gunshot echoed in the distance. I stopped and glanced in both directions. Still quiet, but I changed my mind about our pace.

I grabbed Bernie's wrist and pulled him forward. "Bomb it."

"Bomb what?"

"Run."

Bernie kept up a strong pace that belied his physique. The three minutes we spent running back to his block went past in a blur. My eyes darted from house to vehicle, garbage on the ground, to a bird flapping in the sky. We made it back to the apartment block and crashed through the door.

I bent double with the exertion and gulped for air as my heart tried to thump out of my chest. Bernie leaned against the wall and wiped sweat from his brow. After catching our breath, we trudged up the stairs, back out onto the roof.

I struggled to get my words out to Jack. "Who was it? Where? Did you hit them?"

Bernie appeared through the door and puffed his cheeks. "I'm too old for this shit."

"I didn't see anyone," Jack said. "Think it came from a few blocks to our right."

"So who fired the shot?" Bernie asked.

I collapsed next to Jack. "Who cares if they didn't see us?"

Music drifted over from the distant Honda.

———

Nothing happened for the next hour. The running engine prevented the car battery draining, as long as it had fuel. I looked at the cheap plastic digital watch on Jack's wrist. Quarter past five. Less than three hours of daylight.

Bernie thrust his finger forward. "Down there. By the row of trees."

I scanned along the trees. A man in a white T-shirt stood behind the farthest one, looking around the trunk toward the parking lot. Something glinted in his hand, possibly a knife or a silver gun. He sprinted to a store entrance, craned his head around and looked again. He waited for a minute before cautiously entering the lot. He checked the bodies on the ground, opened the driver's door, and pointed his weapon inside.

"Don't turn the music off," Jack said.

The man didn't adjust the volume. Instead, he crouched behind the car, turning our trap into his trap, exactly what I wanted.

"Working like a charm," Jack said.

Feeling pleased with myself, I turned to Bernie. "What do you—"

He stared at the other side of the parking lot, open mouthed and wide eyed. "Oh, God . . . I think we've fucked up."

"What?" I said and scanned the area below us.

He grabbed my shoulder and pointed down. "Behind the van, over there."

Two people stooped behind a blue van—one male and one female. Both carried guns.

"Bollocks. Let's hope they're just having a look," I said.

"Reckon its Lea Ash?" Jack said.

I shook my head, not as a negative response to Jack's question, more about our plan putting others in danger.

The pair moved behind the next stationary vehicle, around forty yards from the parking lot. Their obvious destination.

"Jack, fire a warning shot," I said.

"We'll compromise ourselves by doing that," Bernie said.

I had to agree. Bringing unwanted attention to our position would risk the relative safety of Bernie's apartment. I didn't have time to run down and head them off, so we had no sensible options.

I looked back to the road. Too late anyway. The man and woman crouched behind a car opposite the lot. I felt helpless as I watched the scene unfold.

The pair slowly entered and headed for the Honda.

I felt responsible and said to Jack, "Sure you can't hit him from here?"

"They're in the line of sight. No chance."

"Come on, come on. He's behind the car. He's behind the car," I murmured to myself.

The woman went to the rear of the vehicle. The man approached the passenger window and peered inside. I took a deep breath.

The man slumped backward with both arms outstretched. The delayed report of a shot echoed up to the roof. The woman remained behind the back of the Honda and hugged the fender. A second shot rang out. She ran around to check on her partner and knelt next to his body. I bowed my head and closed my eyes.

"What do we do now?" Jack asked.

Bernie jabbed me with his finger. "Harry, what do we do?"

I had to do something.

"You two stay here and keep lookout; I'm going to get her. Direct me if she moves. Jack, if you see a killer nearby, hold your rifle above your head with both hands."

Before Bernie or Jack could argue, I ran for the stairs and quickly descended, jumping down three at a time, skidding around corners until I reached the bottom.

Once outside, I sprinted directly toward the parking lot. I knew from our first trip that it took three minutes, and hoped the woman stayed by her dead partner. It seemed unlikely that she would, given that I could still hear the music blaring, but I knew finding her once she went into hiding would be difficult and dangerous, especially on my own.

Just before I reached the parking lot, I looked up at Bernie's apartment block. Jack held his rifle above his head with both arms.

I waved an acknowledgement and raised my gun. Jack pointed toward the trees, the ones where the first killer approached. I quickly moved to the parking lot. The woman knelt about twenty yards away, still by the body of her partner.

"Lea Ash?" I said.

Her head shot up, "Who the fuck are you?"

She raised a silver Beretta and aimed at my face.

I put my finger to my lips and gestured to my left. "There's another coming. Kill the music."

"Stay the fuck back." Her gun shook in her trembling hands. "How do you know?"

"We'll have to do this quickly. Look up there. You see my brother holding a rifle above his head? That means he can see a killer."

"Could be a dummy. Others have tried to fool me before." She stepped toward me, keeping a two-handed grip on her gun. "You don't fool me."

I shot a glance at Jack. He waved frantically and pointed to his left.

"A dummy with two mechanical arms?" I snapped. "Kill me later, but for now, there's danger coming our way."

She followed me with her gun as I jogged straight past her and ducked behind the driver's door. Her partner's body was propped against the rear passenger door with a neat circular wound in his temple, a single stream of blood ran from it, down his neck. I took the revolver out of his limp hand; finding it empty of rounds, I quickly discarded it.

She stepped around the car, keeping me in her sights. "Get your hands where I can see them."

Frustration welled up inside. A killer approached and she wouldn't let me out of her sights. "Get around, now. I could've killed you when I first came here."

I looked back to Jack. He aimed his rifle to the left of the parking lot. If he prepared to compromise our location by firing, an adversary must be close.

Using my moment of distraction, the woman ran around the side of the car and put her Beretta against the side of my head.

"How do you know my name? Are you one of them?" she asked.

I couldn't blame her for acting this way and needed to convince her quickly. "We were the ones on Twitter. I read your messages."

"Were you watching when Chris was shot?" she said.

I ignored her question after hearing footsteps approach.

A large man in a dirty white vest, holding a steel pipe, strode around the corner and paused. He fixed his eyes on Lea and advanced.

He pointed at me. "Don't trust that man, missy, he killed my friend."

He must have heard some of the argument and tried to use it to his advantage.

"Is it true?" she said and bumped the Beretta's muzzle against my cheek.

I thought I might have to shoot both of them. "If I fucking killed his friend, why didn't I kill myself straight afterward?"

"I believe you," she replied without hesitation.

She backed away and aimed her Beretta at me. The man reached within ten yards of her.

"Will you help me kill him?" she asked.

What was she doing?

"Don't do this," I said.

I placed my finger on the trigger and prepared to snap up my hand and fire.

As the man got within five yards of her, he raised the pipe behind his head.

In one crisp movement, Lea spun and shot him in the face. The round passed through his cheek. He collapsed backward and made a strange snorting noise.

We looked at each other. The man continued to snort. I moved over to him, pointed my Glock at his forehead and pulled the trigger, putting him out of his misery.

My trap proved effective, but I stood in the middle of it. Three fresh bodies lay on the ground; one not a killer.

We needed to get out of here. The music and the shots would only attract more. "We've got a safe place. Are you coming or not?"

She glanced back at her fallen partner and sniffed. "Okay, let's go."

As we made our way to Bernie's, I considered giving her more reassurance, but we were still in the open, and the threat level remained high. We reached the building's door that I had foolishly left open after rushing out, and I led her to Bernie's basement apartment.

I took the key from under his doormat and ushered her through his door. "Wait here. I'll grab the other guys."

She wedged her foot in the door as I tried to close it. "Don't leave me on my own, please."

"I'll be back in a few minutes," I said. "Nobody can get through the door once you lock it. I'll knock three times."

I eased her trainer out of the way with my boot and closed the door. The lock snapped. I grabbed the rail and dragged myself up the staircase.

"Where's the girl? What happened?" Bernie said.

I explained events and thanked Jack for the warning.

"I was seconds from taking a shot," he said. "Good thing she did."

"I don't think we can tell Lea she walked into a set-up," I said.

"Why not?" Bernie said. "Our intentions were good. It's not like we knew she would show."

"We told her to come to Elmhurst, and our trap has killed her partner. How would you feel?"

"If I was in her shoes, I'd be pissed off," Jack said, "Let's just say we heard the music and came to the roof for a look."

"Are we all agreed?" I said, looking at Bernie.

He shrugged. "Whatever."

I returned to collect Lea and bring her up to the roof. We still had a couple hours of daylight left to continue to observe the parking lot. I wrapped my knuckles on the door three times on the door.

Lea's voice came from behind it, "Is that you?"

"It's me. Harry. Open up."

The door creaked open. Lea looked either side of me. "You said there were others?"

"Come to the roof. We use the place as a lookout. You'll be safe."

I led her up the stairs; climbing them was starting to feel like Groundhog Day. She silently followed to the top.

Jack and Bernie both stood to greet her. I introduced them, and they warmly shook Lea's hand.

"Sorry about your friend," Jack said.

Lea walked to the edge of the roof and gazed at the parking lot. She sat down with her back against the wall and held her head in her hands. Jack, Bernie, and I looked at each other.

"How long were you watching?" Lea asked.

"Watching what?" Bernie said.

"Where do you think? Did you put the music on?"

A tear dripped from her face. Her immediate interrogation took me by surprise.

"We heard the music and came up here," Jack said. "By the time we saw you, it was too late."

She gave Jack a suspicious look and shook her head. "Too late . . . Right."

"We would have warned you if we could," Bernie said.

"Lea, we've all been through hell during the last couple of days," I said. "But for now, we want to keep watching the parking lot to see if others get drawn in."

"Drawn in?" she said.

"Somebody created a lot of noise down there. It's attracting attention. We want to see if we can learn anything else about the way the killers operate."

"You call them killers?" Lea asked.

"Do you have a better name?" I said.

"We didn't have a name for them . . ."

I thought about how to tell our story to Lea when we got downstairs, and wondered what she had been through. Comparing notes would be interesting.

"Down by the trees again, the same place we saw the first one," Jack said.

Lea jumped to her feet and stared at Jack, anger etched across her face. "The first one? What do you mean *the first one*?"

Jack didn't look at her, instead, he peered down his rifle sights at the killer below. "Er . . . I meant the first killer we saw from up here . . . the one with the pipe that came to attack you."

"So where was the second one, if he was the first?"

"We've only seen one killer from here. This one is the second," Bernie said, rather unconvincingly in my opinion.

"Why was it too late when you saw us down there?" She kept her focus on Jack. I could tell he wanted the roof to swallow him up. "How did you know it was too late?"

Seeing us all stunned and unable to answer, she spun her accusing hand toward Bernie. "He said he couldn't warn us. That means you knew there was something to warn us about."

I felt increasingly ashamed but stuck to our lie. "We were speaking with the benefit of hindsight. We had no idea until the shooting started."

"She's approaching the parking lot," Bernie said.

Strangely, having the distraction of a killer below came as a welcome relief from our rooftop interrogation.

A woman inspected the bodies and looked through the Honda's window. She retrieved the pistol from Lea's dead partner, and disappeared behind the car. The soothing tones of Celine Dion continued to drift over to us on the gentle breeze.

"See that, Lea?" Jack said. "This is the view we had when we came onto the roof."

I wished that Jack hadn't added an extra coating of sugar onto our bullshit. It sounded as if we were trying too hard. Lea struck me as being clever, and I felt sure she would see straight through us if we went any further.

"Can we just forget it?" I asked.

She narrowed her eyes. "Easy for you to say. I've been to hell and back."

"Yes, it *is* easy for us to say," Jack said with an irritated edge to his voice. "We've had a picnic since getting off the plane. Why don't you ask Bernie about his wife?"

Bernie's head dipped and he turned away. Lea took a step back and her expression softened. It wasn't the most subtle thing Jack could have said, but at least it shut everyone up. I leaned my elbow on the wall and continued to observe below.

———

The sun dipped behind an adjacent apartment block. Seven o'clock and another killer had yet to show. We managed an hour's respite from Lea's questioning. She sat cross-legged on the opposite side of the roof. Every time I glanced over my shoulder, she shook her head.

The killer remained behind the Honda. She craned her neck around the hood and waited.

"Here's another one," Jack said, pointing to his right.

A man sneaked through vehicles toward the parking lot, taking a route similar to Lea and her dead partner. She nudged between Bernie and me, now interested in the action below.

"How do we know either are actually killers?" Bernie said.

Lea rolled her eyes. "Do you want to go down and ask politely?"

Bernie opened his mouth to say something, but stopped himself. A wise move I thought.

The man stopped ten yards short of the Honda. He held something behind his back, possibly a knife, I could see from here. The woman sprang out and fired a single shot. The man's right shoulder jerked back, but he remained on his feet. He rushed toward her. She fumbled with her weapon. Before she managed to resolve whatever issue she had, the man plunged something into her midriff. She fell backward; he crouched on her chest, repeatedly stabbing down.

He picked up her weapon and started fiddling with it. Clearly more competent with weapons, four seconds later, he shot himself in the head.

"Probably had a stoppage in the chamber," Jack said.

"What do you make of that?" Bernie asked.

"What do we make of what?" Lea said. "Couldn't you guess that would happen?"

"Yes, but we—"

"Are you surprised by what you saw? Did you expect anything else?"

I disliked her bullying tone, especially against a nice guy like Bernie. "No, not really, but we're learning all time. The more information we gather, the better. I'll explain it all downstairs."

At least, I would explain most things.

With light rapidly fading, I turned to Bernie. "Back to your place, mate. Let's get those candles on the go."

6
BOTH SIDES

With no electricity, candles suited our needs, providing a low ambient glow.

"Anyone fancy half a can of cold chili and a cigarette?" Jack said.

A few days ago, his offer would have seemed laughable and a bit odd, considering he was a guest here too. Now it sounded welcoming, and nobody refused.

I went to help Jack in the kitchen area and left Bernie and Lea sitting opposite each other on the couches. Both remained silent, exchanging awkward glances and false smiles. I hoped they'd strike up a conversation so I could talk to Jack about what had happened during the day.

We took the food and drinks over to the couches. Jack sat with Lea, and I squeezed down next to Bernie. Spoons clinked on porcelain bowls for the next two minutes as we hungrily devoured our dinner. After we finished, I collected the bowls and washed them in the sink. At least we still had running water, although I thought we should start using purification tablets.

Jack passed around a packet of Luckies while I poured four glasses of pop. It felt the right time to share our stories and learn a little bit more about Lea. She looked about twenty-five years old, had chestnut-brown hair in a tight ponytail, a pretty but sensible face, and wore combat trousers and a red sweater.

I passed her a fizzing glass. "So, tell us about your experiences since landing . . . if it's not too painful."

"You don't have to tread on eggshells around me because I'm a woman," she said.

"When we landed here, we trod in a massive pile of dangerous dog shit," Jack said.

I wondered whether Lea's smile was because she enjoyed the comeback or because she thought we were a trio of clowns.

"I'd prefer to hear your side first," she said.

We told Lea what had happened from our arrival on the tarmac to just before we set the trap in the parking lot, which of course we left out. She seemed unsurprised by what had happened with the steward and Maureen, but the man in the cell peaked her interest. She hadn't had the chance to speak to a killer the way we did, and it probably helped her piece a few things together.

Bernie spoke with emotion about Linda's death, and I could see genuine concern on Lea's face as his voice wobbled.

I continued with events after returning to the plane, how the captain had been shot at, and how we managed to convince a killer to shoot himself. Then, reluctantly, and rather sheepishly, I rushed through the part about the girl and the recycling bin.

Jack talked coldly and robotically about our experience at the Queensboro Bridge and the shoot-out afterward with the same girl. I knew he hid his real feelings, and the other two also probably noticed. Nobody changes from a gardener or plumber to a cold-hearted killer in forty-eight hours, whatever the circumstances.

Jack was a part of the Parachute Regiment, one of the first deployed to Afghanistan. He never really discussed any experiences of active service other than throwaway jokes about women and drinking—a defense mechanism I also used to avoid awkward conversations. We talked privately about incidents; some things were best kept behind closed doors.

Finally, I told Lea about our shopping trip but cut out the bottle stamp. The unnecessary action still played on my mind.

Lea sipped her drink and relaxed back. "Did you learn anything else?"

Bernie answered before I could speak. "They don't seem to acknowledge that the world around them is in total chaos. We—"

I cut him off before he talked us into trouble. "Jack had invites on Twitter to parties and an offer of free football tickets. Killers trying to lure their prey. I mean, who could realistically believe the Yankees were playing today?"

"I got a few weird messages. Quickly figured their nature. You seen anything online?"

Jack shook his head. "Nowt."

She frowned. "Excuse me?"

"He means 'nothing,'" I said.

"So, what's your story?" Bernie said.

"I'm from Michigan. Boarded a flight from Detroit to JFK to meet up with an old college friend in Manhattan on Friday. Haven't seen him for years, but really needed his advice. I split up with my partner, Martina."

Lea paused and raised her eyebrows. I wasn't sure what she expected us to say.

"Did you notice anything on the plane?" I asked.

"No, it's a short flight. A bit of turbulence, but nothing out of the ordinary until the captain told us we were diverting to Newark. People started whining about it. The plane landed but stopped short of the terminal. The whole place looked deserted, and loads of passengers started to panic . . ."

"What did your captain say?" Bernie said.

"We were told the place was on temporary lockdown due to a terrorist attack, and we needed to sit tight until it was safe to disembark. We all believed it at first. Why would we doubt it? Could there be any other explanation?"

The last comment hung in the air as Lea seemed to search our face for answers.

"It closely mirrors our experience. What happened next?" Jack said.

I emptied my glass and held in a burp. My father taught me that manners were free, but having no manners carried a cost.

Lea continued, "We spent the first night on the plane in total darkness. I sat in a window seat next to a couple of teachers. Chris and Mike from Detroit. They debated the quality of local schools, mixed with stupid stories about kids they taught. I kept quiet and only spoke when they asked me a couple of questions about my own life. Their constant droning almost made me scream."

I was starting to wonder about the relevance, but kept quiet. Bernie was less obliging. "You wanted to scream because people were talking? Come on, Lea."

I jabbed him with my elbow.

She glared at him. "Some people are so concerned by their own little nests that they are oblivious to what's going on around them. Listening to Chris and Mike, I knew they were so secure in their own little world. I wished I could feel the same, but somehow I knew that it was a whole lot more serious than a lockdown."

"Fair enough. Crack on," I quickly said before Bernie could reply.

"I managed a couple of hours sleep, once they finally shut up. At first light, we still didn't have a clue. With passengers now thoroughly pissed, the captain made an announcement. He told us we had no contact with anyone on the ground, with the exception of a few other planes that landed around the same time. The whole plane erupted in shouts and screams. Tons of passengers went for their overhead luggage. Some started fighting and doing other crazy

113

shit. It settled down after repeated pleas from the stewards and the appearance of an air marshal."

"We never had one of those," Jack said. "Or anyway, no one revealed themselves."

I wondered when the story would get more interesting. So far, it sounded like a carbon copy of our experience, only from a different point of view.

She continued, "The air marshal spoke with authority and told us that he would go to the terminal building and use their long-range radio. He jumped from the front entrance, and disappeared inside the terminal. He never came back."

"Sounds like we had more luck than the air marshal," I said.

"You think?" Bernie replied.

I thought about Linda and shook my head.

Lea glanced between us, probably waiting to see if I was going to answer Bernie with a verbal reply before she carried on with her tale. I didn't.

Her cigarette hissed as she crushed it against the bottom of her empty glass. "A group forced their way out of the plane after deploying a slide. They ran for the perimeter fence. The captain repeated his pleas for everyone to remain seated, but all control had been lost. Others made a break for it. Chris and Mike were annoyed at the behavior of the other passengers, but they agreed to form a small group with some of the surrounding people and head toward Manhattan. Most lived there and knew the area. I joined them, thinking it was better than sitting on the plane. I think at least half of the passengers stayed, scared that they might walk right into a terrorist trap."

"I wonder who gave them that idea," Jack said.

Bernie shuffled on the couch.

"Go on," I said, putting aside the fact that Bernie's theory might have been responsible, after being transmitted between the two planes. He didn't need extra stress after his last couple of days.

"Twelve of us headed out. Most started to panic once we left the airport. Bodies were everywhere. Chris thought it must have been a dirty bomb, which made sense at the time. We were walking along an overpass when a guy in a flashy suit appeared from behind a car. He offered to lead us to safety . . ."

"I think I know what's coming," Bernie said.

"An old lady from our group approached him. He pulled half a brick from inside his jacket and smashed her skull open. He was like a fucking wild animal, screaming." She paused for a moment, probably reflecting on her first experience of a killer. "Before anyone could blink, he threw himself off the bridge head-first onto the highway below."

"That figures," Jack said.

"Yeah, it does now, but back then, I stood in shock. The lady's husband fell to the ground, clutching his chest. We couldn't bring him around. He might have had a heart attack or something. Mike threw up all over my shoes. We were stuck in the open and scared. Two couples ran back toward the airport."

"Why did they do that?" I asked.

Lea hugged herself. "No idea. Before they reached the end of the overpass, another man appeared. He pushed one of the females straight onto the road below. Her partner started throwing punches, but he killed him too . . ."

Jack sat forward. "Wait a minute, this madman killed two people?"

"The guy had a knife and stabbed him in the neck a few times."

"What did he do after that?"

"He ran away. God knows where."

"That doesn't make any sense."

"None of it makes any sense, Jack," I said. "Maybe he was only half affected?"

"Why would anyone be only half affected? We haven't seen that anywhere else."

"I don't know, but it doesn't really change anything. He still killed."

"I don't get why he ran away. What happened next?" Bernie asked.

"Your guess is as good as mine. The other couple huddled against the wall. I think they just froze or couldn't take it anymore. They told me they were going it alone and waved us away. Only six of us made it to Manhattan."

"What was that like?" I said.

"What do you think? A woman came sprinting out of an alley waving a bread knife and headed straight for us. I turned and ran as fast as I could. Had no idea where I was going. When I stopped to catch my breath, only Chris and a lady called Deb were with me. The others must have made off in other directions."

"Shit, what happened next?" I questioned.

"The woman with the knife flew around the corner. A man stepped out of an entrance to an apartment block and hit her in the face with a baseball bat. He kept swinging like a fucking machine, smashing her head all over the sidewalk. I tried to thank him, but he ignored me, picked up the dead woman's bread knife and sawed at his own throat until blood pulsed out. He dropped to his knees and fell face first onto the sidewalk."

"Did you start to see a pattern?" Bernie said.

"I wasn't really thinking straight, but looking back I can. We ran into the apartment block and found a door open on the second floor. We snuck inside and searched for any signs of life. Lucky for us it was empty, so I locked the door."

"Is that where you tweeted from?" I said.

"Yeah, it had all we needed while we figured out what to do. Chris kept speculating about Mike, and Deb wouldn't stop talking about conspiracy theories. In the end, we both told her to shut up."

"What happened outside?" Bernie asked.

"We kept away from the windows, didn't want to attract any unwanted attention."

I nodded. "Smart move."

"We kept the lights off and the curtains closed. I made us dinner, but before we finished, somebody banged on the door—"

"Here we go," Jack said.

"Chris looked through the spyglass and saw a man in a blue uniform. He said he was building security, visiting apartments to check if everybody was okay."

"Right," Bernie said, shaking his head.

"We didn't know, did we? In hindsight, we should have ignored him, but at the time, we were desperate to reach out for any kind of help. Chris put the chain on the door and opened it up. Next thing, there was a huge crash. The door flew open and sent Chris flying backward into Deb and me. The man stepped inside. He had a large tool or something above his head, you know? Like what a mechanic has."

"A wrench?" Bernie replied.

"Whatever. He swung it down toward Chris's face. He rolled out of the way to avoid being hit, but exposed Deb, who took the full force of the blow to the side of her head. I wriggled backward to get away. It took me a few seconds to get my feet free from under Deb's body. The man continued hitting Deb's head with the tool. Chris tried to grab his leg, but the guy kneed him in the face. The man checked Deb's pulse. I don't know why; he totally crushed her head. He ran out, and I heard a window smash."

Lea lit another cigarette and took a long drag.

"You're lucky to be alive. What happened after that?" I asked.

"The guy jumped out head first onto the sidewalk," she said as smoke billowed from her mouth. "We saw him when we left the apartment to come and meet you. Chris blamed himself for Deb's death. If he hadn't rolled away, she would still have been alive, he said. I tried to reason with him, saying it would have been him if he didn't roll. He wouldn't listen. He kept repeating it over and over again until late into the night. He wrapped Deb's body in a blanket from the spare room and sat with it all night. I don't think he knew her at all, but he started losing it big time."

"I suppose different people react in different ways," I said without giving it much thought.

Lea stared at me while taking another deep drag.

"I didn't get much sleep that night. Felt too scared to close my eyes. Next morning, we were both completely beat. I thought another psycho would turn up at any moment. I checked Twitter and saw your reply. Your tweets stood out as genuine among all the other crazy shit. I needed some confidence that I could actually get through all of this in one piece. That's why I replied and agreed to meet you at the bridge."

She flicked ash into her glass. Bernie grunted in quiet disapproval, but I doubt he cared too much. What difference did it make?

"What about Chris?" Jack asked.

"He didn't want to leave the apartment, but I convinced him that we needed to find more people if we wanted to survive. He eventually agreed. I found a map in a drawer, and the bridge wasn't far—"

"I've been waiting to hear this," Bernie said.

Lea rolled her eyes. "We crept toward the bridge, jumping at every distant sound. Within fifty yards, I saw a man walking across from the Manhattan side. He got into a car and started weaving his way to the other end. There was no way I could warn you."

"We probably wouldn't have recognized a warning even if you tried," Jack said.

"We waited to see what would happen, as I knew you might be at the other end. I heard a shot and a long blast of a horn. We sprinted back to the apartment, and I still didn't know if you had survived or were even genuine."

She stubbed out her cigarette and sat back.

"Well, here we are. What did you do after that?" I said.

"Back at the apartment, I sent another tweet and prayed for a reply. Chris paced around the room, saying that we were going to die and we had no hope. He wouldn't eat, and seriously considered wandering the streets to find Mike. We agreed to stay in the apartment purely because it seemed safer than our other ideas."

"What other ideas?" Bernie said.

"Not that many, really. We were thinking about getting a boat and anchoring in the harbor or heading to the end of Long Island. Once you replied on Twitter, I wanted to hook up in Elmhurst. I had a map covering the area and was just about to send you another tweet confirming I was on my way, when the power died. Chris refused to leave at first. I ended up slapping him; he risked both our lives by wanting to stay. If he wanted to do something stupid, I told him, he could do it after we had found other people."

"He sounds like a pillock," Jack said.

"Pillock?" Lea asked.

"Just a silly person," I said. "How did you convince him?"

"When I asked him what Mike would have wanted, he agreed to leave with me and head to Elmhurst. We picked up two guns from dead cops on the bridge."

"You know how to use one?" Jack said.

"An ex had a weird obsession with them and used to take me to a range."

"And when you crossed the bridge?" Bernie replied.

"We headed to the center of Elmhurst and heard music a few blocks away. Chris decided it must have been you guiding us in. I fired by accident. Chris went totally crazy."

"I think we heard it," I said, thinking about the shot that caused Bernie and me to start running from the scene of the trap.

"You know the rest."

While telling us her story, Lea showed she obviously had strength. Otherwise, she wouldn't have made it this far, and the incident in the parking proved it. She had acted decisively when the danger became clear.

"Why didn't you run from the parking lot?" Jack asked.

"I thought I was on my own. I figured I'd been fooled on Twitter by a crazy, and Chris's death was my fault. I didn't know what to do next."

"Hey, don't think like that," Bernie said. "How can any of this be your fault?"

We waited for Lea's response, but she didn't give one. Perhaps she still didn't trust us. I could understand that. But her options were limited. Leaving our group and making her own way would be a lot more dangerous than staying.

I poured us a shot of vodka as a nightcap, and we discussed our plans for the morning. Bernie wanted to find a camping stove, to make hot food and boil water. Jack and I were happy to go along with his suggestion but were a little wary of heading anywhere that would take us around the parking lot. Lea remained mostly quiet but didn't seem all that eager to revisit the parking lot either. Bernie played the gracious host and offered Lea his bedroom; she gladly accepted and disappeared, closing the door. Relegated to the living room with us, he took a pillow and blanket and settled on the floor between the couches.

"What do you think about Lea?" I asked.

"Bit of a loose cannon," Jack said. "We need to make sure she's strapped to the deck."

"I like her," Bernie said, taking me by surprise. I'd assumed he didn't. "If she sticks around, she'll give us balance."

I blew out the candles and rolled onto the couch. "Agreed. Let's sleep on our next moves."

The room filled with Bernie and Jack's annoying asynchronous snoring. I lay awake, thinking about our future options. Between the four of us, we had a reasonable mobile team capable of getting somewhere safe with readily available supplies. I wrestled with the problem of where to go as I fell asleep.

———

I awoke to see dawn seeping through gaps in the blinds. I checked my watch. Five past six on Monday morning. Bernie continue to snore on the floor, and Jack curled in a fetal position on the other couch.

I stood, yawned, and stretched. My thighs felt tight from running the day before. I nudged Jack. "Get up. Let's go to the roof for a chat."

Jack's eyes fluttered open. He swung his legs off the couch and stretched his arms over his head. "Did you say the roof?"

"Yeah, come on," I said.

We grabbed our weapons, falling back into habits learned in the army, and silently left the apartment. We hadn't had the chance to talk in private for the last couple of days, and I wanted to get his thoughts on Bernie, Lea, and our current situation. I also wanted to check on Jack's general state of mind. I didn't like what I'd seen in the local supermarket. It wasn't like him.

As Jack neared the blue metal door leading to the roof, he stopped, retreated a couple of steps, and dropped to one knee. "I closed and bolted the door last night. There's no way it opened by itself."

"Might be Lea? We didn't check the bedroom," I said.

"Or a killer."

I jerked my gun up and aimed at the door. "Whoever it is, they will have heard us coming."

Jack wrapped his hand around his mouth. "Lea . . . Lea . . ."

Nobody replied.

We couldn't just turn around and leave. If our apartment haven wasn't safe anymore, we needed to know. I felt committed to investigate and snuff out any threat.

The door was slightly ajar. Bright light shone through a gap.

"Kick it open and cover me," I said. "I'll go in low so we both have a shot."

Jack nodded and shouldered his rifle. "Ready?"

I tensed, ready for action. "Go for it."

He thrust his boot against the middle of the door. Its hinges screamed as it swung open and thudded against something outside. A man cried in pain as the door bounced back toward us. Bernie slept downstairs. This man probably waited to ambush us.

"Come out with your hands up," I said. "We're both armed."

"So am I. Throw down your weapons, place your hands over your heads, and step outside," a voice shouted back.

"Bullshit," Jack shouted and turned to me. "Let's just bolt the door and leave the prick to die on the roof."

That would mean losing our observation post but would solve the immediate problem. The door stopped halfway after hitting the man and rebounding. I kept low and slowly stretched out my arm to grab the handle. As I did, I looked at the gap underneath the door and saw the edge of a shoe. The man stood against the door outside.

I shifted the Glock into my left hand, dropped to the ground, and fired at the black leather shoe from almost point-blank range. The man screamed and fell to the floor. The top of his head appeared around the front edge. I aimed and fired twice again. The first round hit the top left side of his forehead. The next hit him directly under his chin. Red mist puffed from the top of his head as the round exited.

I waited for twenty seconds. He didn't move. When I did eventually walk out and look around, a nasty surprise waited. Another body. This one hacked to death with a sharp implement.

A horrible thought descended. "Have I killed an innocent man?"

"Define innocent," Jack said. "Was he innocently hiding behind the door?"

We inspected the man I had shot for clues.

Jack stooped over him, then looked at the other corpse. "He'd be covered head to toe in blood if he did that."

An MP40 lay behind the door. I slipped the magazine out of the grip and thumbed out eight rounds, confirmed the matching caliber, and loaded them into my own.

We walked over to the other body, a young woman. Somebody had really gone to town on her chest and face. She had numerous puncture wounds. More than enough to kill her five times over.

"Look here," Jack said and pointed to a trail of blood leading to the edge of the roof.

I followed the droplets to the area where we'd sat the previous day, and looked over the edge of the building. A woman sprawled on the pavement below: another suicide mission completed successfully.

I felt certain the man waiting for us behind the door hadn't killed the woman on the roof, but this confirmed it.

"Three of them up here," I said and looked around the other apartment block roofs in the close vicinity, shuddering at the thought of us being unaware of potentially hundreds of prying eyes. "Just how many of these people are still around?"

"Don't know. They might have seen us up here or maybe they came up to try and spot a victim."

Whatever had happened, three killers had visited the top of our apartment block between dusk and dawn. Like Bernie, I didn't believe in coincidences.

I peered over to the parking lot. The music no longer played, but four more bodies lay around the Honda.

Jack shook his head. "I don't think we can stay here any longer."

I agreed. With dwindling population numbers, killers would be actively looking for prey. The city seemed like the wrong place to be.

We took the opportunity while we were still on the roof to discuss Bernie and Lea. Bernie had yet to fire in anger, except at us. But he didn't shy away from going in first as he had proved in the police building at the airport and at his local store. He had also provided a sanctuary by taking us back to his apartment.

Lea had shown good assertiveness and survival instincts by making her way to Elmhurst to find other people. She'd slickly dispatched a killer yesterday and had shown little remorse, although the memory was ingrained in her mind.

We'd all seen and done things lately that would haunt our memories forever. Jack and I both agreed that the four of us had the makings of a good team.

"We need to get back and brief them," Jack said.

I groaned. "Bernie's not going to be pleased about leaving."

Jack made for the stairs. I gripped his arm. "Are you okay?"

"What do you mean?"

"I mean, do you feel okay? Yesterday . . ."

He shook off my grip. "I'm fine."

We clambered down the stairs and knocked on the apartment door three times. Bernie opened it almost immediately, his face like thunder. Lea stood behind him, looking ready to pounce.

"Where the hell have you been?" Bernie said. "We both woke to the sound of gunfire."

"It's a long story," Jack said. "We'll tell you over breakfast."

I poured two cans of tomatoes into four bowls and served them up. While Bernie and Lea slurped from their bowls, we told them about the man on the roof and the extra bodies.

Lea placed her bowl on the floor and wiped her mouth. "We should head out to the countryside today. I know a great farm in Orange County. Visited it last summer with my girlfriend."

"I know the area," Bernie said. "But, we don't have to leave the apartment for at least a few days."

"I'm with Lea," Jack said. "It's coming up to three days since this thing started, and there's no end in sight. Let's get out of here."

A single sturdy door had gone from making us feel safe to giving us the feeling of being trapped. Killers could already be heading our way after hearing the shots from the roof. If we had to shoot more of them, we might run out of ammunition and be sitting ducks. Personally, I agreed with Jack and Lea but kept my thoughts to myself. It now seemed like wishful thinking that we could go undetected in Bernie's apartment and sit this thing out.

Lea's idea had plenty of appeal. The countryside would surely be quieter. If we found a decent house in a remote place and built it up defensively, our prospects would be better. Traveling carried the most risk; we would almost certainly have to tackle killers on the way.

Bernie looked to me. "What do you say, Harry? You agree with me, right?"

I pushed my feelings of guilt to one side. "You're out-voted three to one, Bernie. I take it you're coming with us?"

"Of course I'm coming. What a stupid thing to say."

Jack slapped his hand on the couch's arm. "That's settled."

I felt pleased that despite his irritation, Bernie went with the majority decision.

"Where's the farm?" Bernie asked.

"Just outside Montgomery, near a big old house. Do you know it?"

"I think I know exactly where you mean. Linda's parents live . . . lived near it. When we drove past, we always talked about our dreams of owning it."

"What's it like for us?" I said.

"Great for what we need. We should go there, not the farm."

"How far from here?" Jack said.

"About seventy miles. Not far."

"Okay, sounds good," I said. "The house it is."

"What is it with you guys?" Lea asked. "The farm's perfect. Better for supplies. Everything."

"We went with your suggestion," I said. "At least give Bernie a choice of location."

She sat back and crossed her arms. "Jesus Christ. Okay."

Bernie failed to conceal his smile.

———

I put yesterday's shopping in my backpack and grabbed my gun from the kitchen counter. Jack slung his pack over his shoulder. Lea had a small daypack and squeezed it shut by pulling the rope.

"No point hanging around," I said. "Ready to move?"

"Won't be a minute," Bernie said.

He went into his bedroom and closed the door. A few moments later, he reappeared with glassy eyes and stuffed a small, framed picture of Linda in his backpack.

Once we left the apartment and headed in line toward Queens Boulevard, I knew we'd made the right decision. The stench of death hung thickly in the air. It would only get worse in the more heavily populated areas. Most corpses were now three days old. I looked at a discolored and unnaturally swollen body, rotting in the morning sun. The city would be unbearable in another two days and probably rife with disease.

Once on the road and heading away from Manhattan, I approached an SUV, parked at the side of the inside lane. Two people lay outside the passenger door, one with gouges in his face and neck. The other, with blood all over his hands, had vicious red-scarred flesh around his mouth and a can of lighter fluid near his hand.

Jack found keys on the ground next to the driver's feet. He used the driver's sweater to wipe crusted blood from the ignition key and tossed it to Bernie. "You know where you're going, chief."

Bernie caught the key in one hand. "To hell in a handbasket."

"Not a handcart?" I said.

He shook his head and jumped into the driver's seat. I sat beside him as he started the engine. It rolled over smoothly, and the dashboard fuel dial swept around to three-quarters full. Jack and Lea slammed the back doors. The SUV definitely belonged to a smoker.

I surveyed the opposite side of the road as we trundled along and turned on to the Long Island Expressway. New territory, but it had a similar feel to Queens Boulevard. Some vehicles used as weapons, others pulled to the side, corpses spread in and among them. I stared at a man with a shredded face. His upper torso was hung through a car windshield. A crow sat on his head. Bernie brought the SUV to an abrupt, screeching halt, causing the crow to fly away.

"Problem?" I said, looking for signs of danger.

Jack poked his head between the front seats. "What's the score, Bernie?"

"Guys, down there to the right. Two men standing outside Aldi."

"They're carrying shotguns." Lea said.

I looked at the front of the store. Two men, probably attracted by our skidding tires, stared at us. They stood seventy yards away and pointed their shotguns in our direction. Around thirty corpses were piled in the middle of an adjacent parking lot.

"Do you think they're like us?" Bernie asked.

"At this range, they could still be dangerous," Jack said. "If they're standing guard, others will be close."

"We can't trust them," Lea said. "Remember that guy on the bridge? He didn't kill himself. There's no way to be sure about anyone."

Lea's earlier revelation suggested that not everyone acted exactly the same way. We thought we had the pattern worked out—kill, then suicide—perhaps there was another trend we had yet to discover. The one common theme was the need to kill. The men below weren't showing any signs of this.

I popped open my door. "We should at least give them a chance."

A door opened behind me. Jack said, "I'm coming with you; show them two of us together."

"Are you sure about this?" Bernie asked.

"I'm not sure about anything," I said.

I slipped out of the SUV, walked to the side of the highway, and waved. Jack stood by my shoulder. We were in an elevated position above the two men, whose shotguns were still aimed in our direction. Electric windows lowered behind us.

I cupped both hands around my mouth. "Lower your weapons. We just want to talk."

"There's four of us here," Jack shouted.

One man lowered his weapon, and I felt a rush of excitement. He said something to the other and walked toward us, cradling his shotgun in folded arms.

"Did you fly from Manchester?" he called out. I was just about to reply, when the man said, "I know you. You're the ones that went to the terminal but never came back."

He spoke in a southern English accent and was quite short, with greasy brown hair and a faded tattoo on his right forearm.

"We did come back. You didn't wait long enough," Jack snapped.

"Where did you go after leaving the airport?" I asked.

The man continued forward, then stopped beneath the road, twenty yards away. "It's been crazy since we left the airport. Thirty of us split from the main group after someone drove at us in a fire truck. I don't know where the rest are."

"There're thirty of you here?" I said.

"Twenty-two."

"What happened to the others?" Jack asked.

The man looked down for a moment. "They didn't make it. We barricaded ourselves in the store. A few people tried to break in, but whenever someone else showed up, they fought each other to death. We haven't seen anyone for the last few hours."

"How did you manage to take a store?" I asked, curious about the strategy. Perhaps it would be something we could employ in future to secure a large amount of supplies.

"We just rushed in, locked the doors, and secured the back entrance. We found a crazy woman inside. She slashed Morgan across the eye. He managed to beat her brains out with a small fire extinguisher."

"That dick from business class. Brown blazer?" Jack asked.

The man nodded. "That's him. He figured that somewhere with supplies would be the best place to hide out. Nobody can get through the back, and we see anyone coming from the front. We started moving the dead an hour ago."

Without warning, the man crouched and aimed his shotgun to the left. A plastic bag drifted along the concrete past him. He looked back at us and puffed his cheeks. "Any idea what's happened?"

"I was about to ask you the same thing," Jack said.

I gestured to Lea and Bernie. Bernie joined us at the edge of the road.

"Did you hear all that?" I asked.

"He sounds legit."

"All right, geezer," the man called up in greeting.

"Is he talking to me?" Bernie asked.

"It's a southern thing, like *mate, mucker, marra*, or *buddy*, as you might say," I said.

"You Brits and your words."

"We've all got them, big fella. Last time I visited the States, I felt too embarrassed to ask what grits meant on a breakfast menu. A bloke on the plane said *janky*—no idea what it means."

"I get your point," he said, turning to the man below. "Sounds like you had a rough time. Are you planning on staying here?"

"Do you have any better ideas?"

"We're heading away from the city . . ."

Bernie paused and looked over the man's head.

Two men bumped out of the store's entrance, carrying out a corpse. I recognized one as Morgan; he wore a makeshift eyepatch. He noticed us and let go of the corpse's arms. Its head hit the ground with a dull thud.

He marched over, stood next to the man, placed his hands on his hips, and glared up at us. "Who are you?"

"I'm Harry. That's Jack, Lea, and Bernie." I said, pointing at each one in turn.

"You're those two cretins from the flight. Thanks for nothing."

"Is he serious?" Jack said.

"Mr. Morgan, come on. These—"

"Oh shut up, Harris, I'll take the negotiations from here. Go and help Tweedle clear the store."

The man stepped back behind Morgan, looked up, shrugged his shoulders, and walked away.

"What do you want?" Morgan demanded.

"We're not here to negotiate anything," I said. "I'm just happy to meet other survivors who haven't got a death wish.

"What are you doing here? Where are you going?"

Morgan's tone irritated me, and his attitude stank as badly as the air, considering our joint situation.

"Away from the city. Can we grab some supplies?" Lea asked.

"I thought you said you weren't here to negotiate anything?" Morgan said, looking at me.

"Fucking hell, Morgan, get a grip. Why—"

Morgan's reaction cut off my reply. He took a pace back, his eyes widening, spun, and sprinted for the store entrance.

He shouted, "Harris, Harris!"

Jack looked at me and frowned. Rapid footsteps echoed below us.

A woman in a green cycle suit appeared from underneath the expressway holding a fire axe above her head. She limped after

Morgan. He disappeared into the store entrance along with the other man, and the door slammed shut. They must have locked it, as the woman rattled the handle a few times. She chopped at it with the axe, cracking the glass panels, but not breaking them.

She paused and leaned on the axe, turned, and looked directly at us.

Bernie gasped. "Holy shit."

I glanced back at the SUV. Something moved in my peripheral vision. I looked along the expressway in the direction we had come from. Around two hundred yards away, a figure darted from behind one car to another.

"Let's get out of here," I shouted.

Jack aimed along the expressway and back toward the SUV.

"She's coming," Lea said.

Footsteps approached below us. The figure moved closer, behind another car.

I jumped back into the SUV and pushed a chunky button to lower my window, making sure I could take a decent aim if required. Jack and Lea trained their weapons out of open windows from the back seats. I looked at Bernie. His hand trembled as he tried to slot the key into the ignition.

"Drive, Bernie, bloody drive," Jack ordered.

"I'm trying," Bernie frantically replied. The engine turned over, and the SUV quickly jerked forward.

I twisted in my seat and looked through the rear window as we moved away. A short, fat man had abandoned stealth and sprinted toward us; luckily, Bernie managed to swerve his way around stationary obstacles on the road faster than our pursuer could keep pace. The man stopped when he arrived opposite the Aldi. He must have seen the woman with the axe. He jumped off the side of the expressway.

I let out a deep breath. "We need to make sure we keep our guard up at all times."

"Imagine if the woman with the axe hadn't shown up," Lea said. "How close would he have gotten?"

"I would have taken him out," Jack said.

Perhaps Jack would have, but it was an important lesson for us to remain vigilant.

———

We drove in silence toward Interstate 684. We agreed for the time being that we shouldn't stop again unless there was an emergency. I maintained a careful watch outside as Bernie slowly picked his way through stationary traffic and over the occasional body along the Hutchinson River Parkway. Once there, the vehicles thinned out, which allowed Bernie to increase our speed away from the city.

"Fucking Morgan," Jack said.

"He was a total douche," Lea said.

I knew the word as French for "a shower" but heard it being deployed as an insult on American TV shows and movies, so got her general drift. A bit like the single middle finger; although that had increased in popularity in the UK over the last decade, I still preferred a two-fingered salute. There's something satisfying about waggling your middle and index finger. People say it was first used by English archers during the Hundred Years' War, waving their bow fingers in defiance against the French upper class. Probably an urban myth, but I liked the story.

"It's people like him that likely caused all this," Jack said. "There he is, trying to take control and create a little empire. We should go back and take him out."

"What? And start killing everyone we meet who annoys you?" Bernie asked.

"You know what I mean, Bernie. If there are people left, we should be working together or the world will end up like a Mad Max movie."

I stayed quiet; even though Jack had a fair point, we couldn't start taking the law into our own hands. Who were we to make the rules? If by some chance we managed to make it through the next few weeks, we could start trying to piece together a community with other survivors. It's human nature to create a pyramid, and at the top are always the wrong people. "Lions led by donkeys" was the First World War epitaph, but the truth lies somewhere in between. In any social group, even a hippie commune, there will be people who try to control things for their own ends. I couldn't think of the sociology we faced, so I changed the subject.

"So what's Orange County like?"

"It's great," Bernie said. "I've always felt at home there, away from the city. Have you visited the fair, Lea?"

"I've only visited a couple of times."

"Who lives on the farm?"

Her window slid down with an electronic whine. "Forget that. Someone's following us."

I adjusted the rearview mirror. A blue car snaked through the traffic about two hundred yards behind us.

"We can't let it follow us, can we?" Bernie said.

Jack lowered his window and shouldered his rifle.

"Try to get a bit further ahead," I said. "Give us enough time to stop and set up an ambush."

"What if they just stop?" Lea asked.

"I can easily take them out from this range," Jack said.

We didn't even know if the person following posed any kind threat, but Jack spoke as if he relished the prospect of shooting. I needed to stay by his side and keep him from making rash decisions.

Bernie sped up, scraping against cars and thumping over debris. By the time the driver of the blue car reacted, we'd gained enough ground to stop and set up our safety zone.

I spotted a good ambush point at the side of the highway. A couple of vehicles wedged together in the outside lane and space on the shoulder. "Stop here, Bernie."

He slammed on the brakes, and we came to a skidding stop just behind what appeared to be a head-on collision.

We took cover behind a red car with a crumpled front end. The windows were so spattered with blood that I could only just see the vague outline of four figures inside.

The blue car, a Buick, came to a stop around thirty yards away. A single woman driver sat with both hands on the wheel.

She tentatively exited and thrust her arms up in the air. "Don't shoot. I'm on my own."

A strange thing to say, I thought. She looked to be a similar age to Lea and wore jeans and a yellow vest. Blood matted her blonde hair on the left side of her head. She didn't appear to be armed and dropped to her knees.

"Why are you following us?" I said.

"I don't know. I've been in an accident," she said, her voice uneven and shaky. "The last thing I remember is a car sliding in front of me. I've been unconscious. When I woke up . . ."

She glanced around the highway. "Oh my God."

"You met anyone else?" Bernie asked.

"Not a single person—at least, not one alive."

I crouched behind the car. "An acknowledgement of events, or a killer's attempt to give us what we want to hear?"

"No idea, but I don't trust her," Bernie said.

"Ask her more questions," Lea said.

Jack looked over his rifle sights. "What's your plan?"

"I don't have a plan. I wanted to find help. This isn't my car. Check the papers inside if you don't believe me."

"They don't prove a thing," Bernie said.

The woman winced and moved her knee. The midday sun reflected off small pieces of broken glass that surrounded her, parts of a shattered window from an adjacent truck. I struggled to think of a way of we could resolve the situation.

"Why not bring her along for the ride?" Lea asked. "I'll keep an eye on her."

"Give over, Lea. Why risk letting her get close?" Jack said.

"Please, guys, stop fucking around," the woman said.

"Let's send her away in the opposite direction. Might give us enough time to shake her off," Bernie said.

"She could easily turn around and start following again," Jack said.

"I'll ask her a few more questions," I said, thinking about the prospect of adding another member to our team. "If she comes for us, we shoot."

All three behind the car nodded in agreement.

I moved into the open and lowered my gun, confident I had cover from the other three. "If you try to kill me, one of them will then kill you, and you won't be able to kill yourself. Do you understand?"

Her shoulders jerked back, and she gave me a wide-eyed look. "Why would I commit suicide? Are you crazy?"

"Strip to your underwear," Jack shouted.

I moved back behind the car. "Jack, what the fuck are you doing?"

"You can be such a skooch sometimes," Bernie said to him.

I had no idea what the word meant, but the context and tone made it reasonably obvious.

Jack glared at Bernie. "I'm making sure she's got no concealed weapons."

Lea shook her head. "Are you trying to get a cheap thrill?"

"Fuck you," the woman said.

"You've got to be kidding me," Bernie said, looking into the distance.

A silver car snaked through the wreck-littered highway toward us.

"This might solve our problem," Jack said.

"What do you mean?" Bernie asked.

"We stay here and let the woman and the other driver talk, watch what happens."

"What if she isn't a killer and the other driver is?" Lea asked.

"We shoot whoever attacks. One of them will slip if they get close to each other."

"You're gonna use me as bait?" Her arms dropped by her sides. "Please, let me come behind the car with you."

"Stay right there or I fire," I said.

The silver car's wheels crunched over broken glass and pulled up alongside the woman. A man with a white beard sat at the wheel. I switched my aim to him. He squinted through his windshield and shook his head.

"What do you reckon?" Jack asked.

The man's window slid down. "What the hell are you doing? Lower your guns."

"One false move and I'll blow your brains out."

"Don't be so absurd, man. Now, lower your weapons."

The woman sprang to her feet and stumbled around to the driver's window. I prepared to squeeze my trigger.

"These fucking perverts wanted me to strip at gunpoint. Please, help me."

I watched in astonishment as the man gestured to the passenger seat. The woman hurried around the car and jumped in. He revved the engine and pulled away.

As he passed us, he leaned out of his window. "You should be ashamed of yourselves."

The woman raised her middle finger out of the passenger window, and I watched the car disappear into the distance.

"What was that?" Bernie asked.

I tried to think of a logical reason behind it. Maybe her accident saved her, although I couldn't imagine why.

"Both from a plane?" Jack said.

"She was in a car crash," I said. "Maybe he flew in on Friday?"

"Or the killer thing has ended?" Lea added.

"Wanna go back to my place?" Bernie said.

"Guys, don't forget what happened on the Long Island Expressway," I said. "Making hasty conclusions could be very dangerous."

"There's no way I am going back to the city," Jack said. "The place is a complete mess and will smell worse than a tramp's armpit in a couple of days."

I looked along the highway for other moving vehicles. Without seeing any, I turned to face the group. "We stick to the plan and keep heading to the countryside. The lower the population in an area, the better."

"You got it," Bernie said and made for our SUV.

Lea shrugged. "Never said anything different."

Bernie drove us away from the scene of the incident, which seemed to have left us all confused. I comforted myself with the thought that it could be a positive sign. The others might have been thinking about the same thing, judging by the silence in the car. A ramping down of the threat level would mean facing up to the state of the world we were left in, which would be a different kind of challenge.

As we turned onto Interstate 84 for the final leg of our journey, Bernie pointed skyward. "A vapor trail. Can you see it?"

A fluffy white line streaked across the sky. A definitive sign that an aircraft had recently been flying above us.

He slapped the steering wheel. "I knew it. I knew we wouldn't be on our own."

"It's one plane," I said. "I wouldn't get your hopes up. If I were the pilot, I'd find a remote island with a runway."

Lea poked her head between the front seats. "Maybe they're from a safe area, searching for survivors?"

"Or invaders on a scouting mission. Checking the results of whatever they initially deployed," Jack said, bringing an abrupt halt to the conversation.

We'd have to wait and see. I certainly wasn't going to go looking for any trouble just to prove a theory, not in the immediate future anyway. I wanted a secure and safe place to live.

——

For an hour, we drove without further incident. Bernie still had to weave through stationary vehicles and corpses in various distorted positions. Birds provided the only sign of life. Some taking advantage of the road kill.

Just after two o'clock, we passed Stewart International Airport. In the distance, a figure moved along the side of the highway. He turned as we approached and waved both arms in the air, clutching a hunting knife in his right hand.

Bernie stopped the SUV fifty yards short. "How do we deal with this one?"

"Get closer. See what he has to say," Lea said. "If he's anything like that lady . . ."

"Spin to your left, we'll broadside him if he attacks," I said.

Bernie crept to within thirty yards of the man, and stopped at a slight angle, allowing Jack and me to aim our weapons with more comfort. The man looked like he'd been dragged backward through a thorn bush and rolled in mud.

"What do you want?" Jack asked.

"Oh, thank you, thank you! You're the first to stop. Can you gimme a ride to Maybrook?"

"Why don't you take a car?" I said.

"I can't drive. Woke up here this morning. No idea how I got here."

I jabbed my gun at his hand. "And the knife?"

"I found it in the ditch. Do you blame me for keeping hold of it?"

"Where's Maybrook?" Jack asked Bernie.

"Not far. You're not thinking of letting him come with us?"

Jack pursed his lips. I thought we needed to stay on red alert, but after the incident with the woman, we had to give people a chance. "Drop the knife and come closer."

He threw his knife to the side of the highway without hesitation and approached the car. "A couple passed by half an hour ago. They didn't stop."

"That's close enough," I said as he got within five yards and raised my gun toward his face. "What have you been doing in the last three days?"

He straightened up and took a step back. "Whoa . . . Easy there. I remember taking a day off, watching a movie, and woke up here."

"Do you know what day it is?" I asked.

"Saturday? I dunno."

Two days out; three days had passed since we'd landed at JFK. He willingly threw down his weapon and didn't have the same sly and deluded edge of a killer.

"We'll take you to Maybrook," I said. "You'll have to come along at gunpoint. We'll explain why once we get going."

Jack opened up his door. The man sighed with relief and clambered in. He sat directly behind me. I pointed my Glock around the side of the seat at his guts. Jack's barrel rested a couple of inches below the man's chin. He smelt like clothing that had been left in a washing machine for a couple of days.

139

"What's your name?" Lea asked.

He glanced down at Jack's barrel and stretched his head back. "Greg. Who are you?"

During the short ride to Maybrook, we gave him a brief outline of our journey since landing on Friday afternoon. He kept exhaling hard and shaking his head. We quickly realized he wasn't a killer, at least not anymore.

"How can you be sure I haven't killed anyone?" he asked. "How can *I* be sure?"

"If you did, you'd already be dead," Bernie said.

"How many survived?"

Nobody could predict with any kind of accuracy.

"We know of twenty-four living people," Lea said. "Most are in the city. We met two on our way here."

"There must be others all over the place," Jack said. "It's only fair to warn you not to get your hopes up about your own family and friends."

Greg bowed his head and closed his eyes. After seeing the carnage around Stewart International Airport, he'd assumed it had been a terrible local accident. If his world wasn't already shattered, we'd managed to smash it with reality in the space of a few minutes. I couldn't think of a reason why we should sugar-coat the truth. We all had to face it and find a way to pull through.

"Seriously? The entire city? Unbelievable," Greg said.

"JFK, Queens, Manhattan, and all the way here. It's all fucked," Jack said.

"Where are you headed?"

"A big old white house on the road to Montgomery. It's—" Bernie said.

"Near a farm," Lea interrupted and finished his sentence.

"I know the place," Greg said. "If home's a nightmare, you might find me knocking at your door."

"Seriously, Greg, be careful," I said. "Maybrook's probably going to look like a war zone, so you need to be prepared."

"And the killers are slyer than a box of monkeys," Jack said. "Don't trust anyone."

"Gotcha. I'll take it easy," he said, attempting to sound calm. I noticed him clasping his hands tightly together between his legs.

We arrived at the exit for Maybrook, and Bernie slowed to a trundle.

"Pull over. I'd like to walk from here and take a look around," Greg said.

Before he left, Greg thanked us for the ride and promised to visit after searching for family and friends.

He probably didn't realize I was more thankful for meeting him.

7
THE HOUSE

We'll be there in ten minutes," Bernie said as he pulled away. "What did you make of him?" Lea asked.

"Nice guy, but dollars to donuts, he's in for some bad news when he gets home," Bernie said. I loved how he liked to see the best in everyone. "I hope he makes it."

"After we set ourselves up in the house, why don't we find a spot closer to town and create a killer trap?" Jack said. "Observe from a safe distance, see how many are about."

Lea sighed. "Haven't you tried this one before, guys?"

We had, but hadn't admitted it to Lea—yet. I didn't see the point in going out to actively get the attention of dangerous people, especially in light of our previous results.

I ignored Lea and answered Jack. "Not for the moment, bro. We've got bigger fish to fry."

We passed the black skeleton of a burnt-out house on our right, and a number of corpses spread around the garden, but the area seemed relatively quiet.

"Over there. That's the farm," Lea said.

A tree-lined road led down to an impressive stone two-story farmhouse with a large wooden Dutch barn, painted red, across a courtyard. Knee-length light-green grass swayed in the fields around it. The place looked deserted and inviting.

"We can have a look later on if you like," I said.

"Didn't I tell you it was great?"

Jack groaned. "Yes, Lea. You told us."

Minutes later, Bernie turned right, and our wheels crackled across a gravel drive.

He slipped the SUV into park and held his hands out, as if presenting the house. "Whaddya think?"

Stunning, in a word. The kind of place that I thought I'd only see on television in a period drama. Set back forty yards from the road and painted brilliant white. Five steps led up to a fantastic old porch wrapped around the front. Six carved Roman-style columns held up the slate roof, and a smart white picket fence encircled the yard. A path made out of small stones ran from the drive to the front entrance and disappeared around both sides of the house. I could definitely be comfortable in these kinds of surroundings.

I carried out a quick risk assessment. A spacious, lush, dark-green lawn surrounded the house in all directions. Trees extended the length of the property's perimeter on three sides. Plenty of places for a killer to hide, but enough distance to take them down if we remained vigilant. Across the road, green fields as far as the eye could see, which didn't arouse any immediate concerns. We could secure an area of the house and maintain watch. Good enough for the moment.

We checked the outside areas first. Jack and Lea headed around the right side of the house, and Bernie and me, the left. We met at the back, having seen nothing to worry about. A large shed stood in the back corner of the garden. I approached and looked through a side window. It contained gardening tools and a stack of plastic pots.

"External house search," I said and started looking through windows.

"Here, in the kitchen," Bernie said.

I peered over his shoulder. Two bodies lay on the kitchen floor, a woman and man. Both had bloody wounds, and a chopping knife lay between them. A half-prepared salad decayed on the counter.

"Let's clear the house and take them out," I said.

"Take them out?" Lea asked.

"Burn them," Jack said.

"After we clear the house, Jack and I will bury them in the back garden. You and Bernie secure the windows and doors."

I opened the back door, entered the house, and crept from room to room, gun in front of me, checking for any killers or survivors. This really was a beautiful place: huge windows letting in warm sunshine, well-kept wood floors that squeaked with just the right amount of character, clean and spacious, big rooms, a wide hallway, and more than three bathrooms with tubs and showers. Every room felt expensive, with fittings and furniture that I'd seen on Celebrity Lifestyle TV shows, the handcrafted sort that only the rich could afford.

The spacious bedrooms looked inviting. Big beds covered in thick quilts, plush rugs on the floor, cozy fireplaces in each bedroom, reading nooks filled with overstuffed leather-covered armchairs. It felt like a long time since I'd slept in a proper bed, and I looked forward to getting some well-deserved rest. We finally returned to the kitchen, and I gazed down at the two victims while shielding my nose from the stench of decay.

"Change of plan," I said to Bernie and Lea. "Why don't you clean the kitchen and find out what supplies we have? Jack and I will take care of the bodies."

Lea flipped open the cupboards below the sink, a standard place for storing cleaning materials. Bernie opened the higher cupboards and placed items of food on the counter. Jack and I dragged the two corpses out onto the back lawn and grabbed two shovels from the shed.

"I bet you thought you'd dug your last garden," I said.

He shrugged. "Easier to burn them."

It seemed like an overly callous thing to do, and the smoke risked drawing attention to our new home. "Let's get cracking. Those two loungers are winking at me."

Jack nodded. "Now you're talking."

He stamped his shovel into the lawn and ripped up a chunk of turf.

I always enjoyed hard, honest work and made quick progress as the earth bore the brunt of my bottled-up emotions from the last three days.

Jack threw down his shovel, stretched his back, and groaned. "Must be roasting here in the summer."

I wiped sweat from my brow and sat on the edge of the grave. "Nearly five o'clock. We don't want to be doing this in the dark."

Lea popped her head out of an upstairs window. "Keep up the good work, boys."

After a five-minute break, relaxing with the sun on our faces, we finished digging the graves to a depth of around four feet and rolled in the bodies.

I straightened the bodies up. At least we could show this couple the respect in death that so many others would never get. "Shall we say something?"

"Rest in peace," Jack said and scraped earth into the grave.

The task became much more palatable once the couple disappeared under a layer of soil. Jack silently plugged away beside me—we still had work to do and could talk properly once we had time to relax.

When I start something, I like to finish it as quickly and efficiently as possible. I'd been like that since a child, like a dog with a bone, when given a task. Get the job done.

We finished at roughly the same time, grabbed our guns, and sat on the two lounge chairs for a well-deserved rest.

"Can you hear that?" I asked Jack as I lay back.

"Hear what? I can't hear anything?"

"Exactly. No gunshots, no screaming, no running."

I shielded my eyes with my forearm and relaxed. Muffled chatter came from inside the house—hopefully, Bernie and Lea organizing our security arrangements.

My eyelids drooped. I stood to avoid nodding off. "Let's get cleaned up and have dinner."

"I could sleep for days," Jack said.

He lazily rolled off the lounger and followed me inside.

In the kitchen, Bernie stood over a large pot of water heating on a camping stove.

"You're Brits," he said. "You wanna cup of tea?"

"Does a shark have a waterproof nose?" Jack said.

Bernie smiled and grabbed a cup. "There're eggs and bread; I'll make you a sandwich."

"Cheers," I said. Lea entered the kitchen and leaned against the counter. "How're the windows and doors looking?"

"Locked the windows, and I placed piles of coins on each frame. Saw it on TV; we'll hear if anyone breaks in, even if they don't smash the glass."

"Front door?"

"Solid. You'd need a sledgehammer."

"Probably sensible that we set up a watch system tonight—two hours each, from midnight till eight. Gives us six hours each."

Bernie placed a steaming cup of tea in front of me. "Are you sleeping downstairs?"

"I fancy one of those beds, but I'll take one of the graveyard shifts."

Lea wanted an early night, so we let her take the last watch. Jack and I said we'd be up late anyway, so we would take the first two. This left Bernie with the four till six in the morning. He didn't care and said he'd sleep like a log, no matter what.

After finishing his tea, Bernie made everyone a fried-egg sandwich, as promised. A treat even more welcome than our hot drink.

Bernie and Lea emptied the cupboards of anything we could use and piled bottles of water, cans of meat, jam, cake, carrots, and potatoes on the table.

Lea ran a hand over the food. "I'll make us stew."

"Sounds good to me," I said. "I'm off to get cleaned up."

The grave digging had reopened the wound where Maureen had slashed me at the airport. I had to keep it clean and dressed to avoid infection. I thumped upstairs to one of the bathrooms and peeled off my shirt and bandage. I washed my hands, wet a sponge, and wiped away the seeping blood.

I checked the cabinets and discovered a small roll of bandages, and wrapped them tightly around the raw slash. I smiled in the mirror when I thought about John Rambo. I wouldn't be doing any needlework on my own body. I had a hard enough time sewing on a button.

Back in the kitchen, Bernie peeled a carrot. Lea leaned over a large pot on the camping stove and dropped in chunks of potato.

Bernie leaned his head toward the back garden. "Jack's outside on the lounger. Go join him if you want."

"Are you sure? Anything I can do to help?"

"What is it you guys say? 'Too many cooks spoil the broth'? Get outta here."

"Cheers, Bernie."

I walked outside and sat on the spare lounger next to Jack. He passed me an open can of fruit cocktail and a spoon.

"I feel like I should be doing something," he said.

"I know what you mean, but we need some downtime."

Jack folded an arm behind his head and carried on reading *Day of the Triffids*, which he'd picked up from a bookcase inside.

I settled back on the lounger and watched a brightly colored bird, busily hopping around a tree. As I wondered what species it might be, the smell of cooking wafted over from the kitchen, and my mouth watered.

I momentarily closed my eyes and tried to capture this single peaceful moment, away from the events of the last few days. I felt calm until I opened my eyes again and caught sight of the two graves in my peripheral vision.

We still needed to stay alert, so I patrolled around the house, enjoying the breeze on my face and the sound of the wind whispering through the trees. With space around us, an apparent lack of people, a reasonable amount of supplies in the kitchen, and a secure house, I started to believe our prospects were looking up.

My long terms plans, pre-flight, were to have security, peace, and a nice family home. Those desires hadn't changed, but bringing them about seemed a lot more difficult in the current world. Before, I'd considered myself a man of principle who would achieve my ambitions through honest hard work, acting with compassion, integrity, and respect. All useless in terms of dealing with a driven killer.

I returned to the lounger and sat facing Jack. "Not a bad place to recharge our batteries. Bernie and Lea seem to be warming to each other."

He lowered the book. "To deprive a gregarious creature of companionship is to maim it, to outrage its nature."

"You've just read that, haven't you?"

He tossed the book at me and lay back.

As natural light began to fade, Lea called from the kitchen, "You guys ready to eat?"

We enthusiastically made our way back inside. She directed us to the dining room.

Bernie leaned over a silver-plated candelabra and used a plastic disposable lighter to get the candles going. "Come in, gents."

I felt like they were making an effort for us. I had no idea why. Neither owed us a thing.

We sat around an oval-shaped oak dining table on posh-looking carved chairs with sumptuous purple seat cushions. Lea set down a bowl of stew and a spoon in front of each us and served herself last. The food tasted good, and we ate in companionable silence.

I stacked the bowls and sat back down. "Once we've acclimatized, I think we should try to find other survivors."

Jack puffed out a smoke ring from a cigar he'd found stored in the dining room drinks cabinet.

"I say we check on Greg; he seemed like a good man," Bernie said.

"I need some special supplies," Lea said.

"There's plenty here," Jack replied.

She reached over and tapped his hand. "Not for what I need."

Jack blushed and changed the subject. "Why not set fire to a car and observe it from a distance?"

Bernie rolled his eyes. "Not this again."

"Don't you ever learn your lesson, Jack?" Lea said.

"I'm going for a wash," Jack said, sounding slightly pissed off.

He dropped his cigar on a wooden floorboard and twisted his boot on it before trudging up the stairs.

"What is it with him and fires and traps?" Lea asked.

"He's just doing what he thinks is best. Give him a break. Who knows the right answer?"

"I know the *wrong* answer," Bernie said.

I've always believed a man should be there to defend himself, so I excused myself from the table instead of carrying on the conversation.

"Tell me about Linda," Lea said to Bernie.

I left them to it and had a dig around a chest of drawers in the corner of the room. I liked that Bernie had somebody to talk to other than Jack and me. Lea was attractive, and I felt sure she could help soothe his mental wounds.

Without finding anything of interest in the drawers, I rifled through cabinets but just found ornaments, coasters, silverware, and china. I decided to go upstairs and use another bathroom.

I filled a sink with water, used the hand soap to wash myself, toweled myself down, and walked to a bedroom in my underpants to find some clean clothes.

I found a comfortable-looking gray velour tracksuit hanging up in a wardrobe—the type I only ever saw in a charity shop back in Manchester. I hopped into the bottoms, feeling grateful for a fresh change of clothes, and put an arm into the sleeve.

Coins spilled and bounced on the wooden floorboards downstairs.

I wrestled on the velour top and grabbed my Glock from the bed. Jack flew out of the bathroom, and we met at the top of the stairs.

"Are you all right down there?" I called.

"We're still in the dining room. Someone's in the house," Lea said.

"Shit, so much for a safe haven," Jack said.

I put my finger to my lips. Somebody creaked across the floorboards. It sounded like they were in the hallway. I descended two steps. The second one groaned. I leaned over the banister and looked below. A figure dashed out of view.

Jack followed me as I dropped down four more steps. I paused to listen. Nothing.

"Stay where you are. I'll shoot," Lea shouted.

I waited, expecting to hear a shot. Nothing happened. "Do you know their location?"

"No," Lea called back. "Think they came in through a living-room window."

"Fuck," Jack said.

"I don't think they've got a gun," I said.

"What makes you say that?"

"They could've just shot Bernie or Lea through the window."

Floorboards creaked to my left. The living room. A formal entertaining area in this house, with two large brown leather couches, a long glass table in the middle, and paintings around the walls.

All natural light had ebbed away, leaving the room dark.

"You two still okay?" I shouted.

"Still here," Bernie said.

"Stay where you are." I turned to Jack. "Let's sort this out."

I climbed to the bottom of the stairs and looked through the gloomy living-room entrance. Moonlight shone through the windows. At least I'd have some visibility.

"Cover me," I said.

I hunched down, edged to the entrance, and took a single stride into the living room, aiming at the open space to my left. My eyes had already adjusted to the darkness after spending enough time out of the dining room. I detected no signs of movement apart from the linen drapes, twitching in the breeze on either side of an open window four yards to my right.

I dropped to one knee and swept my gun around the room. The person had to be in here somewhere, unless they'd escaped back through the window.

"You see anything?" Jack said.

The left-side drape flapped to one side. A slim figure ran at me.

I dropped to my back and fired. Jack's muzzle flashed. I heard his bolt snap back and forward.

The figure screamed and dived. I quickly rolled to my left.

A mason's hammer thudded into the floorboard where my head had been.

I fired at the head. The figure's body jerked and relaxed.

"Clear," I said.

"Bernie, Lea," Jack said.

Lea tentatively walked around the corner, holding a candle. Bernie followed, and they stood over the body. I'd picked myself off the floor and got a better view of our attacker under the candle's glow. A young male in a basketball shirt, tattoos covering both arms.

"Your coins worked, Lea," I said.

"Kinda wish they hadn't."

"Meaning what?" Jack asked.

"Meaning, he wouldn't have shown up."

She handed Bernie the candle, closed the window, and collected the coins that were scattered across the floorboards.

Bernie nudged the body with his foot. "We're gonna have trouble defending this place from psychos."

"Take it easy," I said. "It's one attack. We haven't seen any evidence to show this place crawling with killers."

"Take it easy? I'm totally wired."

"Whoever takes watch, sits on the porch by the open door. We can see anyone approach from the front. If someone tries to come through a window, we'll hear smashing glass or coins dropping."

———

We all sat on the porch until just after eleven in the evening. Nobody wanted to sleep, not after suffering the recent shock of our intruder. Jack and I dragged the body around the back of the house. If it carried on like this, we would soon have a heavily stocked cemetery.

Bernie cracked first. He yawned and groaned, rising out of his wicker chair. "I might try to get some shut-eye."

"I'll clean up," Lea said.

They both disappeared through the door. Jack followed them and returned a minute later with a bottle of whiskey and two glasses. "Fancy a nightcap? I need to unwind."

"Just a small one," I said, conscious that we might have to react at any moment. Every dark tree surrounding the property had changed from being part of the pleasant surroundings to being a perfect hiding place.

We sat in comfortable peacock chairs by the side of the door, with a small table between us. Jack chugged his whiskey in one gulp and topped himself up.

"Go easy on," I said.

"All right, mum," he said.

I wondered if he'd started suffering from post-traumatic stress disorder. Self-destructive behavior such as drinking in dangerous situations and avoiding talking about events like the shooting in Elmhurst were both symptoms. I decided to get him talking about our situation. I had no idea if would help, but bringing things out was the opposite of letting things fester, and I had no better ideas.

"I don't think Dave and Andy had much of a chance in Manhattan," I said.

"I'm almost one hundred percent sure they died on Friday."

"Family and friends? Do you think anyone back home made it?"

Jack poured another whiskey. I gave him a disapproving look.

"I think we should assume they didn't pull through. Why are you talking about it now?"

"Just chewing the fat," I said.

We sat quietly for the next few minutes. I reflected on the future possibilities and decided to push any long-term goals to one side and concentrate on our short-term survival. We could get through to the other side if we took it in bite-sized chunks and didn't try anything stupid.

At some point, survivors would start clustering and building strength, but a bigger unknown threat loomed over us: Who had done this, and why?

"Reckon we should recruit Greg if he's still about?" I said.

"Don't see why not. There's more than enough room here."

Jack swallowed his whiskey in a single gulp and slammed his glass on the table. He avoided eye contact and refilled.

"You're no use to me hammered if a killer turns up," I said.

He shook his head and sighed. "Do you think Bernie and Lea will stick around?"

"I think Bernie might. Not sure about Lea. She's an independent sort, and I still don't think she trusts us."

"You're probably right—"

A floorboard creaked behind the front door. Jack jumped to his feet and peered through the fly screen. "Lea, is that you?"

She rattled it open, walked out, sat on the wicker chair, and turned away from me.

"How long have you been there?" I asked.

"A few minutes," she said without turning around.

"I'm off to get a cigar," Jack said, escaping our awkward situation.

She'd probably heard everything. As far as I could remember, neither Jack nor I had said anything bad about her. I'd speculated about whether she trusted us, but that was it. I decided to get things out in the open before we went any further.

"Lea, I've a confession to make, and you're not going to like it."

She spun to face me and grimaced. "Do you think I didn't know you started the music?"

"P-pardon me?" I said.

"You three couldn't act to save your lives. I knew straight away on the roof of Bernie's apartment block. You were all sheepish and pathetic."

She gripped the chair's armrests and maintained an icy stare.

"I take full responsibility," I said. "Don't blame Jack or Bernie. I had an idea to draw killers to a certain spot, away from us. It's fair to say it went badly."

Jack staggered out and flopped in his chair. He sensed the tension on the porch, bent down, and started unfastening and tying his bootlaces. Twice.

"You've spent over a day with us. Surely you can see what we're all about," I said.

Her face softened and she shook her head. "You should have told me right away. I would have understood. I'm not a total bitch."

"Are you sure? You were going mental on the roof," Jack said.

"Course I'm sure. I can understand what you did, but show a little faith in me."

"We do," I said.

"You think that I'll pack my bags at the first opportunity. I heard you from behind the front door."

Jack frowned. "That's a bit sneaky, isn't it?"

"Who are you to talk about sneaky?"

I didn't want us going down the same rathole again, so I passed Lea my glass. "Join us for a drink."

For the next hour, taking us past midnight, Jack, Lea, and I had our first straight talk. She understood the way we'd reacted after we explained—the car, the music, and the awful turn of events. We were miles from home and any kind of comfort zone.

Show me somebody who claims to act perfectly in an unexpected apocalypse scenario, and I'll show you a liar.

We speculated on potential locations for survivor groups, and knew one place. Unfortunately, none of us could stomach Morgan.

A spray of automatic gunfire echoed in the distance.

"How close was that?" Lea asked.

"A few miles at least," Jack said, "There's bound to be a lot of frightened and confused people walking around."

"Let's not get too jumpy. We'll deal with any immediate threats," I said.

Lea stood and stretched. "I'm hitting the hay. Thanks for the chat."

"No worries," I said.

After five minutes, Jack's eyelids sunk.

"You want to get forty winks? I don't mind staying up," I said.

155

He rubbed his hand with his thumb and index finger. "I've got a better idea. Fancy a walk to that farm we passed? I'm in the mood for a bit of exploring."

"That's the booze talking, Jack. Leave it till the morning."

"We'll be fine. Come on."

Jack stood and picked up his rifle. "Let's see if we can get some fresh supplies. There might be chickens, vegetables, and all kinds of stuff. Are you game?"

"It's not a case of being bloody game," I said, barely able to conceal my anger. "We're on lookout. Are you forgetting what happened three hours ago?"

He ignored me and unsteadily thumped down the porch steps.

"Jack, come back!"

He continued across the garden.

"Shit!" I ran inside and heard clanking in the kitchen. I ran through the hallway and skidded through the entrance. Lea was washing our bowls in the sink. "Listen to me. Jack's heading for the farm. Can you keep watch while I convince him he's making a big mistake?"

She dropped the dishcloth and grabbed her Beretta from the counter. "Why the hell is he doing that?"

"Dunno—a mixture of booze and stress. Thanks, Lea."

I kicked the fly screen open and sprinted across the garden. Since landing, Jack's behavior had become increasingly erratic. I felt compelled to follow and couldn't let him go out on his own. With threats still out there, I would just have to deal with the fallout.

I caught up with him, purposefully striding along the road. "Why didn't you listen?"

"I knew you'd follow. What have we got to lose?"

I didn't answer him, but losing our lives through reckless actions was an obvious answer.

Jack continued forward. I felt committed to his silly idea, rather than having an argument on a dark countryside road. As we neared

156

the property, a light twinkled from a farmhouse window. Possibly a lantern, flashlight, or alternative electricity source.

We crept along a tree-lined road that led to the farm's gate. The hum of a generator came from inside the large Dutch barn. I headed for it, using it to shield any noise of our approach. I pulled myself flat against the barn's side and edged around it. Jack followed. I kept catching whiffs of alcohol but resisted passing comment.

I pointed to the farmhouse window. "They're not exactly keeping a low profile."

"How shall we handle it?"

"I thought you were the one—" I stopped myself and decided on a more positive approach. Now that we were here, the best thing would be to correctly execute a plan. "Sneak up to the window and have a look inside. If someone's in there, I'll knock on the door. You keep watching through the window to see if they pick up a weapon."

"If they shoot first?"

"I'll stand by the side of the door. You crouch below the window. If they want to try it, they'll be fools. We have the element of surprise here. If it's an armed group, we come back in the morning with a white flag."

He nodded. "Okay."

We crossed to the window, keeping low across the courtyard, and looked inside. A stocky middle-aged man with a bulbous nose sat on a recliner, reading a book. I slipped across to the door, banged the side of my fist against it three times, and moved to the right side, keeping my gun pointed at the shoebox-sized window pane.

Jack shot me a glance. "He's coming straight to the door. Didn't see a gun."

"Who's there?" a high-pitched voice called from behind the door.

"Your new neighbors. Two of us here," I said.

"Two of you? What do you want?"

Jack scrambled up to the opposite side of the door. "We don't want any trouble. This is the first place we've seen with lights on since the power went out."

"Do you know what time it is?"

I checked the luminous hands on my watch. After one o'clock. I took a deep breath and moved left, making my profile visible through the opaque window.

The man took a step back. I leaned forward and saw my breath condense on the glass. "We've come to warn you about killers in the area."

"How do I know I can trust you?"

"We could say the same thing," Jack said.

I held my gun up to the glass. "I could've just shot you through the door or through the window while you were reading a book."

"You were watching me?" He said, sounding increasingly nervous. "We can talk here."

Jack kicked the bottom of the door. "Let us in or I'll smash the bloody door down."

I frowned at him and shook my head. Jack could handle a few drinks, but he'd never acted like this before. If we'd found another genuine survivor, I could understand the man's reluctance, especially now that his home had been threatened.

Surprisingly, after another ten seconds of silence, I heard a bolt scrape along its latch, and the door creaked open, throwing artificial light across the yard.

The man shrank back from the entrance and extended his palms toward me. "I don't want no trouble. Please, come in."

I switched my gun to my left hand and extended my right. "Harry—and that's my brother, Jack."

Relief washed over his face, and he attempted to smile as he weakly shook my hand. "Jerry Caisley. This way."

He led us to the living area and wearily gestured to the couch. "Would you like a drink?"

The place had an eighties feel. Fake wooden beams on the roof, a dirty jade carpet, a cassette player propped on a plastic table with five tapes stacked next it. Strange fantasy-style ornaments filled his dark wood display cabinet: dragons, elves, and wizards.

Jack slumped on the couch and looked around. "Got anything cold?"

Jerry pottered away and quickly returned with two chilly cans of coke. He moaned like a man twice his age as he sat in his lazy boy. He took off his glasses, breathed on them, and dried the lenses on his sleeve.

Jack popped open his can and took a couple of loud gulps.

Jerry replaced his glasses and relaxed his hands on the lazy boy's arms. He quickly went from being scared to relaxed. For a moment I thought it odd, but if two men approached me in this current world, and shook my hand, I think I'd have the same sense of relief.

"What's a pair of Brits doing all the way out here?"

"Just trying to find a safe place," Jack said.

"You noticed anything funny during the last few days?" I asked.

He drummed his fingers on the arm and glanced at my pistol. "I'd love to know what *you've* been doing. How did you end up at my farm? You say there's only two of you?"

"That's right. Harry, you tell him the story."

I wondered why Jack had omitted to tell Jerry about Bernie and Lea, but went along with it and would find out later. I told Jerry about our experiences since landing at JFK, our meeting Maureen, and what had happened in the police building. I skimmed over the details of our time in Elmhurst and described our trip to Orange Country.

Jerry's shifty stare gradually turned to a wide-eyed look of horror. He retrieved a handkerchief from his pocket and mopped his brow. I couldn't see any sweat. Maybe it was a reflex to the disturbing events.

"When did you see the vapor trail? Did you see anything in the sky?"

Jack shook his head. "Today, and no."

"I see," he said and steepled his fingers to his mouth. "The guy you met from Maybrook? Did you get a name?"

"Greg. Do you know him?" I answered.

"Greg from Maybrook? Can't say I do. You're at the Watsons's place?"

"Big white house half a mile up the road?" Jack said.

"That's the Watsons's." He looked at me. "I noticed you're wearing the old bastard's clothes."

I nearly spat my coke out. My father had taught me from a young age to never speak ill of the dead. Although there are obvious exceptions, like Osama Bin Laden.

"A bit harsh, isn't it?" I asked.

Jerry sighed. "You try being his neighbor for ten years. See how you like it."

He seemed to be getting a lot of information from us without giving much in return. I wanted to know his story, so I ignored his apparent hatred of Mr. Watson. "Take us through your experiences since Friday."

He pressed a button on the side of his chair. A footrest smoothly whined out. He balanced his tartan slippers on top of it and readjusted himself.

"There's nothing much to tell. I felt a small earthquake or something last Friday. I went outside to look around, and somebody bashed the back of my head. I came around facing a dead man." He shuddered and hugged himself. "It was like he died staring at my face."

"Did you know him?" Jack asked.

"I don't really mix. Not really a people person. That's one of the reasons I moved out here. Not that Watson respected—"

"Did you feel any strange urges?" I asked.

"Did I want to kill anyone? No. I moved the body away from the house and called the police. They didn't answer. I tried chatting to my online buddies, but nobody's responded since I felt those tremors."

"So you just sat tight?" I asked.

He poked his glasses against his nose. "If something dangerous was going down, I didn't want to get caught up in it. After a couple of days, the power failed, and I fired up the backup generator. You're the first people I've seen."

I felt a tinge of jealousy. Apart from being smacked over the head, he'd had a pretty easy ride compared to us, although I couldn't begrudge anyone for that. I became conscious of time and checked my watch. Past two o'clock, and Lea would still be on watch. I decided to go back and relieve her.

"Can we come and see you later? Say lunchtime?" I said.

"Sure thing. See you then."

He showed us to the door. Jack wedged his boot in when Jerry tried to close it. "Stay alert. We got attacked a few hours ago."

Jerry rapidly nodded and eased Jack's boot outside with his slipper. "Okay, okay. Good night."

We trudged up the farm's road and turned toward the house.

"He wanted us away in a hurry," Jack said.

"Probably because you stink like a barmaid's apron."

"Whatever. It's the way I deal with it."

I stopped him and put on my 'Jack, I'm being deadly serious' face. "Just make sure it's not at anyone else's expense, right?"

Jack groaned. "I get it."

"Last question, I promise. Why did you tell Jerry there's only two of us?"

He spun and started walking for the house. "Because we know nothing about him. I'm finding it hard to trust anyone at the moment."

Due to my suspicions over Jack's state of mind, I decided to leave things for a while and hoped my words had sunk in.

When we arrived back at the house, Lea sat in the wicker chair on the porch. I waved as we crunched up the stone path. She scowled in reply.

"Where the hell have you been?"

"The farm," I said. "Met a bloke called Jerry."

"Do you know him?" Jack asked.

"Why would I know him?"

"Because you said you'd visited the place."

Lea rubbed her face in frustration. "What is it with you two?"

She looked tired and in a mood similar to when we first met her on the roof. I didn't have the energy to deal with it at the moment. "Go to bed, Lea. We'll take it from here."

She shook her head, snatched a blanket from the chair, and headed inside.

Jack and I stayed out on the porch, trying to keep ourselves awake. We talked through all the events since landing to see if we had missed anything of note, but we couldn't think of anything new. Eventually, Jack fell asleep.

I thought about Jerry's farm and his great set-up. Maybe he could help us get power to our house with a generator. He could be a very useful person to know in the area.

Just before four o'clock, Bernie's shift, I shook Jack's shoulder.

"Time for beddy-byes."

He licked his lips and blinked. "How long have I been asleep?"

"Less than an hour. Up you go."

He disappeared inside. I had a quick patrol around the property to check for danger. After finding the place quiet, I climbed the stairs and located Bernie's room by listening for a noise similar to someone sawing a log.

I gently knocked on the door and popped my head in the room. "Bernie, you okay to take watch?"

"Gimme a minute."

I hung around on the landing until he shuffled out of the bedroom.

"You must be maxed out. Take my room."

"There's enough for all of us," I said.

I found an empty bedroom, stripped, and jumped in bed. My head sunk into a feather pillow; I pulled the heavy, soft duvet over my body and almost immediately fell asleep.

———

Daylight streamed through the bedroom blinds, and I contemplated turning over to snooze. However, as I remembered last night's events, I threw back the duvet and rolled out of bed. My window had a view of the front driveway area, and all seemed quiet. I pulled on the retro tracksuit and searched downstairs, finding Lea and Bernie in the dining room.

"Morning, Harry. Sleep well?" Bernie said.

I gripped my wrist and remembered I'd left my watch on the bedside table. "What time is it?"

"Nearly eleven; we decided not to disturb you."

He poured a coffee and slid the cup toward me. I appreciated the fact that Lea and Bernie left me to sleep, and I felt reasonably refreshed. Shortly after, Jack thumped downstairs and joined us at the table. He looked rough as a bag of spanners, but I had little sympathy.

"Everyone still good with visiting Greg?" Bernie asked.

"Fine by me," I said, "but I need a wash first. By the way, Bernie, Jack and I have a lunchtime appointment."

Bernie smiled. "Lea told me all about it. You were nuts to go out last night."

She glared at Jack from the other side of the table.

Jack avoided eye contact and sipped his coffee. "I'll tell Jerry the truth. It's my responsibility."

"Who wants breakfast?" Bernie said, thankfully changing the subject. "Sorry, Harry, got no grits on the menu today."

Jack rose from the table and picked up his rifle. "I'm not hungry, and somebody needs to keep a lookout."

He left the room with a coffee mug in his other hand. Bernie frowned. "What's his beef?"

"Nothing for you to worry about. Breakfast would be great. Make Jack some too, and I'll take it out to him."

Bernie used the last of the eggs to make a huge omelet. I ate half and took the rest out to Jack, who did have an appetite. I hoped his behavior stemmed from feelings of guilt about last night, rather than it being another sign of him slowly spinning toward a drain of despair.

We washed in different bathrooms and met in the midday sunshine outside the SUV. At least we had the weather on our side, and Tuesday was shaping up to be another beautiful day.

"Jerry can wait," I said. "I think he lives like a hermit anyway."

"I'll go and introduce myself," Lea said. "Leave you to your boys' reunion?"

Bernie had found a local map inside and stuffed it next to the handbrake. He started the engine and put the SUV in drive. "We stick together. Best way of staying safe."

We headed to Maybrook down a quiet country road and approached the outskirts of the village along Homestead Avenue. I looked for signs of life and for the address Greg had given us. Bernie pulled over and checked the map.

Lea jabbed her finger at window. "We're already here . . . Aristotle Drive, right?"

She pointed down a street of large detached houses, all painted light green. Out of my slightly open window, I heard the noise of a vehicle approaching.

I looked back through the windshield. A black Range Rover approached from the opposite direction.

Jack noticed it too. "Get down!"

I closed my window.

Bernie cut the engine, and we ducked.

"Are we just letting them drive right by?" Lea said.

"I want to make sure. Do you want a killer slamming into us at high speed?" Jack asked.

"I'm still spooked from last night. I agree with Jack," Bernie said.

"What's the rush?" I said. "We let it sail right by, and then we find Greg. If they're local, I'm sure we'll bump into them again."

I leaned above the dash to check the progress of the oncoming vehicle. Three hundred yards away. Two hundred. One hundred. Slowing down.

"It's stopping around here," I said.

"They can't have seen us," Bernie said.

"What's it doing, Harry?" Lea asked. "Take a look."

"Turning into Aristotle Drive . . . two people inside . . . They've stopped outside the second house on the left. Have a look, but keep down."

The other three shuffled into position.

Nothing happened for two minutes. Eventually, two men jumped out, wearing black pants and sweaters. The first man, overweight with a buzz cut, carried a silver revolver behind his back. He approached the front door of the house. The other, a man with a ZZ Top–style brown beard, crouched in front of the garage, providing cover. The overweight man knocked on the door.

He shouted something against the door. The whole picture looked similar to the way Jack and I had approached Jerry's. After a few minutes, the door opened. Greg stood in the open entrance.

The man whipped the revolver from behind his back, pointed it at Greg's face, and pushed him to the front of the garage. ZZ Top tied his arms behind his back and kicked him in the back of the leg, causing him to drop to his knees.

"What the hell . . . ?" Bernie asked.

"Lower your window—see if we can hear them," Lea said.

Bernie twisted the key to activate the electronics. I gingerly hit the button. The window slid down an inch.

"I've told you, I've got no idea. What do you want?" Greg asked.

"Tell us the location, and we'll let you live," revolver man said.

"What location? I don't know what you're talking about."

"This is your last chance. I'll give you exactly five seconds," ZZ Top said.

"Please, there's nobody left alive. I've— "

"They're bluffing," Jack said.

The overweight man pressed his revolver against Greg's forehead and fired. Greg toppled backward and lay motionless on the ground, revealing a red splat on his white garage door.

"What the fuck?" Bernie said in quiet amazement.

The men shiftily glanced around, presumably to see if anyone else had noticed the gunshot. We ducked back down.

"Who are they looking for? Why did they kill him?" Lea asked.

"We can't take on that rifle in a firefight at this range," Jack said, "unless I hit him with my first shot."

Hurried footsteps slapped against the road surface. The Rover's engine roared. It sped past us in the direction of the house.

"Why did they kill him?" Bernie asked.

"We should warn Jerry," I said. "If they're going around picking off survivors, he's probably next."

Bernie sat at the wheel and twisted the key. "To Jerry's farm?"

I thought for a moment. "Take us home, and Jack and I will just cut across the fields."

"Stay out of sight," Jack said. "We'll take the flare gun and fire if we see any danger coming toward you."

"Shouldn't we all stick together in case—" Lea said.

"No time to debate it—sorry," I said and slapped Bernie on the shoulder. "Pedal to the metal."

With a plan quickly formulated, Bernie sped back to the house and parked the SUV in the back garden, where it would not be visible from the road. I grabbed the flare gun and loaded a cartridge. I realized that all the times Bernie had flashed it around in Queens, it hadn't even been loaded.

I think Bernie realized too and gave me a sheepish look; I returned a smile.

"We'll keep watch from the upstairs front window," Lea said.

She disappeared with Bernie through the back door.

Jack and I moved off quickly. We jogged across the front lawn, vaulted the fence on the far side of the road, and bounded across a green field. We kept low as we hurried along, straddling more fences and trying to remain hidden from the road until we reached the outskirts of Jerry's property.

Jack shouldered his rifle and jerked it toward the left edge of the barn. "We'll go the same way as last night. In case they're already here."

"Okay, follow me."

I slowly edged my way along the side of the barn and craned my head around the corner. A black Range Rover was parked in the courtyard outside Jerry's front door.

"They're already here," I said.

"Can you see any movement?"

I looked around again. "Figures through the window. Three of them."

"Are they threatening him?"

"I don't know. Looks like they're talking."

"Ambush?"

If we managed to catch them off guard, we could disarm them at gunpoint. But if things didn't go according to plan, they had the advantage of an automatic rifle, if ZZ Top knew how to use it properly.

"Let's wait. They didn't fuck about with Greg."

"What about Jerry?" Jack asked.

"We hardly know him," I said, surprising myself with my detachment. I wondered if I had started sacrificing some of my morals in order to ensure the survival of our small group.

We barely knew Bernie and Lea, but they were now the closest thing we had to a family. Keeping that family safe was the priority for me. If we did take these people on, I wanted to make sure we had the upper hand.

The conversation inside continued for another two minutes. Then the men left the room. "I think they're coming out," I said.

A bead of sweat rolled down my temple, and my heart thumped against my chest. I caressed the Glock's trigger with my finger.

Revolver man and ZZ Top walked out the front door, followed by Jerry. I heard Jerry laugh as he climbed into the back seat of the Rover.

"He looked the opposite of frightened," I said to Jack after the Rover rumbled away.

Jack tilted his head and frowned. He opened his mouth as if to say something but didn't.

"What are you thinking, Jack?"

"We told Jerry about Greg in Maybrook last night."

"And?"

"What if the fat fucker told them about him? What if they're coming for us next?"

I looked back in the direction of the house. "The Watson's place."

Jack sprang to his feet. "Let's go."

"Wait two seconds."

I pointed the flare gun skyward and fired. A red projectile whooshed high in the air, and I hoped that Bernie and Lea would see and understand the warning.

I ran as fast as my legs would carry me along the road. We had no time to tactically advance through fields. The Range Rover was parked thirty yards short of the property and looked empty. Using the cover of the trees around the driveway, we snuck up behind it. Through the glass, I could see figures standing roughly in front of the house. Bernie knelt on the edge of the lawn; the overweight man pointed his revolver at the back of his head. ZZ Top aimed toward the house. Jerry stood next to him and whispered something into his ear.

I ducked back behind the Range Rover.

"Christ, what the fuck do we do now?" Jack said.

"Whatever we decide, we need to do it quickly."

Jack bent to catch his breath.

I squatted down and looked below the Rover. We had a shot from here. But only with Jack's rifle. The group on the lawn were tightly clustered. I could accidently hit Bernie from this range.

"Prone position Jack," I said. "Take out ZZ Top."

"Easy from here. Then what?"

"Revolver man behind on Bernie. Hopefully, they'll freeze."

ZZ Top shouted, "Come out, Lea. Someone is really eager to see you."

I wondered why they knew her name. Maybe Bernie had told her to keep down, or they had asked him their names before pointing a gun at his head. We didn't have time for any intricate planning. The situation could escalate at any second, and we needed to act.

Jack lay down by the side of the Range Rover to make himself a smaller target for any return fire. He glanced up at me. "Ready?"

I nodded. Jack aimed and fired.

ZZ Top staggered back. He detached from the group and dropped to his knees. He clutched his chest and rasped.

Jack reloaded.

169

I fired three shots in ZZ Top's direction, no longer worried about hitting Bernie. One punctured his neck, and he dropped to the ground with a gurgled scream.

Jerry and the revolver man spun to face us as we trained our weapons on them. Bernie tried to get up. Jerry put his arm on his shoulder and forced him back down. "Back on your knees."

The other man mouthed obscenities at us but kept his revolver aimed at Bernie's head.

"You said there were only two of you," Jerry said.

"You told us a pack of lies," I said.

"Hit on the head and waking up next to a corpse? You pair of gullible pricks." He glanced at ZZ Top. "We just want to talk."

Jack stood and aimed over the hood of the Rover. "We saw what happened to Greg in Maybrook. I take it you gave away his location?"

Jerry sneered. "If you fire one more shot, you can kiss your friend good-bye."

"You've one revolver, and we're both aiming straight at you," I said. "You're in no position to negotiate."

Bernie peered over at me and faintly shrugged. I hated seeing a bloke like him being reduced to a scared expression.

"Are you okay, Bernie?" I asked.

"They took me by surprise. Jerry came to the door, shouting for you to help him. By the time I saw the flare, it was too late. Sorry, guys."

"There's nothing to apologize for."

Jerry glared at me. "There're more coming this way. Give yourselves up now, and I'll let all three of you leave. We only want the bitch in the house."

I shuddered to think what a vile creature like this would do with a woman.

"Last chance, Jerry. You seem to be in charge, so you're next," I said.

He grabbed Bernie by the back of the collar. "You haven't the guts. You're too worried about your friend."

"He's your last bargaining chip. Use it wisely."

He let go of Bernie's shirt and took a sideways step. "We can wait here until the heavy artillery arrive. You seriously don't want to be around for that."

"Do not take another step toward that rifle," I said. "Let Bernie go, and you both walk away."

"We'll exchange him for the woman. You three leave in that heap of shit on the drive."

They must have seen Lea through a window. Jerry's spitefully cool negotiation skills chilled me, but not half as much as the thought of what he would do to her.

"No chance," I replied. "Let Bernie go now, or we'll shoot."

I covered my mouth with my hand and leaned toward Jack. "Take revolver man out."

He hunched over his rifle.

Jerry said something to revolver man, who nodded and stiffened his posture.

"No!" Bernie shouted.

Revolver man fired at the back of Bernie's head from close range. A puff of red mist appeared in front of his face, and he sank to the ground. I stood in momentary shock. Jerry and the assassin used our hesitation to run toward the fields.

Jack and I fired simultaneously. One of us hit revolver man in the thigh, and he dropped to his knees, gripping his leg. I ran out of ammo.

Jerry scrambled over the fence and ran through the field in the direction of his farm. He disappeared after dropping into the long grass.

Jack slid his bolt forward and fired at revolver man. The force of the impact ripped his jawbone from the right side of his face. He slumped lifelessly against a fence post.

I ran to Bernie, shouting his name. I pulled up short, realizing we could do nothing. He had a nasty exit wound on his forehead and parts of his brain splashed across the lawn.

Jack joined me over his body. "Oh my . . . No . . ."

Lea ran out of out of the house. "Is he dead? Is he dead?"

When she reached us, she clamped her hands over her mouth and inhaled sharply.

I swallowed hard and composed myself. The image of Jerry sitting on his lazy boy, spinning us bullshit, ran through my mind. I squeezed the Glock and snarled.

"Jerry," Jack said through gritted teeth.

"I'm going to find him if it's the last thing I do," I said.

"I'll be right behind you," Lea said.

I dropped the Glock on the grass and picked up ZZ Top's AR-15. I carried out a standard British army make-safe procedure on it, placed the loose round back into the top of the magazine, and slammed it home before putting one in the chamber.

"To the farm," I said.

We climbed over the fence on the opposite side of the road and jogged through the fields toward his farm.

As we neared the barn. I said to Lea and Jack, "I want him alive."

"Fuck that," Jack said, "he's going to have a long, slow, painful death."

"Fine with me," I said, "but we get him to talk first. He's got some serious explaining to do."

8
THE BARN

I leopard-crawled the last thirty yards to Jerry's barn. He would expect us to follow, so it would be foolish to walk through the main entrance.

As I pressed myself against the its wooden exterior, I heard a muffled voice coming from inside. I turned to Jack and Lea and put my finger to my lips. They joined me against the wall and listened through gaps in the timber cladding.

"Control, this is NY three. Do you copy?"

A crackly voice replied, "This is Control. Please reconfirm the numbers."

"This is NY three. Three of them, two Brits and they're all armed."

"What happened to NY patrol six?"

"Those fuckers shot them. They'll be coming here soon. I'll hide in the barn until you send reinforcements."

Not the slickest voice procedure I'd ever heard. Jerry sounded in a flap, and rightly so. We were coming for him.

"I'll take the front with Lea," I said to Jack. "You take the side door."

Lea and I scampered round to the large double doors at the front of the barn. One door hung slightly open. I guessed he'd entered in a panic and forgotten to close it.

"Wait here and keep a lookout for any hostiles," I said.

She nodded and crouched by the door, facing the road.

I pressed the AR-15 into my shoulder, took a deep breath, and slipped through the gap. Jerry sat with his back to me, wearing a headset and leaning into a radio transmitter.

"Thanks," he said. "Tell them to come here first but to be on the lookout."

"Roger. Control out."

Jerry ripped off the headset and turned around. I stood five yards away and aimed at his twitching face.

"Hello, Jerry. Fancy seeing you here."

He glanced to his left, at a rifle sitting on top of a pile of supplies.

"You know the script if you try that," I said.

Jerry started to edge backward. The side door creaked open behind him. He spun around. Jack lurched forward and smashed the wooden butt of his rifle into Jerry's forehead. Jerry dropped to the floor and curled into a ball. Jack followed up with two firm blows to the top of his head until Jerry lay motionless.

I crushed his glasses with my boot.

Jack grabbed an axe from a dusty workbench and raised it above his head.

"Jack, no," I said. "We need him alive."

Jack dropped the axe, bent over, and checked his pulse. "He's out cold."

I scanned the barn and noticed a heavy old table against the rear wall.

"Jack, give me a hand pulling that table into the middle of the barn. Lea, you find some rope."

"What are we going to do with it?" she asked.

I could see pure anger in Jack's eyes, and I felt the same emotion, but I had to remain calm and find out what Jerry knew.

"It looks like it weighs a ton. Flip it on its side, and we'll tie him to it."

174

Jack and I scraped the heavy table into position and tipped it over. Dust shot from the floor as it crashed on its side. Jerry groaned.

We grabbed an arm each, dragged him across the filthy ground, and propped him against it. Lea brought some thin orange rope she'd found wrapped around a barrel. I cut four long pieces and tied each of Jerry's limbs tightly to individual table legs. It worked out a lot better than I'd originally thought. He had a little wiggle room but wouldn't be escaping unless he changed into the Incredible Hulk.

With Jerry secure, I had a closer look around the barn. An unusually high number of boxes of water and cans of food were stacked against the left side. He'd been preparing for something.

Jack grabbed the AR-15 off a box of canned peaches and checked it.

Five respirators and an equal number of ear protectors sat on the workbench where Jack had grabbed the axe. A large, black metal object sat in the right corner of the barn, rectangular in shape, about half the size of a single bed and with a chrome pole protruding out of the top.

"We need to get back outside," I said.

"Why? Is there something in here?" Lea asked.

"No, nothing like that. Jerry called us in to *Control*; they might send backup. Talked about patrol numbers."

"I heard that," Jack said. "Let's set up an ambush near the entrance. I bet they'll drive right in here if they're as stupid as patrol six."

"What do you mean 'stupid'?" Lea said.

"They drove right up to Greg's house. At our place, they didn't shoot Bernie straight away. If I were them, in a hostile situation, I'd have taken Bernie out immediately and picked off Lea from outside with the rifle."

"Charming," she said, looking slightly surprised.

"Whatever," I said. "We don't want them catching us with our pants down."

Jerry opened his right eye and moaned.

Jack picked up a dirty rag from next to the generator and stuffed it into his mouth. Jerry weakly struggled against his restraints.

Jack leaned next to Jerry's ear. "Just you wait."

As we walked away, Jerry spat out the rag and shouted, "Fuck you!"

Jack turned back, ran to the table, and smashed his fist into Jerry's left eye. His head bounced back against the underside of the table and flopped down. He grabbed Jerry's hair and forced the rag back into his mouth.

"Steady on, bro," I said to him outside the barn. "I'm not saying we obey the Geneva Convention, but we need to get him talking."

"I'm doing this for Bernie."

"There's plenty of time to avenge him, but we need to be clear headed and act in our interests."

A faded red wooden fence, in need of a lick of paint, and trees lined the sixty-yard road to the farm's entrance. I spotted three decent-sized oaks within a few yards of each other on the left side of the house that would provide a good hiding place to spring our ambush. Waiting on opposite sides would restrict our arcs of fire.

I checked my watch after twenty minutes of silently waiting. Half past two. I thought about how long to wait before returning to interrogate the weasel in the barn.

"What are we gonna do about Bernie?" Lea asked.

"We'll get payback—don't worry about that," I said.

She shook her head. "No. I mean we can't leave him on the lawn."

"We bury him after we finish," I said.

Jack held his arm up. I simultaneously heard the buzz of a distant vehicle.

It continued to approach, the buzz growing increasingly louder.

I held my rifle against my chest and tensed.

A minute later, I caught sight of a black roof speeding along the country road toward the farm.

"Jack, you and I empty our mags into the windows and doors. Lea, finish them off if necessary. Got that?"

They both nodded.

The Rover reached Jerry's entrance, its brakes squeaking as it slowed to a stop. I glanced around my tree. Two people in the front seats. A man wearing thick-rimmed glasses and a thin-faced woman. Both wore black. Not hard to recognize the pattern emerging.

We faced a coordinated effort, perhaps a gang taking advantage of the situation on the ground, but I had the feeling we weren't exactly dealing with elite soldiers.

The Rover slowly advanced along the farm road. The woman in the passenger seat held a rifle across her chest in a two-handed grip. From that position, she wouldn't have time to react. Maybe she naïvely thought a Rover's body provided a level of safety. I've seen hundreds of movies where people duck behind vehicle doors for cover. The truth is that they only offer concealment.

I took a deep breath. The driver's window came level with me. "Now!"

I rolled around the tree and fired repeated shots into the driver and passenger. In my peripheral vision, Jack did the same. The driver's window shattered and collapsed. Both people danced in their seats as multiple rounds zipped into them.

The driver slumped sideways toward the passenger. She hung forward against her seatbelt, motionless. The Rover veered off the road and came to a crunching halt against a tree. Lea ran to the passenger's window and fired two shots. A spray of blood covered the interior of the splintered windshield.

She looked back at me. "Her eyes were moving."

I kept my rifle shouldered and rushed to the Rover. Job done. "Let's clear this up in case any others turn up."

We dragged the corpses out and placed them into the backseat before taking the magazines from their rifles and reloading ours. The matching rifles, AR-15s, along with the black clothing, confirmed these people were probably all part of the same organized group.

I put the Range Rover into neutral, and we rolled it around the side of Jerry's farmhouse, out of view from the road.

Jack searched the trunk but found nothing. Lea found a hand-held radio with a flat battery in the glove compartment.

"Back in position in case any more of these amateurs show up," I said.

We waited by the trees, but no one else appeared. I wondered who these people were. The killers we'd encountered had been extremely dangerous, and a serious weapon had been used to create them. A complex and coordinated attack of this scale would require huge resources and skills. However, I had my doubts this group was responsible, judging by the members' level of competence. It was time to make Jerry talk. We needed answers, and I wanted them now.

Lea volunteered to keep watch from outside the barn in case anyone else showed up. Jack and I agreed, both feeling confident about dealing with any similar threats. With a couple of loaded rifles, we could take out any other patrols, even if they knew we were here. The evidence so far suggested that we were far more dangerous.

Jerry had spat out the rag and narrowed his eyes when I entered his barn. "You don't know what you're dealing with. Trust me."

I resisted a strong urge to punch Jerry in the mouth. His words, not his actions, would dictate his fate. "That's what I'm here to find out."

"Do you want the good news or the bad news?" Jack asked.

"If I were in your shoes, I'd untie me and get away from here as quickly as possible."

I crouched in front of him. "Why would I do that?"

He snarled and his hands jerked forward against the rope. "You're won't get away with this."

Jack stood behind me. "Your latest patrol is dead. That's four down. Don't become the fifth."

He looked to his left and slyly raised one corner of his mouth. "Maybe we can come to a compromise?"

I sighed. "Drop the idea that we're reasonable people. You ended any chance of that by killing Bernie."

Jack put on his worst German accent, "We have ways of making you talk."

Jerry's face dropped. "What? What are you going to do?"

"That depends on how cooperative you are," I said.

Jack turned to me. "Do you think Jerry will enjoy waterboarding?"

"No, but there're quicker ways of making this coward talk."

I started to look around the barn for a tool to threaten him with. I had no intention of playing the role of medieval torturer but would use the implied threat and slight force if required.

I heard two thumps behind me and glanced over my shoulder. Jack pulled his boot away from Jerry.

Jerry grimaced and spat on the ground. "You asshole."

I found a pair of rusty bolt cutters and dropped them in front of him. "Where would you like me to start with these?"

He attempted to appear sincere. "I've got information. We can make a deal."

Jack snatched the bolt cutters from the ground. "We don't make deals with terrorists."

Jerry tried to twist his foot around as I untied his shoelace. I slipped off his shoe and ripped off his sweaty blue sock—all part of the act to scare him.

The radio crackled, and I immediately spun to face it.

"This is Control. NY three. Please confirm the patrol has arrived. We have lost contact."

Jerry nervously looked at the radio. "If I don't respond, they'll know something's wrong."

"Should we respond? You could pretend to be Jerry," Jack said. "It's worth a shot."

Jack wrapped his hand around Jerry's mouth. He shouted and blew against it.

I sat on a stool in front of the radio, placed on the headset, and pressed the transmit button.

"This is NY three. The patrol has arrived," I said, attempting to mimic Jerry's Boston accent.

"You're not NY three. Confirm your call sign," a crackled voice replied after a brief pause.

"I'm NY three. The patrol is here at the farm."

"What's the pass code for today?"

I looked back at Jack, who shrugged his shoulders. With our cover blown, I dropped the pretence. "Jerry's told us all about you. I know where you are, and I'm coming for you."

I waited by the radio for a minute but received no reply.

"Oh dear, Jerry," I said. "Control thinks you've talked, and for all they know, you might be already dead."

Jack removed his saliva-drenched hand, wiped it on his shirt, and picked up the bolt cutters again. "Mark my words. Control won't be saving you from these."

His previously defiant and sly expression changed to one of concern. "They're in Michigan. I only follow orders. They made me do it."

"Made you do what?" I said.

"The first activation. You can't fight them."

"Fight who?"

He nervously glanced at the radio, probably to check if I'd left it on transmit. "There's a huge network. I'm only a small part, irrelevant to them, but I stayed alive by doing what they told me."

"You're far from irrelevant in our eyes, Jerry," Jack said.

"You saw the consequences of the first activation on Friday. That's what you're up against."

I knelt in front of him, feeling slightly confused. "What's the first activation?"

"You can't stop them, even if you knew."

He turned away from me. I snatched the bolt cutters from Jack, placed the two blades around his big toe, and gently squeezed.

"No, no—wait," he stammered. "Anthony knows more than me—he's higher up the pecking order and knows a lot more detail. I only found out on Thursday evening."

I struggled to control my anger. He knew about Friday and now tried to sell someone else down the river to save his own skin.

Jack kicked the table. "You knew this would happen and went along with it?"

Jerry closed his eyes and nodded. "They made me do it."

I squeezed a little tighter. "This Anthony character, what does he know?"

He grimaced and looked at his toe, then me. "He lives in Pennsylvania and always has the inside scoop. If you want to know what's happening next, untie me, and I'll take you to him."

Jack pointed to the large object in the corner of the barn. "Is that thing part of it?"

"They call it a device. It's part of the North American grid. That's what transmitted the first activation. Don't ask me about the technology, but it works."

"We'll smash it up then," Jack said.

Jerry tried to blow his sweat-soaked hair away from his eyes. "Wouldn't make a difference. The radius of each device overlaps to ensure all areas are covered if one malfunctions."

"Where are the other devices? Do you have a map?" I said.

"I'm a grunt. Anthony has one in his garage. He's the one you need to be attacking with bolt cutters."

Jack started pacing around the barn, rubbing his hands through his hair. The more information we prized from Jerry, the more I felt an increasing responsibility to do something about it. We might possibly be the only ones alive who had the opportunity.

"Who's behind all of this?" I asked.

"You seriously don't want to—"

Jack sprinted across the barn and smashed Jerry in the temple with his rifle butt. Jerry dangled limply against the restraints, out cold again.

I stood and held my arms out. "What the fuck, Jack? We were just getting somewhere."

"I couldn't resist," Jack said. "After all he's done, he thinks he'll worm his way out by dropping his mate in the shit."

"He's not worming his way out of anything. Just go easy until we get what we need."

I could understand the intent behind Jack's action, but it wasn't a smart move. If he killed Jerry, we might never find Anthony and gain more information. I needed to start managing his actions more closely.

With Jerry in cloud cuckoo land, I decided to inspect the device. It didn't appear to be anything special. The black rectangular base looked similar to marble mounts used by sculptors and came up to my knees. Jack tried to push it over so we could check the bottom for markings. He strained against its chrome pole but the thing didn't budge.

We both heaved against it and managed to topple the thing over. It crashed against the dirty floor.

Lea poked her head through the door. "Everything all right?"

"Have you been listening?" I said.

"It's unbelievable. Do you trust him?"

I shrugged. "Strange thing to lie about."

"Let me know if you need me," she said and slipped away.

I crouched next to Jack and looked at an array of serial numbers stamped into the metal on the bottom of the device.

"Do you think it's code?" Jack asked.

"I'm guessing whoever made this wouldn't exactly advertise themselves. Maybe you're right. We'll ask him when he wakes up."

Jack felt around the base for any seams or hinges. He picked up a wrench from the floor and thumped it against the base. It gave off a hollow clank.

"I'll smash it open. See if we can find a clue inside."

He found a long-handled axe in the corner and attacked the device, grunting with every swing, but he only managed to make small dents along the bottom edge.

"Christ, it must be made of titanium," he said.

"You keep going at that. I'm going to explore around the barn."

I left Jack, chopping away, and went back to the radio. I recognized it as HF because of the frequency range on the dial. This meant Jerry might not have been lying about Control being in Michigan. Distance was no object with these, especially during daylight, as radio waves bounced off a thicker ionosphere. It thinned at night, making transmission more difficult, but still possible.

A sheet of white paper lay on the desk next to the receiver, covered with childish drawings of naked women with oversized breasts. Almost definitely, Jerry's perverted handiwork.

I held it up toward Jack. "Looks like we've got a talented artist on our hands."

Jack stopped chopping and squinted at the sheet. "He's got serious issues."

I read the back of the paper as I showed him.

'Genesis Alliance—Voice Procedure for Operatives.'

The page contained instructions on how to hold radio conversation, along the lines of very basic military practice. The name at the top interested me the most: Genesis Alliance.

"Any luck with that thing?" I said.

"Breaking into Fort Knox would be easier."

"Leave it for now." I moved back in front of Jerry and grabbed his chin. He rolled his head and murmured like a teenager after too much booze. I said to Jack, "Don't pulverize him unless I say."

"Why are you going easy on him?"

"I'm not, but we need to know what he knows."

Jack took a bottle of water from the stockpile, opened it, and poured it over the top of Jerry's head.

Jerry convulsed and blew water away from his face. "Where am I?"

"In your barn. Who is Genesis Alliance?" I asked.

His eyes widened, and his restraints twanged tight. "Who told you about that?"

"The sheet of paper by the radio. Did Genesis Alliance plant the devices and set off the activation?"

"Maybe."

Jack stood over him with balled fists. "They already think you've squealed. No point holding back on us."

He groaned, probably as his memory fully returned and he realized the gravity of his situation. "They placed the devices, activated them—the whole nine yards."

"We need more than that," I said.

"I'm a pawn. Let me take to you to Anthony. He's a key player."

"I'll decide on that after you tell us everything you know," I said.

"I don't know much more than what I've told you."

He must have realized by now that we were not joking, but he still withheld information, like how he joined Genesis Alliance and why he had a device on the property that had led to the death of millions.

I picked up the bolt cutters and squeezed them around his toe again. "Try harder."

Jerry gasped, tried to pull his foot away and spoke quickly, "They activate the devices remotely. Anthony knows the exact location of Control."

"What's the distribution area of these devices?"

He looked straight into my eyes. "They built a global network. We're just one small part of it."

The bolt cutters fell from my hand, and I stared at his twitching face.

Jerry had confirmed our worst fears about the scale of these events. Jack, now standing behind Jerry, shook his head repeatedly.

I jumped to my feet, grabbed Jack by the arm, and led him out of the barn. We stood with Lea a few yards from the entrance.

"Did you get all that?" I asked.

"Anthony in Pennsylvania and something about Michigan?" Lea said.

I looked back into the barn. "We need addresses from him. As much as I hate to say it, he's probably telling the truth in terms of him being a minion."

"There's no way he's close to running the show," Jack said.

"Are you gonna kill him?" Lea asked.

The thought of it appealed to me, but I'd calmed down since Bernie's shooting and didn't want us turning into murderers. "We'll leave him here. A killer might find this place and give him a nice ironic death. Let's keep our consciences clean and use that option when necessary."

"You flew from Detroit, Lea; how far is Michigan?" Jack said.

"It's a huge place. He could mean anywhere," Lea said. "Pennsylvania's on the way."

"Let's just take a step back for a minute," I said. "He told us that he could lead us to Anthony, who knows more information. That should be our focus."

Lea screwed up her face. "He could lead us? You're not thinking of bringing that piece of shit along for the ride!"

"I didn't say that. Let's get back in there and get him talking. We decide our next moves based on his information."

Happy at least to have a vague plan, Jack and I entered the barn. Jerry snapped his head around as we approached. "I heard every word. I'm not giving you the address."

Jack picked up the bolt cutters and towered over him. "I'll give you thirty seconds to tell us Anthony's address."

"It's my insurance. If I take you to his place, it keeps me alive. Once you get your hands on him and hear what he has to say, you'll be thanking me."

He put the bolt cutters around Jerry's little toe and clenched his teeth. Jerry screamed as Jack drew blood. I winced but resisted pulling him back. A firm bluff was fine, as long as he didn't start snipping toes off.

"Stop! Fucking stop! I'll talk." Jack loosened the blades. Jerry composed himself. "Genesis Alliance is dedicated to ensuring the survival of the human race. There's around two thousand of us in North America."

"I want Anthony's address," I said.

"That's my insurance. I want out, and I'll lead you to everything you need to know."

"We'll get it out of you," Jack said.

His face stiffened with resolve. "You won't . . . What have I got to lose? If you kill me, you don't find out. If you leave me here to die, you still don't find out."

I mulled over the option of taking him on a road trip. If it came to it, we could always use him as bait for a killer, if attacked, or dump him on the side of the road if he became too painful.

"What's this bullshit about the survival of the human race?" Jack asked.

"They're deadly serious. If you believe Anthony, Genesis Alliance has saved the human race. I went along with it to stay alive."

Jerry didn't appear to be lying, but I struggled to absorb his latest revelation. "You instigated a kill-suicide compulsion to save us? Are you completely mad?"

"It's not me, it's them. You've seen the effectiveness of the technology firsthand. I was only a tiny part of a much bigger picture. That's the corporate bullshit they told me—Anthony knows more."

We needed to know more. I looked down sternly. "How did you end up with a device in your barn?"

"The smaller ones were delivered from Michigan to people like me. The larger ones were constructed by a special team from Genesis Alliance." He rolled his eyes. "Anthony told me about a huge one in Africa. How many times do I need to tell you about that guy?"

"Do you know the timetable?" I asked.

"At the risk of sounding like a broken record . . ."

Jack squeezed the bolt cutters again. Blood trickled down Jerry's foot.

"I haven't been fully briefed on the next steps. The key to the success of the organization is in the drip feeding of information. Genesis Alliance can't afford to have hundreds of people walking around with the full timetable. We get told one step at a time. I have radio contact with Control but get the specifics off Anthony; he emailed me on Thursday night to tell me about Friday."

I snorted in disbelief. "He emailed you about the activation?"

"What's so strange about that?"

"How did you end up joining Genesis Alliance?" Jack said.

"And keep it all a secret?" I added.

"Anthony recruited me after I responded to an ad on the Internet looking for a homeworker in a remote location. He sent a link and I registered my details. When he came here, he showed me a photograph of the last person who stepped out of line, and told me I was committed to the team. What would you do in my shoes?"

"Tell him to go fuck himself," Jack said.

"Did you realize what the consequences of your actions would be?" I asked.

"Depends how you look at it. I saw the consequences as staying alive. It was happening with or without me."

Jack pressed his forehead against the side of Jerry's head. "At the expense of millions."

"How did Genesis Alliance know this would work?" I asked.

"Anthony told me about some tests they ran in West Africa."

Jack stamped on his ankle. "Why didn't you tell the authorities?"

Jerry squirmed in pain. His left hand trembled. He may have been going into shock.

"And have my throat cut like the man in the photo?" he said in a strained voice. "I only know certain members of the organization, like Anthony. The anonymity protects us all to a certain extent—like in situations like this."

"What do you know of the origins of Genesis Alliance?" I asked.

"I've told you, I wasn't in it from the start. Some questions we weren't allowed to ask. Anthony tells the regional coordinators only what they need to know."

"Regional coordinators?" Jack said with a look of disbelief. "You make it sound like you were setting up for the Olympics, not attempting to wipe out our species."

"How did you avoid the effects?" I said.

"Anthony put a weird gadget against my head. It was all part of the induction."

"Do you know anything about it?"

"Nothing. Whenever I asked him a question, he'd say, 'Loose lips sink ships.'"

"That's all you know?" Jack said. "Seriously?"

"That's it."

I decided to scare him a little more. I shouldered my rifle and turned to Jack. "We're done here. You don't have to stay and watch."

Jerry struggled wildly against his restraints. "The activation failed in Northern England. We had two device errors. I heard it on the radio."

Jack motioned toward the barn door, and we joined Lea outside.

188

"Lea, did you hear that?" Jack asked.

"What does one unaffected area in England mean for us over here?" Lea said.

I pondered her question while feeling a sense of relief that some of my family and friends might still be alive. Short term, Jerry's new piece of information meant nothing for us. If we wanted it to mean something in the long term, the best way to achieve this would be to follow the Genesis Alliance trail. Who else could make an impact or even knew they existed, outside someone in their ranks?

"Forget about England," I said. "Our priority should be finding and interrogating Anthony. If Jerry's telling the truth, we'll get deeper into their organization."

Jack took a step back. "Hang on a minute. Since when did this become our problem?"

"Think about if we were standing here and another one of those activations went off. It's not like dealing with a patrol. We could end up killing each other. That's very much our problem."

"Why don't we go back and talk to Morgan and his group? We could put a small army together."

"Jack, you're not thinking. If we stop and turn back now, there's probably more chance of us being caught up in another one of those things, on ground level this time. Plus, I reckon they'll be expecting us to run away and not be coming for them."

He kicked a stone along road. "We need to make sure we take them all out."

I gave him my 'Stop and think for a minute, Jack' look. He leaned against the fence and shook his head.

"You're serious about bringing Jerry along," Lea said. She turned away and I heard her breathe, "Unbelievable."

"He's not going to spill the beans," I said. "He knows we need him to find his boss."

"Give me five minutes with him," Lea said.

I noticed her knuckles whiten as she squeezed her Beretta. She spun and headed for the barn. I quickly moved in front of her. "We're not shooting him. We need him for the moment."

"Beat the information out of him—or something. I don't want to be in the same space as that maggot."

She tried to edge around me. I stepped in her way again. "Keep a watch out here. We'll tie him up and raid his supplies."

I slung my rifle and entered the barn. Jack joined me, and we carried eight boxes of water and canned fruit outside. Lea continued to fidget. I didn't want two loose cannons on the team. I thought she would see the logic in our plan, but it just seemed to get her goat.

The sundial in Jerry's courtyard claimed the time to be around four o'clock. It felt about right. I decided we should grab two more boxes of mineral water due to my growing distrust of the water supply; diseased corpses might be floating anywhere in the system.

"One more each, Jack—that'll fill up the trunk."

The rope restraints creaked as Jerry leaned forward. "What are you going to do with me? You can't leave me here."

"You're coming with us. You better pray you remember Anthony's address."

He sighed with relief and shiftily smiled. "There's something else you should know."

"Oh yeah, what's that?" I asked as I picked up a box.

Lea slipped through the barn door as I tried to exit. I bumped into her. She softly placed her hand on my shoulder. "Please. Leave him here. I can't stand him."

"He's coming with us," I said and looked over my shoulder. "Spit it out."

He glanced at Lea. "Why don't you ask her how long she's worked for Genesis Alliance?"

Lea ducked past me and raised her Beretta toward Jerry.

9
TRIP

Jerry's revelation left me stunned. Jack, on the other hand, dropped his box and swung his rifle toward Lea almost immediately. No matter how hot Jack got, I was glad to know he would always back me up.

"Drop your weapon, now," he shouted.

Clicking into gear, I threw the box to one side, crouched, and raised my rifle. "Put it down, Lea, don't make any silly moves."

Lea threw her Beretta to the dirt and bowed her head.

I leaned forward and grabbed it. "Start talking."

She looked at me with all the innocence of a killer. "He's lying. Can't you see he's trying to get us to turn against each other?"

"No, I'm not. She's visited here before," Jerry said, gazing at her with all of his previous cockiness. "With another dyke."

"What's he talking about?" Jack asked.

"He's lying, Jack. Do you seriously trust him?"

Lea flew from Detroit on Friday, led us to the farm, and Jerry's goon asked for her during the standoff outside the house. Too much of a coincidence. In fact, it seemed totally obvious when I thought about it.

"They asked for you at the house. Jerry said he would leave us alone if we handed you over," I said.

"They were probably perverts. You've seen what Jerry's like, he—"

"That bitch was here last year. How else did you find the place?"

"You said you visited here before," Jack said to Lea, glancing at me. "And he told us he's lived here for ten years."

"Put your hands on your head," I said.

"I haven't been a danger to you so far, have I?" she pleaded.

I shook my head in disgust. "Bernie might not agree with that—if he were alive. Hands on your head."

Jerry sneered. "Don't trust that dyke an inch. She's in this way deeper than me."

I edged around to the table and knelt beside him. "If you call her that one more time, I'm going to blow your brains out. Why didn't you say anything before?"

He jabbed his head in her direction. "Anthony told me she dates Control's niece. I didn't want it getting back to him that I'd talked. If I gave her a pass, she might have returned the favor. Seems I've nothing to lose now."

Lea's eyes narrowed. "Why would I talk to Ron about an insignificant shit like you?"

Jack and I exchanged surprised glances. At least she'd stopped pretending.

"Who's Ron?" I asked.

"Guys, I can explain. I never meant for Bernie to get killed. I'll tell you what I know; it's not what you think."

"Cover me," Jack said. He patted her down for weapons and backed a few yards away. "She's clean."

Jerry tried to brush my leg with his fingers. "Don't trust her. She'll get us all killed."

I moved back a step. "Shut up. You don't get a say in this."

"Are you going to tell us who Ron is?" Jack said.

"She knows Control. Anthony told me—"

I pushed down the urge to kick him in the face. "Shut the fuck up for a minute. She can speak for herself."

The rug had been firmly pulled from under our feet, and I wasn't sure how to move forward from here.

She twisted a ring on her finger. "It's true what he said about Martina."

"We want to know about Ron and the part you have played. Fuck Martina," I said.

Jerry laughed. "She does."

I picked up the Beretta and smashed the grip against Jerry's fingers. He squealed and struggled against his restraints.

"I didn't know any of this was going to happen. Please, hear me out for fuck's sake!" Lea said.

I kept her in my sights while I thought of a solution.

"If that Range Rover we shot up still drives," I said to Jack, "bring it around to the barn doors so we can load it up with supplies. We can transfer them to the undamaged one, outside our house."

Jack grunted and disappeared out of the side door of the barn. Lea leaned against the counter and held her head in her hands.

"I just want to find out if Martina's alive," she quietly murmured.

"Wait for Jack. We both deserve to hear this."

I felt angry with myself for not lining up a few obvious details. I didn't pay any serious attention to Lea when she told us that she'd visited the farm back at Bernie's. She even pointed the place out when we arrived. I also never stopped to think about one of the patrol calling her name and quickly justified it because of the urgency of the situation. The pace of events had swept me along, and I'd only focused on survival.

I nearly kicked myself for feeling guilty over our white lies about the Elmhurst parking lot trap, even though our actions had been well intended. I'd even apologized to her, and she'd begrudgingly accepted.

Anger bubbled up inside me again. I guessed Jack would be feeling the same, which was the last thing I needed. I wanted to know the level of her manipulation.

The Range Rover rumbled outside the barn door and stopped with a squeak. Jack entered the barn with a face like thunder.

"I've been thinking," he said. "That first patrol may not have been the clowns we thought they were. They didn't shoot first because they were trying to take her alive."

"When I saw her at the Watsons's," Jerry said, "I recognized her as one of the dykes who came here for a meeting. I thought it might get me some credit with Anthony if we captured her."

I slapped Jerry across the head. "Stop calling her that—I mean it."

Lea lowered her hands from her face. "Guys, don't jump to any conclusions."

"Don't worry," I said, "you'll get your chance to tell us everything on the long road trip to Pennsylvania. But first, we're going to load the vehicle and bury Bernie."

Jack and I could pass judgment after we heard her story. If she turned out to be a part of all this, we could always use her as a leverage in the future.

Jack kept his rifle aimed at Lea while she and I loaded the bullet-riddled Range Rover with boxes of bottled water and canned food. Between us, we had two rifles with full magazines, two pistols with six rounds each, and a bolt-action rifle with seven loose rounds. I'd left the flare gun behind the barn when I'd fired it to warn Bernie and Lea about Jerry, but we decided not to waste time looking for it.

"Right, Jerry. I'm going to cut you free from the table and tie your hands behind your back. If you try anything funny, you get to suck on a bullet. Do you understand?"

"You don't have to tie me up; you can trust me more than you can trust her. I've given you information."

"Lea hasn't tried to kill us," Jack said.

Jerry groaned. "Yet."

I cut Jerry's hands free with a hunting knife that I found by the radio. He massaged his wrists and let out a deep breath.

"Put your hands behind your back," I said.

He shook his head but complied. I bound his wrists tightly together. I half-expected a struggle, but it seemed that most of the fight had left him.

After I cut his feet free, he unsteadily rose and stretched his legs.

We led Jerry and Lea at gunpoint to the open doors of the Rover. "Jack, you get into the back with Jerry. I'll drive."

I wanted to sort the situation out with Lea sooner rather than later. Controlling two prisoners would be a logistical nightmare. I considered putting Jerry in the trunk but decided against it for the time being.

I passed my rifle to Jack and kept Lea's Beretta in my left hand. We drove back to the house in silence. Jack held his rifle to Jerry's head. Lea sat silently in the front, probably deciding how to frame her story.

I pulled up level with the undamaged Range Rover. "Lea, help me move the supplies to the other Rover."

She quietly transferred boxes, and we quickly completed the task. I didn't breathe a word to her after we finished, and she stood between the two vehicles with her hands on her hips. I looked through the back window of the bullet-ridden Rover.

"Everything still okay?"

"He's been as good as gold," Jack said.

He leaned over and flicked Jerry's ear.

Jerry pressed his lips together and dived toward Jack. He head-butted him in the side of the face. Jack dragged him across the seat and repeatedly swung his fist at the back of Jerry's head.

I yanked open the rear door, and dragged Jack out. "Leave him. He's not worth it. I'll sit with him for the trip."

"Be my guest. I'd probably end up choking him," Jack said and passed me my rifle.

I gripped Jerry's collar and pulled him out.

"He provoked me," Jerry said.

I ignored him and faced Jack. "Take the Rover around to the side of the house. I'll bring these two."

Jack glared at Jerry before jumping in to the freshly stocked Rover. He bumped across the lawn, past Bernie, and steered around the left side of the white house. I felt like I had to keep giving instructions to maintain control and to stop the group going into meltdown.

"All right, you two. Let's grab Bernie and carry him around the back," I said. "Jerry, stay by my side. I'm not letting you out of my sight."

Lea immediately walked over, gazed down at Bernie's body, and pressed her hand against her chest. Jerry followed, cursing under his breath as he limped.

Bernie lay in the same position, on his side with his eyes and mouth wide open. She leaned down and closed his eyes. I grabbed his collar with my left hand, and Lea took his legs, and we carried him around the side of the house. Lea buckled and dropped to one knee, probably struggling with the weight. Jerry loudly tutted. She altered her grip on the bottom of Bernie's chinos, clenched her jaw, and we continued to the side of the Watsons's graves.

I grabbed the two shovels from the shed and threw one at Lea. "Start digging."

She didn't hesitate. Not wanting to untie Jerry, I slung my rifle and joined her. Jack shoved Jerry to his knees.

Twenty minutes later, Jack grabbed my shovel as I raised it for another thrust. "I'll take over. You keep an eye on dickhead."

Thankful for a rest, and with the hole nearly deep enough. I sat on the grass and pointed my rifle at Jerry from the hip. He was the reason we were digging this grave, and I should have made him work at gunpoint. Too late now.

He opened his mouth to say something. I raised my left palm. "Not now. Don't you dare say a word."

To Lea's credit, she didn't complain even though we left her to dig without a break. After forty minutes, with the sun starting to dip, I rolled Bernie into the grave and straightened him up.

I paused above the grave, bowed my head, and replayed moments through my mind that I had spent with my friend.

Jack let out a loud sigh. I looked at him, and he nodded. I hit the shovel into the pile of dirt and threw some in the grave. Lea, with dewy eyes, helped me, and we silently filled it.

The quietness could have made Bernie's burial quite solemn, but tension rather than grief, as well as thoughts about the inevitable confrontation to follow, dominated the atmosphere. I had no idea what Lea planned to say, but if her story wasn't good enough, she would be in for a very uncomfortable ride—perhaps in the trunk with Jerry.

Jack threw the shovels in the shed and returned with a grim look. "I don't want to hang around here any longer."

I knew Bernie's death had cut him deeply. It cut us all, apart from Jerry. Lea looked ready to pounce on him at any moment. I expected her to take a swing at him with the shovel. Sadly, she didn't.

"Straight to Pennsylvania" I said, agreeing with Jack that we had nothing left for us here but bad memories. I didn't care what Lea thought of the idea. "What's the address?"

"Oh no," Jerry said with an irritating laugh. "You must think I'm stupid. You get the exact address when we get close. If I give you it now . . ."

"Give us a clue, for God's sake."

He sucked on his teeth. "Head for Hermitage. That's all I'm saying."

"You're not leading us into a trap, are you?" Jack said.

"Do you think I'm fucking telepathic?"

Jack screwed up his face and stepped toward Jerry, but managed to hold himself back from whatever physical pain he intended to inflict. Jerry and Jack had quickly built up a mutual and passionate hatred of each other. Understandable, considering the circumstances.

"Are we driving through the night?" Lea asked. "It's a helluva long way."

"We? There is no 'we' at the moment," I said. "You sit in the front with Jack where I can see you. I'll take the back with Jerry."

She muttered something under her breath and slumped into the passenger seat. I pressed Jerry's head into the back and shoved him in before going around to the other side and climbing in.

Jack fiddled with the satellite navigation system. "Hermitage, right?"

Jerry thudded his head against the front headrest. "How many times does he need to be told?" Jerry said.

I pulled him back in the seat. "Jerry, do you ever stop?"

Jack found Hermitage, and Sat Nav started calculating. It registered as a six-hour drive. Wishful thinking due to the state of the roads, but at least we had something to aim for. With renewed focus, we left the property. I looked back at the white house, radiant in the early evening sun as we turned onto the road, and wondered if I'd ever see the place again.

———

Jack merged onto Interstate 84, and we headed west. Once again, we snaked through stationary vehicles in the road, bounced and crunched over debris. Jerry stared in horrified awe at the state of the highway. What had he expected to see?

I reached around Lea's seat and tapped her on the shoulder. "Start talking."

"You need to hear me out before passing judgment," she said.

"You've got an opportunity right now. Jerry, you can keep your mouth shut."

"How do you know Ron or Control or whatever he's called?" Jack said.

"You already know that. His niece is my partner."

"Whatever—get to the important part," I said.

"That *is* the important part to me; I left Martina after we had an argument. I'm just praying Ron kept her alive."

"Kills his own family, eh?" I said.

"I doubt it, but Ron's very weird."

"Come on, Lea, we don't give a shit about his personality. Give us details," Jack said.

"I met Martina two years ago. She moved in with Ron after her mom died of cancer. She doesn't know her dad."

Jerry sneered. "Sounds just like a Jackie Collins novel."

"This is your final warning," I said. "Any more spiteful crap, and you're spending the rest of the journey in the trunk. Got it?"

"Okay. I used to love fairy tales as a kid."

I pushed the muzzle of my rifle into his side. He grimaced but remained silent.

"I take it you know the location in Michigan?" Jack asked.

Lea let out a heavy breath and rubbed her hands along her thighs. "I do, but I don't know any details beyond my job."

"Tell us about that then," I said.

"After we'd been together a few months, Martina scored me a job working for Genesis Alliance."

"Doing what?" I said.

"Ron needed an administrator and logistics coordinator. Easy work and it paid well. Ron was a bit overbearing but who hasn't had an odd boss?"

"Anyone who turns people into murdering, suicidal maniacs is more than a bit odd," Jack replied. "What did the job involve?"

"Ron owns a small warehouse on the edge of Monroe; he would tell me when and where the containers needed to be shipped. My job was to arrange a courier to ship specific units to nationwide locations. I could do it all from home."

"Did you distribute devices around the world?" I said.

"Very rarely. I thought GA mainly operated here. The description on the packing slip was always 'Scientific Testing Equipment.' I'm not interested in science. It was just a job. Would you question it?"

"No," I admitted.

"Why would I be suspicious? I visited the warehouse once. It had a security guard and looked like nothing special. Tons of large boxes stacked in columns."

"Was that all you did?"

"I had to do some other general admin work. I looked after the company's online banking. At first, I couldn't believe how much money went through the account. I asked Ron about it, and he told me it was normal for an import/export business to have that kind of turnover. I don't really know much about business, so I just went with it."

It all sounded normal so far. I would robotically carry out those tasks for half-decent money, and not expect it to lead toward an apocalypse.

"Tell us more about Ron," Jack asked.

"He's a creepy bastard. But he kept giving me pay raises, and I took lots of vacations. I didn't want to cause trouble as I was making good money. Martina really loves him."

"Creepy in what way?" I said.

She shuddered. "I went away with him to one of his meetings in Florida. I didn't attend the meeting, but he tried to book us into a double room and said it was the only one available. When I checked with reception, they had a few spare ones, so I took one of those. He got wasted in the hotel bar that night and tried to persuade me to go up to his room; he offered me fifty bucks to give him a back massage."

Jerry laughed. I looked across at him.

"I didn't say a word," he said.

"Carry on, Lea. How did you meet Jerry?" Jack said.

"It's pretty much like he said. Ron took me to a few meetings. One was at Jerry's barn. Martina came down with me, and we had a weekend in Manhattan afterward."

I turned and stared at Jerry. "So he knew Ron too?"

"Not that well. Ron called the regional coordinators 'bottom feeders.' Jerry's probably met him once or twice."

"Hear that, Jerry?" Jack said. "You're a newt."

Jerry stared out of the window and didn't acknowledge him.

Lea continued, "I took bank details from people after the meetings and set up payments to them through the company account. Jerry's account received thousands of dollars from Genesis Alliance. He was one of the people I met who stuck in my mind."

"I can understand that," Jack said.

"How many were on the payroll?" I asked.

"I can't remember exactly. Maybe a few hundred? I tried to keep clear of Ron after what happened in Florida. That's why I tried to get Martina to come along. She started a new role in the company, covering Latin America, and was often on trips abroad. It put a strain on our relationship."

"Do you think she knew more about this? Did you tell her about Ron?"

"We didn't really talk about work. I found it pretty boring. She might know more since she and Ron are close. I was scared that if I told Martina about him, she'd dump me. She worships Ron, and if I made it a choice between him or me . . ."

"Can you think of anything suspicious?" Jack asked.

"No, that's about it." She looked across to him. "Would you have guessed what was going to happen?"

"Probably not. How did you end up on a flight to New York? I'm surprised Martina would let you go if she had any feelings for you."

"I had a massive argument with her on Thursday night. Ron planned a company party somewhere out of town. I refused to go, and she went crazy. I booked a New York flight to go and see a friend for the weekend. I needed a shoulder to cry on. Martina called me Friday morning and was really pissed. I was already at the airport."

"What did she say?" I said.

"She wanted me to go straight to Ron's house. She said I was letting down the company at an important time, and they needed me back in Monroe. I hung up and switched off my cell."

"Sounds to me like she knew what was going to happen."

"I don't want to believe that yet. When the plane landed and I saw what was happening, I didn't connect any of it with Genesis Alliance. I'd only shipped boxes and set up some payments."

"And your mate?" Jack asked.

"I was going to try and find my friend in Manhattan; I hoped he could help me. That's why I joined the group on their trek into the city. I quickly realized my friend was probably dead."

"Did you hear from Martina?" I said.

"I received two direct messages from her on Twitter. In the first one, she told me not to tweet anything about GA and asked me to stay indoors for the next seventy-two hours. That's when I first started to become suspicious. I replied, asking what was going on. The second message told me not to answer the door to anyone and to keep it locked."

"Sounds like she definitely knew what was going on," I said.

Lea twisted around and peered at me through the gap between her headrest and the seat. "You don't know that. She might have asked Ron after it all started."

"Yeah, right. Come on, Lea, you're blinded by love. Are you trying to convince me or yourself?" Lea seemed to be giving this woman far too much trust. She sounded like Ron's apprentice.

She shook her head and sighed. "This is where you guys came in. After Chris got killed and you turned up at the parking lot, I thought you might have been one of them. I needed help to get to Jerry's farm. If Genesis Alliance had anything to do with this, I thought he might have some answers. It was the closest meeting place to Bernie's I could remember. I still didn't believe it, though. I also wanted to get back to Martina."

"So you used us?" Jack said.

"We all wanted to leave. All three of us wanted to find out what's happening, right?"

"It was four of us."

She raised her hand to her face. "I'm as upset about Bernie as you are. Give me a fucking break."

"Hold on," I said. "Why didn't you go straight to the farm when we arrived in Orange County?"

"I planned to sneak out and confront Jerry if he was still alive."

"When?"

"I was making my way out the first night, but you two were outside chatting. You weren't leaving the front of the house any time soon, and you were giving me whiskey. I watched you leave the house from the upstairs window and started to get nervous. When you told me Jerry was alive, I wanted to sneak away the next morning, but Bernie wouldn't go to bed after his shift."

"Why didn't you tell us any of this?" Jack asked sharply.

"I tried to convince myself that Genesis Alliance had nothing to with it. If it was true, it meant that I'd played a part in the deaths of all those people. When Jerry attacked the house and they killed Bernie, I couldn't deny it to myself anymore."

Lea leaned back in her seat, closed her eyes, and puffed out her cheeks.

Jerry slowly clapped his feet. "Ten out of ten for acting. What a crock of shit."

I ignored him and thought about Lea's story.

If it was true, and it was certainly plausible, I could understand Lea's actions. Most people had ignored an inconvenient truth or two before, especially if it meant having an easier life. Perhaps not ignoring something as big as the plans of Genesis Alliance, but who was I to judge? After mulling it over, I felt satisfied with most of what she had to say, but also annoyed at the depth of her lies.

As far as I was concerned, we had a bigger target in Hermitage and needed to stay together as a team.

"So what do you think?" I asked Jack.

"I was about to ask you the same thing."

He didn't sound too upset. I guessed he thought the same as me. Trapped in a moving vehicle together with Lea, we couldn't openly discuss our opinions.

I tapped her on the shoulder. "Don't worry about it. I can understand why you did what you did. Let's move on and make sure we take care of business."

I still had reservations about Lea, but she was an angel compared to Jerry and had never been a direct threat since we met in Elmhurst. I wanted to keep a level of trust in survivors, rather than paranoia. Everyone acts differently in stressful situations, and I reminded myself of that when listening to her story.

"Don't beat yourself up about Bernie," Jack said. "You didn't know it would happen. We've all made mistakes since Friday."

She took a piece of paper towel out of her pocket and blew her nose. "Thank God. I knew you'd understand once I'd explained."

Jerry shuffled over to me. "You guys really are stupid. She won't let you screw her, you know?"

"Jack, pull over. I've had enough of him," I snapped.

He leaned away. "What are you going to do?"

"I'm going to gag you; you've had plenty of warnings."

"I promise, I won't say another word. Don't you think I've had enough?"

The Range Rover stopped.

I opened up the back of the vehicle, took out a folded bed sheet from the corner, and cut a long piece from the edge. Jack held Jerry's shoulders firmly against the seat as I tied it around his head, covering his mouth.

Jerry gave a muffled shout—probably an insult, but the gag did its job. Jack climbed back into the driver's seat, and we pulled away. I had an idea that might rid us of the annoying twat.

"Did you go to a meeting in Hermitage?" I asked.

"If I could remember the address, do you think I wouldn't tell you? I sent a couple of deliveries there but never visited. Anthony's part of Ron's management team; he came along to the team-building event at Splash Universe a few months ago."

"Splash Universe?"

"It's a water park."

"Jesus. A team-building day at a water park, to organize the end of the world?"

"No, it was an attached hotel that was part of the complex. We had a weekend there, and I didn't hear any talk of killing people. Looking back, it feels a bit ridiculous, but at the time, it was just a company event. That's how Ron ran things. He's normally pretty casual, but only if you play by his rules."

"What do you mean?" I said.

"I only saw a couple of people piss him off during the last two years. They'd just be disagreeing with him over some minor detail, and the next thing you knew, they were fired."

"Getting the bullet from Genesis Alliance isn't the worst thing in the world," Jack said.

"I said 'fired' because that's what I thought at the time. Nobody ever saw them again. Your description may be more accurate."

"What do you remember about Anthony?" I asked.

Jerry moaned furiously for a few seconds. We all ignored him.

"I didn't talk to him. He stayed in Ron's huddle at the bar most of the time. He kinda looks like Larry David. Do you know him?"

"The skinny, bald guy with glasses?" Jack said.

"That's the guy. He didn't acknowledge anyone outside the inner circle, but it suited me. I used to laugh with Martina about Ron's freaky associates."

We were starting to build a small picture of Genesis Alliance, although it still didn't make sense. To find out more about Anthony, I would have to get Jerry talking again, a difficult task to manage when he seemed to thrive on insulting Lea and winding us up.

The satellite navigation system chose a route that kept us on the interstate all the way to Hermitage. The smell of decomposition rose in strength when we passed areas of higher population and became almost unbearable as we approached Scranton. We decided to keep the windows up and use the air conditioning.

Shortly after getting onto Interstate 81 at ten in the evening, we came across a demolition derby–style pileup. Jack turned the Rover around and took us back to the previous exit. He flicked on the high beams, illuminating more debris, allowing us to go slightly faster in the dark.

Sat Nav automatically recalculated our route, and we ended up looping around on the Pennsylvania Turnpike and merging onto Interstate 81 again just past Dupont.

"Jack, are you still okay driving?" Lea asked, finally feeling confident enough to start conversation. "Shall we stop for the night?"

"I grabbed seven hours last night; I can go for another few hours."

"Give me a shout, Jack. I'd like to get to Hermitage by first light," I said.

So far, we were in good shape for a dawn raid.

Lea and Jerry were still a concern, and I wanted at least one of us awake at all times, especially when nearing a wolf's lair. I believed Lea to be almost genuine, but her link to Genesis Alliance and Ron's niece made me question what decisions she might make. If it came to Jack and me or Genesis Alliance and Martina, I still wasn't sure which way she'd go. We still needed Jerry the snake. He knew about Hermitage and probably a lot more.

I hoped there would be no major blockages from here to Hermitage, including human ones.

"Pull in at the next station," I said. "We can get some Red Bull and food."

"Sounds good to me," Jack said, "although the last two I've seen have been smoldering ruins."

Half an hour later, we passed a sign indicating a station one mile ahead.

Jerry couldn't be left on his own, and neither could Lea. I quickly formulated a plan.

"Jack, pull over."

He looked in his rearview mirror, smiled, and slammed on the brakes. Jerry woke up with a muffled scream after flying forward and bouncing face first against Jack's seat. Our Rover stopped at the side of the road.

"Jerry, I'm going to tie your legs together. You're staying in here. Jack, you take Lea, go into the store, and grab as much stuff as you can. See if you can find a tube to siphon gas from other cars, and grab a flashlight. Use your imagination. I'll have a look around outside to see if I can find anything."

I took the rope from the trunk, held Jerry down with my knee on his chest, and bound him tightly. He shouted through his gag, but I ignored him and placed him in reverse fetal position on the back seat.

I reached under the seat, fished out Lea's Beretta, and held it over her seat.

"Thanks," she said.

Jack raised his eyebrows but said nothing.

He swung our Rover into the station a couple of minutes later and stopped by a pump. I guessed he did it out of habit, since they wouldn't work without electricity.

Jack and Lea got out of the car, disembarking into the gloomy forecourt, and headed toward the store.

I tugged at Jerry's ropes and checked that the knots were nice and tight. Confident I had him well secured, I stepped out of the vehicle and scanned the immediate vicinity. Finding nothing apart from dark pumps, plastic gloves, paper towels, and a dirty sponge close to our Rover, I decided to relieve myself in a bucket of sand.

I swept my rifle around in the dark, listening for any suspicious sounds. Two minutes later, Jack and Lea emerged from the store and jogged over with four plastic bags stuffed with goods.

"Decent score?" I asked.

"Everything we need, including these," Jack said.

He opened his bag to show me the contents.

A bright light shone on my face. I pulled my rifle into the alert position, dropped to one knee, and prepared to fire. The light went out before I could lock on to its location.

"What the hell was that?" Lea gasped.

I edged behind a pump and peered into the gloom.

"Get behind the Rover," Jack said.

Jack crouched next to me and pointed to the left of the store. "I think it came from around there."

"Who's there?" I shouted. "We're not here to hurt you."

No response.

"Were you trying to signal us?" Jack called out.

After a few seconds, a gruff male voice said, "Drop your weapons, and we'll come out. We don't know if we can trust you."

"How do we know if we can trust you?" Jack asked.

"We only want to talk," the man said.

"How many of you are there?" I said.

"Me and one other."

I looked at Jack and Lea, both concentrated on the area the voice came from.

"Come out," I said. "You're safe. We want to meet other survivors."

Slowly, from behind the store, two figures appeared through the dark. A man and woman. They stopped ten yards away.

"This is as far as we're coming. Do you know what happened?"

"Want the long version or the short version?" Jack said.

The man took another step forward. "What? . . . The short version. We're desperate here. Are you part of a resistance?"

"Afraid not. Everywhere is total chaos. People turned on each other, and most are dead. We've met survivors in the last few days, so you're not completely on your own."

"What happened to you?" I asked.

"We came across each other in the state park. After talking, we both realized we had lost a few days. After deciding to go to the hospital together, we saw dead bodies and other crazy shit. We're flying solo here and would sure appreciate some help. The army or whatever."

"Head east—that's your best bet," Lea said.

"Where are you going?" the man replied, sounding suspicious. Not a huge shock considering we were traveling west.

"Michigan," Jack said. "But we heard on a radio transmission that a group is forming in New York."

I immediately grasped that Jack had told these people a lie for their own good. It would be unfair to expect them to risk their already fragile lives by helping us capture Anthony. Being a bigger gun than Jerry, he might have more goons around him. I hadn't thought of that before.

"Did you get any details? What's the government doing about it?" the woman asked.

"Forget about the government," I said. "They're probably all dead. We know there's a group holed up in Aldi on the Long Island Expressway. Head toward Manhattan. You'll find it."

"That's miles away. We met two men—"

The man pulled her back by the shoulder. "Leave it. They don't have the first damn idea."

"Guys, forget about the army, government, or any of that shit," Lea said. "We have to make our own way. Head to New York."

"Whatever. Maybe we'll see you around," the man said.

Both turned and disappeared into the gloom. I wondered why they'd bothered attracting our attention in the first place.

Jack stood and brushed dust off his knees. "Let's get out of here. Chances are there's going to be a few more like them. We can't help everybody."

Lea trundled after him with slumped shoulders. "I feel sorry for the lady. He was a scumbag."

"Scumbag? That's a bit over the top, considering . . . ," Jack said.

"Jack. I know one when I hear one."

"The social rules have changed," I said. "They're frightened, lost, and don't have the faintest idea what's happening. It's not exactly easy for us, and we have a better understanding."

I heard a thud behind me and turned. Jerry lay on his front outside the open passenger door. He must have managed to open it and wriggle out.

I rushed over, hauled him to his feet, and pushed him back inside. I knelt over him and untied his blood-drenched gag.

He smiled at me with glistening red lips. "You should have snatched her."

"Snatched who?" I said.

"The woman. We could've taken turns on the back seat."

"You're a piece of work," I said and wondered if he really meant it or he just wanted to annoy me. Whatever his intention, I refused to take his bait and shoved him across the back seat. "Sit back and be a good boy."

"You don't realize what you're missing. Anthony told me how much lonely pussy would be out there after the first activation. You need to—"

"You know the drill," I said. "Loudmouth, gagged mouth."

Jerry nodded. I slammed the door, and Jack accelerated away.

After picking our way along the highway for another half an hour, I noticed headlights dazzling in the distance behind us. "You see it, Jack?"

"Yep, got my eye on it."

The vehicle continued to follow our route through the debris for another twenty minutes, past one o'clock on Wednesday morning. Not completely surprising to see another driver on a major highway, even in these circumstances, but I wasn't quite ready to trust in coincidence.

It gained on us and flashed three times.

"We can't let them follow us all night," Jack said.

"Pull over," I said. "I bet you a penny to a pound it's the couple from the station."

Jack slowed to the shoulder. The vehicle flashed again.

"Let me do the talking," Jerry said. "You're too soft."

I ignored him and continued to watch out of the rear window. The car's headlights jerked up after it bounced over a piece of debris on the road. Sparks shot through the air after it hit the side of something and veered to the left. They were in a rush to catch up.

Jack stopped when he found an open stretch of road. Less cover for our followers if they really wanted to get close. Jack and Lea flew out and ducked behind the hood. I cut Jerry's legs free to make it easier to move him, and dragged him outside by his collar and stabbed my rifle in his back.

The car, an Audi with a diesel engine, pulled alongside. The passenger-side electric window smoothly descended, revealing the man from the station.

"Thanks for waiting," he said.

"What do you want?" I asked.

"We've decided to come with you."

Jack lowered his rifle and walked around the front of the Rover. "What do you mean 'come with us'?"

"We had a chat after you left. You seem capable. We think we'll be safer together."

Although extra numbers could be handy, we would have to go through our story, which would expose Jerry and Lea. Others might not be as forgiving or keen to cross swords with Anthony.

"You can't come with us, but we'll meet you here next Sunday," I said, hoping to appease them with my suggestion.

"Why not?" the man said.

"There's trouble ahead," Jack said. "It's our fight. After that, we'll come back."

"There's trouble in both directions. The other men we met were looking for two Brits and a woman. They had a Rover too. Friends of yours?"

"That's one of the reasons we followed," the woman shouted from the driver's seat. "I had to tell you."

Another patrol. I remembered Jerry on the radio at the barn, giving our brief description. I wondered how many resources Genesis Alliance could throw at us, especially once they realized we'd wiped out their Orange County operation.

Jerry let out a satisfied grunt. I twisted his collar tightly around his neck.

"No friends of ours," I said. "Did you say they headed east?"

"A few hours ago. Do you have a spare gun?"

I wondered if our detour at Scranton had avoided a highway shoot-out. Whatever had happened, we'd avoided them.

"Sorry," Jack lied, "we don't have any to spare. We wouldn't want to expose you to any unnecessary danger."

212

"Who do you think you are? John Rambo?" the man said, his voice brimming with sarcastic disdain.

"Fuck you," Jack said and spun away. I think tiredness must have gotten the better of him.

The man sprang out of the car and hurried up to Jack with clenched fists. They stood inches apart and eyeballed each other. I caught the faint whiff of booze.

"Say that to my face, you pussy!" he said.

I couldn't believe the situation unfolding and wanted to douse it as soon as possible. With the news of a patrol on the road, we didn't need to hang around the side of the highway making new enemies.

Jerry kneed me in the thigh and tried to burst free from my grip. I kicked the back of his leg and he dropped to one knee.

"They're holding me hostage. The one that you called a pussy is a rapist; I've seen him do it to three women. This one too." The man glanced around the Rover, but he seemed far more interested in Jack. "Look at the blood around my mouth. That one tortured me."

He spluttered the last few words after I scrunched his shirt around his neck.

I leaned next to his ear. "Shut up, Jerry."

"Hey, what the hell?" the man said, looking at me.

"Ignore him," Lea shouted. "Do you think I'd be traveling with them if they were rapists?"

The situation descended into a tailspin. Two survivors, most likely tired and stressed, were probably now in an even bigger state of confusion.

"Let's all calm down and talk it through," I said.

"Come on, Mark. It's not worth it," the woman shouted from inside the car. "We need to find a place for the night."

He didn't respond to her. Instead, he focused on Jack.

"Are you going to say it to my face?" he slurred and poked his finger into Jack's chest. "Pussy."

I knew what Jack's response would be. I let go of Jerry, sprinted over, stood between them, and pushed both apart with the palms of my hands. "There are going to be no roadside fights tonight. It's people like Jerry we should be angry—"

"He's making a break for it," Lea said.

I turned to see Jerry running for the opposite side of the highway. "Jack, tell him about Jerry while I go and catch the bastard."

He disappeared through some trees on the far side of the road. I slung my rifle across my back, sprinted across the lanes, leaped over the barrier, and headed for his entry point.

I plunged down a short, steep slope and skidded to a rustling stop at the bottom, just avoiding a head-on collision with a pine. I paused to listen for his footsteps on the forest floor.

An owl's hoot broke the silence.

He hadn't had the time to get far and must be behind a tree in close proximity.

Moonlight shone through the gaps in the canopy, giving a reasonable amount of night vision. I waited for him to make his move.

My heart rate quickly settled, and I relaxed my breathing. I heard a faint sound of panting to my left. Jerry, being out of shape, had a much longer recovery rate.

I moved closer and ducked behind a tree. Peering around it, I identified a thick trunk, the only thing in the near vicinity that would hide his bulky frame.

A twigged snapped under my boot as I advanced.

He made a run for it.

I bounded after him, throwing branches out of the way. I stooped below a thick one and came up a few yards behind him.

He glanced over his shoulder. I dived and rugby-tackled him to the floor. I thrust my knee into his back, pinning him on his front. His chest rapidly heaved up and down below my weight.

"Try that again and you won't make Hermitage," I said.

He wheezed and swallowed hard. "Just testing you, that's all."

I dragged him to his feet and led him back to the highway. The car had gone.

Jack and Lea waited outside the Rover. They both looked relieved to see me shove Jerry across the road.

"Thought he might outrun you," Jack said.

"Yeah, right. What happened with those people?"

"He left in a massive sulk and headed east. Said if he ran into the other patrol, he'd tell them our location."

"He had piles of money on the back seat," Lea said.

"What a goose," I said. "That's only good for having a fire."

"Don't be surprised if there's more than one patrol coming for you," Jerry said.

I opened the back door and hustled him into the back. "You need to work on your fitness."

Lea took the wheel to give Jack a break. We could still make Anthony's by first light.

———

During the night, we were forced into swapping vehicles twice as our attempts to siphon fuel proved unsuccessful. For tactical reasons, we selected cars parked at the side of the road. The owners had probably come to a halt and left to hunt or join an existing fight. We rolled along toward Hermitage in a Chevrolet, Jerry repeating annoyingly that we were heading in the right direction, even though Interstate 80 led all the way to the small city.

This stretch of highway in Pennsylvania turned out to be the fastest of the trip. Lea swept around single abandoned vehicles and only had to slow at five crash scenes. All were passable—the benefits of being near no major cities.

Jack kept shouting and swearing in his sleep. Something about *killing them all.*

I reached under the passenger seat and pulled out a rolled-up road atlas. I flicked to the page covering Hermitage and held it in front of Jerry. "Can you pinpoint Anthony's on here?"

He turned away. "I'll tell you exactly when to stop and even give you an undercover approach."

I wondered what to do with Jerry after our morning raid. We couldn't let him ride off into the sunset because he'd likely return for revenge. I decided to cross that bridge when we came to it.

The first signs of dawn appeared in the sky at five thirty on Wednesday morning. We passed a sign for Hermitage.

"Slow down," Jerry said, scanning along a wooded area as Lea cruised along. He knocked his head against the window. "There— the gap in the trees. Stop."

Lea screeched the Chevy to a halt on the quiet shoulder. Jack jerked awake.

To our right, overhead wires ran through a thirty-yard break in the trees, crossed a small road, and continued into the distance.

I got out, stretched my legs, and looked up. Thick dark clouds spanned the sky, and I wondered how long the weather would hold. A moderate stench of death hung on the gentle breeze, nowhere near Scranton's terrific fetor.

Jack and Lea disembarked to survey the scene. Jerry shuffled to the open door. I helped him out, and he limped to the edge of the road.

"Remember our deal?" he asked.

"Deal?" I said. "We kept you alive to bring us here."

He moved in front of me and tried but failed to look sincere. He also needed to brush his teeth. "I want assurances if I tell you the final part. What happens to me?"

I hadn't made my mind up and decided to lie for the sake of brevity. "We go our opposite ways and forget each other existed."

"Works for me. Head through the gap for just over a mile. It leads to Hogback Road. Turn right, and his is the first place on the left. You can't miss it."

I turned to Jack and Lea. "You get that?"

Jack nodded. "Hogback Road, first on the left."

Jerry turned his back to me. "I've done my part. Cut me free."

"Not yet. We need to find out if you're telling the truth."

He spun round and gave me a sour look. "You promised—"

"Your words carry no stock. Once we establish Anthony lives there and has information, you can go on your merry way."

He muttered something about me being a cocksucker and leaned against the Chevy.

Lea rummaged in the trunk and produced three cans of baked beans and plastic spoons. "Here you go, boys. Get some energy inside us."

The ring pull made the cans easy to open, and as I chewed the first mouthful, I thought of Bernie and his apartment. I imagined destroying the local Genesis Alliance faction and getting some revenge for his death and for all the others in the world.

My mind switched from Hermitage. We had to find out GA's future plans. If they'd carried out the first activation, a second could just be around the corner.

Jerry hungrily watched me finish the can. I tossed it at his feet. "You get fed when we return."

He kicked the can along the road and bared his yellow teeth.

Lea stared toward the opening in the trees, apparently lost in her own mind.

"A penny for your thoughts," I said.

She flinched back into reality and gave me a docile look. "I'm thinking about Martina and what we do after this."

Jack threw his can to the side of the road. "It depends what we find here. This bloke might have all the answers."

217

I held out my hand and raised Lea to her feet. "This is our primary objective. Push all other thoughts aside. You don't want to compromise any of your actions."

"I want to see Martina, but—"

"Forget about her for now. It's reasonably safe to assume that Anthony will be armed if he's at home. He could call for backup, so we need to be quick once we get there."

"How shall we take the house? A pincer movement?" Jack said. "He might be expecting something if he's monitoring or ordering the patrols."

I liked the strategy, a favorite of the army when capturing an enemy position. If the property had the cover of trees to one side, we could feint at the front and take him out with a flanking maneuver.

"You're gonna have to explain that to me in English," Lea said.

"I approach the front of the house, keeping a reasonably safe distance and acting like a confused survivor. Hopefully, it catches his attention, and we flush him out. Once he appears and focuses on me, you move in from the side."

"What if he shoots you?"

"He doesn't know who I am or if I've got heavy backup around the corner. If I make him think I'm alone, we'll snare the bastard. I'll take your Beretta and conceal it in a plastic bag. Make it look like I'm carrying looted supplies."

"Then what?" Lea asked.

"We take him, dead or alive. It depends on the situation," Jack said.

I felt a speck of rain hit my cheek and glanced up at increasingly angry-looking clouds. "Easier to do this when it's not bucketing down. Let's get going."

"He might be asleep," Lea said.

I put a reassuring hand on her shoulder. "We had a saying in the army. Improvise, adapt, and overcome. We'll be fine."

"Just remember: Jerry told us about this place. Be ready for a nasty surprise," Jack said.

"I'm still here," Jerry said.

"Good point," I said. I walked over, grabbed him in a headlock, and forced him into the back seat.

"What the fuck are you doing?" he cried.

"Remember what you said about insurance? This is mine."

I tied his ankles together and looped a piece of rope from them to his wrists. I slammed the door and watched him flip around like a fish out of water.

"Are we seriously letting him go?" Jack said.

"No idea. What do you reckon Lea?"

"He's no use as a bargaining chip."

I took Lea's Beretta, slipped off the mag, and thumbed out four rounds. Should be enough with the cover of two fully loaded rifles. I reloaded the magazine, put one in the chamber, and placed it in a plastic bag among three packets of pretzels. When I approached the house, I wanted to look as nonthreatening and clueless as possible, with a gun hidden but close to hand.

Jack gave Lea a quick lesson on how to use the AR-15. We were ready for launch.

I confirmed our approach while thumping came from inside the Chevy. "We follow the wires until we can see Hogback Road. From there, we creep through the trees and survey the ground. Ready?"

Jack and Lea shouldered their rifles. I picked up the plastic bag containing the Beretta.

We marched off the highway in an extended line, crossed another minor road, and entered the wide trail below the overhead wires. A rumble of thunder echoed in the distance.

Dense woodland covered our flanks. My boots flicked up dew from the short grass, soaking the bottom of my velour tracksuit. After reaching a dogleg, I paused and raised my hand. Jack and Lea stopped on either side of me. I edged forward and looked around it. Hogback Road lay about half a mile ahead.

I gave a crisp indication to my left. "Through the pines from here, guys."

The breeze through the trees created a light background noise, enabling us to move quickly without fear of being heard from a distance. I darted from pine to pine, with the other two following.

Five minutes later, we reached the edge of the road. I crouched behind one of the tightly clustered pines. According to Jerry's directions, Anthony lived in the first property on our right. I gazed in that direction. The tree line stopped forty yards ahead, a positive sign that somebody lived here. I wondered if he'd been sent any kind of warning.

I waved Jack and Lea forward. "I think that's the entrance to the place over there."

"It's quiet," Jack said. "Let's go for it."

Without wanting to waste any time, I ran in a low position diagonally over the road and into woodland on the opposite side. I slowed my pace and reached the edge of a property. Concealed from the road, no neighbors, a good place to hatch our plan.

I peered at a two-story rectangular brick house with timber boarding around the first floor, set back a hundred yards from the road. A gravel drive ran from the front to a double garage at the side. A black Range Rover was lazily parked on the overgrown front lawn. Our cover ran the full length along the left side of the property, perfect for a flanking move.

We crouched in a huddle.

"We stick with the plan," I said. "You get into position, and I'll casually saunter over and see what happens. I don't plan on getting too close, and I'll try to keep the Range Rover between myself and the house. If there's no sign of him, we move in from different directions and carry out a house clearance."

"If the shit hits the fan, we'll RV back at the Chevy," Jack said.

"RV?" Lea asked.

"Rendezvous—meet back there. Harry, give us five minutes to get there and find a decent angle to attack."

"Will do. Good luck."

"Cheers, same to you."

Jack and Lea disappeared among the trees, and I waited.

I watched the second hand rotate around my watch five times, then took a deep breath and went for it. My pulse raced as I hit the road. I tried to appear as casual as possible, appearing in front of the property, stopping, and looking toward the house.

I wandered down the driveway and searched for signs of movement behind the windows, but they only returned dark reflections.

Something moved in my peripheral vision. I kept my head straight but turned my eyes left. Jack and Lea crept from the trees and stood with their backs against the garage wall, out of view from the house.

I pulled out a bag of pretzels, opened it, and chucked one into my mouth. If Anthony was watching, he refused the bait. I decided to provoke a reaction. I walked to the Range Rover, pressed my left hand against the driver's window, and looked through; the keys were in the ignition. I tried the driver's door and heard the house's front door open behind me.

"Stop right there. Put your hands up."

I pretended to drop the bag of pretzels in fake surprise, slipped the bag off my wrist, and placed it sideways on the ground next to me. I raised my arms and slowly turned around. During the turn, I glanced over at the garage. Jack held his thumb up and started to edge backward.

"Don't shoot. I'm trying to find people . . ."

Lea's comparison of Anthony to Larry David proved quite accurate. He tucked an AR-15 in his shoulder and glared through the sights at me. He advanced forward in a pair of black and white striped pajamas and gray slip-on shoes.

"Find people or take their wheels?"

"I've got a car a mile down the road. Do you know what the hell's going on?"

"What are you doing here?"

"No idea. One minute, I was on holiday at the Great Lakes. The next, I'm on the side of a highway, surrounded by corpses. Where is this place? Ohio?"

He lowered the rifle slightly and looked over the sights. "I can tell by your thick accent you're not from around here."

Over his shoulder, Jack moved across to the house. Close enough for an accurate shot to blow Anthony's brains out. If I sensed he had an itchy trigger finger, I planned to duck and tie my bootlaces, giving Jack a clear shot.

"Have you been out and seen anything? It's crazy out there," I said. "I've only met two other people."

"Who were they?" he asked and jabbed his rifle forward. "Answer me."

"A couple heading to New York. Both frightened and tired. They thought it might be a dirty bomb attack or something."

"Why didn't you go with them? Why did you come here?"

"They were on a motorbike. They said it was easier to travel that way. I've been to a few houses around here . . ." I frowned at him. "What's with all the questions anyway?"

"You can't stay here. I can't help you."

I tried to look offended and picked up my bag. "Thanks for nothing."

He slung his rifle by his side, turned, and walked back to his house. I glanced across; Jack and Lea were both pressed against the wall.

"Hold on—can you help me with directions? I'll just get my map," I said.

Anthony spun around and shrugged his shoulders. "Sure, but make it quick."

He yawned and gazed up at the sky after a distant rumble of thunder.

During his brief moment of distraction, I pulled the Beretta out and pointed it at his face in a single movement.

"Hello, Anthony."

His eyes widened, and he staggered back two paces. His hand grasped the stock of the AR-15, slung by his side.

"Don't even think about it," I said.

Jack appeared behind him and moved around to his side. "One more false move, and you're dead. Your turn to reach for the sky."

He held up his hands. "You've got this all wrong. That's not my name."

"The AR-15, the black Range Rover, the questions?" I said. "Fuck off. You're Anthony from Genesis Alliance."

Lea jogged over and stopped behind him. He jerked his head to one side as he heard her footsteps approach but kept his eyes on me.

"I don't know what you're talking about; I'm just a regular guy who got through all of this by staying inside."

"Is there anybody else in the house?" Jack asked.

He shook his head. "Just me."

"Put your hands on your head and kneel," I said.

He dropped to his knees and locked his trembling fingers over his smooth dome.

"There's someone you might like to meet."

I gestured Lea forward. She stood beside me and faced him.

He gasped. "Oh shit."

"That's him. That's Anthony."

Jack smashed him in the face with the butt of his rifle.

He collapsed on the grass and moaned. "Who are you? What do you want?"

"You'll find out soon enough. Tie him up," I said.

Jack bound his wrists together and pulled him up to his feet.

"Where shall we do this?" Jack asked.

I looked around his property for an ideal location. "The garage. I'm sure he'll have a few tools in there we can use."

"You can thank Jerry for giving away your location," Jack said.

Anthony scowled and spat blood on the ground. "The fucking lizard. I knew it. Where is he?"

"We have him. But that's the last thing you should be worrying about," I said.

"You need to talk, Anthony. These guys are serious," Lea said.

"I'm a small player, I can't tell you anything."

Jack shoved him toward the garage. "Time to make you squeal."

I swung one of the large double doors open and looked inside. A device sat in the far right corner, similar in size to the one in Jerry's barn. Typical garage contents were cluttered along the left wall: a mower, a hoe, and a barbeque grill on wheels. On the other side, he had stacks of food, water, and a desk with a radio on top. I wondered if Jerry styled his barn on Anthony's garage. I found an impressive-looking hunting knife and a fully loaded Ruger LCR sitting on the desk.

I held up the Ruger. "Jack, seen this?"

"Nice one. I'll take that," he replied.

I placed both weapons in my bag and studied a whiteboard hanging above the desk. Spidery writing in blue marker pen scrawled across it, but the text didn't mean anything to me. It would be easier to make Anthony talk.

"Sit him down," I said.

Jack thrust his knee into the small of Anthony's back. He arched forward and fell to his knees.

Anthony shot Lea a desperate glance. "Get these two to back off, and I'll talk to Ron for you."

Lea shook her head and took a step back.

"Just to be completely up front with you," Jack said. "Jerry talked after we used bolt cutters on his toes. Don't even think about wasting our time."

He squirmed. "Are you going to kill me?"

"We're not murderers like you," I said. "Tell us the Genesis Alliance plan, or consider picking up your teeth from the ground with broken fingers."

I felt we needed to up our verbal and physical game with Anthony. Being higher ranked than Jerry, I suspected he would be more in line with the Genesis Alliance ideology and a tougher nut to crack.

Anthony closed his eyes and rapidly shook his head "I can't, he'll—"

Both him and Jerry seemed terrified of Ron. I wondered what kind of character could evoke such fear in an already crazy world.

"If that's how you want to play it," Jack interrupted. He reached into my backpack and pulled out the can of pepper spray. "Any plastic bags around here?"

Lea found one full of seeds, emptied it, and handed it to Jack. He stood behind Anthony and twisted his ear. "Last chance. Tell us about Genesis Alliance."

"I can't. Please, you must understand—it's far bigger than you imagine."

Jack sprayed the can across Anthony's face and covered his head with the plastic bag, holding it airtight around his neck. Anthony bucked violently and sucked all the air out of it, causing it to tighten around his face. After twenty seconds, Jack released him, and he collapsed on the floor, gulping for air.

He looked up in fear, with bloodshot, streaming eyes. Jack picked up a roll of masking tape from the garage floor and held it up. "I'll tie his legs together. Harry, hold him there."

I sat on Anthony's palpitating chest while Jack slapped tape around his ankles and knees.

"Do his hands," I said.

I flipped him over and forced his wrists together behind his back. Jack secured them, and we turned him back on his front.

He coughed twice and grimaced. "You won't get away with it. They'll kill—"

Jack knelt over his body, dragged him up by his pajama lapels, and head-butted him on the bridge of his nose. Anthony fell back with a grunt.

He lay back with his mouth wide open, moaning and cursing. I picked up the can of pepper spray and squirted it down his throat.

Anthony retched three times and spat out of the corner of his mouth. "Stop . . . Oh my God! . . . Stop."

"What do you want to know? I'll talk."

"Lea, pass me that toolbox," Jack said.

She stood at the garage door, looking nervous, but we had to go with the nuclear option. A patrol could turn up at any minute. We didn't have time to soft-soap him. Besides, I felt little sympathy for a man who had played an active part in the death of millions. I doubted many felt pity for the Nazis hanged after the Nuremberg trials. This was our courtroom, and we continued our cross-examination.

"Are you going to talk?" I demanded.

"Just go. I won't say a word." His voice cracked, and he squeezed his eyes tightly shut. "They'll hunt you down."

Lea placed the toolbox next to Jack and stepped back. He opened it up and ran his fingers over the contents.

I glanced at Lea. She slowly nodded.

Jack grabbed a hacksaw and rolled up the left leg of Anthony's pajama bottoms. "This is coming off below the knee."

"You wouldn't—you can't," Anthony gasped.

"Want to put a bet on that?" Jack snarled.

He gritted his teeth and sawed at Anthony's calf. I thought it a great bluff until Anthony screamed and bolted stiff. I leaned over Jack's shoulder. He had already cut an inch deep and had no intentions of stopping.

I reached to pull him away.

Anthony screwed up his face. Saliva sprayed through his clenched teeth. "*Stop!* I'll talk. I'll fucking talk!"

I knelt next to his head and held the pepper spray over his eyes. "What's happening next? Is there going to be another one of those activations?"

"Yes, tomorrow—but I can help you. Get me that—"

"Tomorrow? What time?" Jack said.

"Eleven in the morning. I found out yesterday."

I checked my watch. Twenty-eight hours to go. We had to stop it. "I don't give a shit when you found out. Is it triggered in Michigan?"

He swallowed and nodded. "Monroe. Did Jerry tell you that?"

"You said you can help. How?" I said.

"I can neutralize you. It's a simple procedure."

"As if I would let you carry out any procedure on me," Jack said. "What about the next activation and the one after that?"

"It's a one-time procedure. Over there, in the corner, the cattle prod. Just zap yourselves on the head a few times."

Jack snorted. "Christ, you must think we're all stupid."

Anthony shook his head. "Far from it. I respect you."

I squirted the can in his eyes. He growled and spun his head away.

"Stop sucking up," I said. "Jerry told us you used a tool on him. Where's that?"

"I don't have it," he said in a slow, croaky voice. "That's the truth."

Anthony's suggestion seemed ridiculous. I couldn't put my faith in him to help us avoid the consequences of a second activation. I had to keep in mind what these people had done and the serious nature of the impending threat.

I thought of what would happen to us and any other survivor if we were hit with another activation. I turned to Lea. "How far is Monroe from here?"

She looked up. "About two hundred miles. We'd easily make it."

"Are you thinking what I'm thinking?" I asked.

"Yeah, we need to deal with the organ grinder, not his monkeys," Jack said. "There's no point wasting our time here. We got what we came for."

"I can help you. Seriously," Anthony said.

"Final question," I said, hovering the pepper spray's nozzle around his eyes. "Why did Genesis Alliance do it, and who are they? First sign of bullshit, and you can guess what happens."

He sucked in a deep breath and gave me an apprehensive look.

"Go on," I said.

"Genesis Alliance has stopped humanity from wiping itself out—"

"By wiping everybody out first?" Jack said.

"You wouldn't understand. Natural resources are running out. States fight each other. Terrorists attack over religious beliefs. A global pandemic may be just around the corner because of the squalid living conditions in overpopulated cities, diseases will spread like wildfire. We needed a reset. A decimation."

"You've got screws loose," I said. "Is this what it's really all about?"

"Don't you even find a grain of truth in our logic?"

"Let me see how this works," Jack said. "I have a friend who's married with three kids. They have another child. Due to his low income and small house, their resources are stretched to the limit, and it leads to arguments. But hey, there's always murder-suicide to trim down the bills and whip things into shape.

He slapped Anthony across the head. "You bloody idiot."

Anthony sighed. "I knew you wouldn't understand. None of you do."

"Who leads this organization, and where are they based?" I asked.

"Ron runs North American operations. I don't know his superior. That's how this thing works—"

"Okay, we know the score," I said. "Jerry came out with the same shit."

"This time we don't need him along for the ride," Lea said, stepping in from the entrance with folded arms. "I know exactly where Ron lives."

"Let's get on the road," Jack said, "after sorting him out."

Anthony nervously looked at Jack, me, and finally Lea. "What are you gonna do to me?"

I found two dog bowls among the clutter along the side of the garage. I filled one with three cans of peaches and poured two bottles of water into the other. I wouldn't leave him to burn to death in his own buildings, but he would watch them turn to ashes.

"I'll give you a clue; we're not taking you to Splash Universe," I said and headed out to the Rover. I placed both bowls on the back seat and returned to the garage. "Put him in the back. He's going to watch his house go up in smoke."

Jack and Lea dragged Anthony by his bound ankles to the Rover and heaved him into the back seat. I took the keys, stabbed each tire with his hunting knife, and then opened the rear door by Anthony's head.

"You've got some food and water. If we don't manage to stop the activation, at least it'll keep you going until somebody shows up and kills you."

He rolled onto his side. "You can't leave me like this."

"Yes, we can," Jack said.

"You'll be digging your own graves. Genesis Alliance is far bigger than you realize. Do you seriously think it stops in Monroe? We're only a small part—"

I ignored Anthony, slammed the door, and passed Jack the Ruger from my bag.

Anthony's breath steamed against the window as he shouted from inside the Range Rover, but we ignored him. I felt light spots of rain on my face and jogged back to the garage.

"Lea, search the house with me," I said. "Jack, smash his radio and have a rummage around. See if you can find any GA notes or handbooks."

I headed into the house with Lea, leaving Jack in the garage. The door opened easily, and I motioned for Lea to search upstairs. The living room had a stone-effect fireplace along one wall, three vulgar orange leather couches, and a cluttered bookcase. I leafed through the bookcase, pulling out random books and shaking them for any hidden papers. It felt like a waste of time, so I pulled the bookcase over and kicked the debris with my foot but found nothing of interest.

The small, cream fitted kitchen smelled of grease and had a pile of dirty plates in the sink. I found some boil-in-the-bag food, which would come in handy.

The dining room on the other side of the staircase contained a table and six chairs. Framed photographs lined the wall. Anthony really loved himself. The one of him on a jet ski, waving and wearing a pair of speedos, turned my stomach. I took down a framed photo of a fishing group. In the center was a man holding up a large fish. The brass plate on the wood frame read "Ron's catch of the day." *Interesting*, I thought and tucked it under my arm.

I kicked over a bureau and rifled through it but found nothing else.

As I walked back to the front door, Lea came down the stairs. "Only the usual kinda stuff up there."

Hammering came from the garage. I found Jack attacking the activation device with a lump hammer.

"Leave it, Jack," I said.

He turned, with sweat pouring down his forehead, surrounded by a mess of smashed pots, tools, and broken glass. "It's as tough as the other one."

"We'll just torch the place," I said.

I tipped a bulky mower on its side, opened the fuel tank, and emptied it onto the garage floor. Enough to get a small fire going. Jack found a large box of matches and tossed them to me.

"Wait here a minute," I said to both.

I jogged back into the house and went straight for the kitchen. I opened the gas supply to the stove, set fire to the curtains in the dining and living rooms, and returned to the garage. Jack had already lit the fuel, and a healthy fire crackled and popped.

Lea waited for us by the road, facing the opposite direction— I figured probably because she thought our techniques for gaining information were questionable. To me, they were completely justified, considering the circumstances.

We jogged along the road and turned through the gap in the trees that led back to Interstate 80.

"What's that under your arm?" Jack asked.

"I'll show you back at the Chevy."

I kept up a strong pace, thudding along the dew-glistening grass, until I saw a plume of black smoke rising from the highway. I skidded to a halt, and Jack crashed into the back of me.

"Look," I said and pointed, realizing the smoke rose from around the position of our Chevy.

"Do you think Jerry—" Lea said.

Men shouted. Close to us. Probably around the dogleg.

"Into the trees," I ordered.

We sprinted to our right. I ducked and weaved between the tightly clustered pines for fifty yards. Then I dropped behind a tree, shouldered my rifle, and observed.

Lea took cover ten yards to my left. Jack scrambled next to me. "What do you think?"

"We'll see in a minute."

231

The shouting continued. Figures approached from the highway. Two in black clothing, advancing through the clearing with rifles shouldered.

Two more followed. Another in black, and Jerry.

He waved his arms in an animated fashion. His voice being the loudest. He pointed forward, and they all started running.

"We could take them out," Jack said.

I looked through a gap in the canopy toward Anthony's house. Black smoke billowed into the sky. "We don't know how many we're facing. They could pin us down. Let's get back to the road before Anthony tells them we've only just left."

"Chased from behind, Ron probably expecting us, killers on the loose, and a second activation in"—he checked his watch—"just over twenty-seven hours."

I sprinted to Lea. "Back to the road and out of here. They're going to be hot on our tail."

"What if there's more on the highway?"

"We'll slip away through the country or city."

With no time to lose, I hunched down and cut a path through the trees. Jack bounded along to my right. Lea followed him. Within twenty yards of the minor road that ran along the side of the highway, I slowed and took more deliberate steps.

Through the trees that separated both roads, I could see our vehicle in flames. Our supplies were gone, but that wasn't our biggest issue at the moment.

I crept further forward. Two Rovers were parked ahead of the burning Chevy. Three men with Jerry. One might still be here. Maybe more, maybe none. I ducked down but couldn't see any feet on the ground around the cars.

Jack and Lea edged alongside me.

"What do you think?" Jack said.

"Looks quiet. If we've got a chance of returning the favor with their Rovers, at least it might slow them down for a bit."

Jack sprinted across the minor road. He leopard-crawled through the trees leading to the highway, stopped, and raised his thumb.

Lea and I dashed across the road. Careful planning would have been great, but we simply didn't have time.

After scanning the road and seeing no sign of life, I walked onto the highway, rifle pulled against my shoulder, stepping as softly as possible. The raging Chevy helped disguise any sound.

Jack patrolled to my right, Lea between us, Beretta outstretched in both hands. He froze for a second and dropped to one knee, aiming at the front Rover. I spun to face it. A puff of smoke rose from behind it and drifted away.

Somebody probably sitting against the wheel having a cigarette.

Lea's shoe crunched on a piece of broken glass.

A man shot up from behind the vehicle.

I opened fire from less than twenty yards. Jack did the same. The man jerked as multiple rounds whipped into his torso. The Rover's front windows shattered. He dropped to the ground.

Jack ran around the front of the Rover, and I heard a single gunshot. The coup de grace. I swept my rifle around the area, looking for any more goons.

Without detecting signs of movement, I moved to the closest Rover and tried the door. Locked. Not everybody left their keys. I retrieved the hunting knife from my bag and stabbed every tire.

I heard crashing behind me. Jack sat in the front Rover and kicked at the bullet-riddled windshield. Lea covered him in a squatting position.

I ran over. "We got keys for this one?"

Lea rattled a bunch in her hand. "Found them on him."

Jack managed to kick four large holes out of the shattered windshield. Good enough to get away from here. I looked in either direction of the highway and couldn't see any other vehicles.

"Let's get out of here," I said.

A loud dull explosion boomed in the distance. Hopefully, Anthony's house, taking them all out.

Jack sat in the passenger seat. Lea started the engine, put the Rover in drive, and punched the accelerator. We skidded away and picked up speed.

I observed through the back window. Tiny figures appeared from the gap in the trees and stood on the highway. They wouldn't get us from a mile unless they had a sniper rifle.

Lea let out a deep breath. "Shit, that was close."

"You're telling me," Jack said. "A few more minutes at Anthony's . . ."

———

Lea hammered it along Interstate 80 for the next hour, while we still had favorable road conditions. I expected us to slow around Cleveland, but Genesis Alliance, including Anthony and Jerry, would face the same problems, if they followed in hot pursuit.

I passed the picture to Jack.

"So this is Ron," he said.

Lea glanced away from the road. "Yeah, that's him."

"Anyone else in the photo you know apart from Anthony and Ron?" I asked.

"That's Martina on the left," she said attempting to sound matter of fact.

I leaned between the seats. "So you think she's still innocent?"

"What if you saw a picture of me with those guys at the team building? Would that make me guilty by association?"

"You have to admit—"

"So, we're really going?" she asked, abruptly changing the subject. "They'll be expecting us after this."

"If they have a way of communicating," Jack said.

"We're on a deadline," I said. "If we don't make it, we might die tomorrow. That's all the motivation we need."

I returned to my observation post at the rear window. I didn't want them taking us by surprise. The wreckages and parked cars became heavier as we began to pass Cleveland. We slowed significantly and had to keep stopping to drive other cars to one side or try to nudge them out of the way.

At one point, the vehicles queued up in lanes as far the eye could see; most had the doors open. Drivers must have been in a traffic jam when the activation struck, all jumping out for a fight to the death. We jogged two miles in rain to get past that obstacle. At the head of it, emergency services vehicles surrounded a pre-activation crash. Paramedics slumped around a gurney.

Just after midday, we stopped in front of seven cars that had crossed the highway, blocking our path. Bodies lay outside the vehicles, but all had corpses inside, as far as I could see, except for one. The car blocking the outside lane appeared to be empty.

I opened the driver's door to get in and start the engine. An arm flopped out. The incredible stench of rotting flesh hit me like an express train. A purple, bloated face of a small lady looked up at me from the footwell.

I staggered back to the car with my hand over my nose and mouth. We'd all gotten used to the smell—it was everywhere—but I'd never received such a powerful blast, and the view had been equally as revolting.

"Car swap time again," I said.

Jack groaned. "Can't you just move that car? What's inside?"

"You don't want to know."

We crossed to the opposite side of the obstruction. Lea found a nice Toyota with a full tank of fuel. I hoped this would get us all the way to Monroe.

The debris thinned out between Cleveland and Toledo, and our pace picked up as sunshine started to peep through the clouds. We were closing in on Monroe and had no plans to stop. We didn't want to give anyone a chance of catching up with us, conscious that they might only be half an hour behind.

I was just about to comment about how we'd gotten past the worst part of the journey when Jack hurriedly pressed a button to lower the passenger window. He spewed vomit against it before it had completely dropped.

I pressed my hand on his back. "What's up? Are you all right?"

"Think I've eaten something dodgy. My guts feel terrible."

"You haven't eaten anything different from us. Have you?"

He threw his head out of the window and retched. Lea passed him a half-full bottle of water from the driver's side cup holder.

He swilled his mouth and spat outside. "Who knows what kind of diseases might be in the air? I'll be okay."

None of us had slept for over twenty-four hours. Driving through the debris on the highway at the highest possible speed required an energy-sapping high level of concentration and alertness. I think we were all running on pure adrenaline, and now Jack had food poisoning? These were definitely not the best conditions to be staging an assault on Ron's house.

"Let's get close to Monroe and get some rest," I said. "We'll go to Ron's tomorrow morning."

"Isn't that cutting it a little close? The activation is tomorrow morning," Lea said.

Jack held his stomach and groaned. "It's probably not a bad idea. I feel like shit. Besides that, it's probably going to be dark by the time we get there. I'd prefer to take the house in the hours of daylight."

"What about the ones following us?" Lea asked.

"I've been thinking about that," I said. "With the state of Anthony's leg, and Jerry having no sleep for over twenty-four hours, do you really think they will move through the night with the same kind of urgency as us?"

Lea shuffled in her seat. "They might radio in. Whatever. I think they'll be expecting us."

"Ron's going to be protected anyway," Jack said. "Besides that, they've got an activation to plan for, and how many are based in Monroe?"

Lea didn't answer.

"If they've got a couple of thousand spread across North America," I said. "I can't imagine the place being a fortress."

"It's gonna be a death trap if we wait," Lea said.

"We need to be in the best possible shape if we're going to beat them," Jack said. "Lea, you might know the area, but we don't. What if something happens to you?"

"We're going in whether we like it or not," I said. "It's a choice of fighting them to the death before eleven, or fighting each other to the death after."

"When you put it like that . . ." she said.

Darkness descended as we skirted Toledo. With no further issues, apart from two stops for Jack to puke by the side of the road, I took the wheel and plowed up the Detroit–Toledo Expressway.

As we neared Monroe at quarter to ten in the evening, I struggled against the weight of my eyelids. Jack and Lea had both dropped off a few miles before, so I bit my lip, shook my head from side to side, and forced my eyes open as widely as possible. When none of that worked, I decided that we needed to stop.

10
MI

I shook Lea awake. She blinked a few times and frowned at me.
"How far is it from here?" I asked.

She yawned and looked around. "Where are we?"

"Close to Monroe. Is there any place you know where we can stop for a few hours?"

We approached a road sign. She squinted into gloomy night. "It's not far, maybe ten miles. Exit here, and we should be able to find a place. I don't think any GA live in Luna Pier."

I pulled off the highway and drove down a dark street, dipping our headlights. Silhouettes of houses appeared on both sides. I parked the Toyota against the curb without feeling particularly fussy about our choice of house. We only needed a roof and a door.

I stopped next to a small, two-story white house with darkened windows. Jack threw off his seatbelt and jumped out. He opened the house's creaking metal gate, approached the front door, and knocked four times. I think tiredness and sickness had overwhelmed him, and his body switched to autopilot.

Predictably, after no answer, we crept around the back and tried to peer through the windows, but blinds prevented us from seeing inside.

"Fuck it," Jack said. "Let's kick the back door in. I'm too tired to start hunting around for the perfect house."

He raised his foot and smashed it against the door. It didn't move. Lea stepped forward, turned the handle, and the door opened.

"Sometimes it's worth keeping things simple," she said.

Jack looked at me and puffed out his cheeks, probably to keep himself from snapping.

We entered the house directly into a small, clean kitchen and continued into the living room. I glanced at a huge LCD TV attached to the wall, the same size as the one in my local pub. I doubted I'd be watching football with a beer in hand anytime soon. A blue leather couch sat opposite, with three green paisley pillows neatly placed along it. Magazines were spread across a glass coffee table. The owners seemingly liked motorbikes.

"So far, so good," Lea said.

"Let's grab bedding from upstairs and sleep down here," I said.

They were both too tired to bother arguing. I led up the squeaky staircase, listening for movement elsewhere in the house. I found three closed doors around the landing, presumably two bedrooms and a bathroom. We took a door each, and I entered a small room with a single bed. Probably a guest room, due to the sparseness of the walls and piles of boxes stacked on the bed. I ripped off the duvet, sending boxes tumbling to the ground and spilling contents of books, records, and a couple of old plastic toy trucks.

Lea shouted from another room.

I dropped the bedding, raised my rifle, and ran for the nearest open door.

Lea stared at two dead bodies, embraced in each other's arms on the bed. An elderly couple dressed in day clothes, they didn't appear to be long dead. Four empty pill bottles sat on the bedside table.

I guessed they'd decided to end it rather than live in this shattered world. The activation probably didn't get them, but the
consequences did.

"Sorry, they freaked me out in this light," Lea said. "I didn't
mean to scare you guys."

"No worries," I said. "I found a duvet in the other room."

Jack edged past me and looked at the scene on the bed.
"Jesus Christ."

We filed back to the living area and sat on the couches in
silence. We were all too exhausted to bother shifting the dead
couple, and we needed some rest. I rose with a grunt and checked
that all the doors and windows were locked. Jack and I pushed a
large dresser and bookcase in front of the internal doors. One of us
would wake if somebody tried to break in.

I took a recliner. Jack spread out on the floor with the duvet,
and Lea pulled a single sheet over herself on the couch.

Ron probably plotted his next moves a mere ten miles away.
I couldn't concentrate on what we might face and how to get around
it. I drifted in and out of sleep until a disturbingly vivid dream at
dawn woke me completely.

In the nightmare, I stood at the head table, preparing to make
a speech. I glanced to my left at my bride, a rotting corpse in a frilly
white dress. I shuffled my notes and looked around a large reception room. My decaying family and friends, in suits and dresses, all
raised their glasses. They started to heckle me.

"Why did you get on the plane, Harry?"

"Why are you still alive?"

"You'll be married to the dead soon."

I awoke with a start and rubbed my eyes, muttering under my
breath, "Fucking hell."

Some claim that dreams can be interpreted. I had no idea but
guessed mine could have been fueled by survivor guilt, a mental

condition that occurs when a person perceives himself to have done wrong by surviving a traumatic event when others did not.

"You all right?" Jack asked.

I sat forward and rubbed my face. "I just had a nightmare about getting married."

"Loads of people have had that in real life."

Lea lifted the sheet from her face. "Mostly women faced with the likes of you, Jack."

We all managed to get at least a few hours of sleep, and I felt a lot better for it. Jack said his guts had improved, and he hadn't vomited since we'd arrived at Luna Pier. We could attack Genesis Alliance with clearer heads and more energy.

I made my way into the kitchen to search the cupboards and found a rare treat in the second one. Something that reminded me of our old ration pack meals. I fished out two cans as if they were heaven sent—Spam.

I opened the fridge and grabbed a sealed, lukewarm bottle of Coke, opened the cans of Spam, found a couple of forks in a drawer, and proudly carried breakfast into the living room.

Jack eagerly grabbed a can and tucked in. Lea appeared less enthusiastic but soon wolfed down large, pink chunks of processed meat with equal vigor.

"Taste as good as you thought it would?" Jack asked.

"It's gross. Anything else on the menu?"

"Sorry, Lea, the kitchen's closed," I said.

After breakfast, we sat around, discussing our next moves. Jack suggested driving to within a couple of miles of Ron's house and approaching on foot. I agreed. It was inconceivable that we could drive right up to Ron's house in an unknown car without being stopped by Genesis Alliance. We would also be less visible on foot and take smarter routes, across gardens, along hedges, or through houses.

"Do you know where we can get our hands on some black clothes?" I asked.

"I know a couple of places in South Monroe we could try. They're both two miles from Ron's, so it fits nicely with Jack's idea."

"We've got the right weapons too," Jack said. "All of them have AR-15s."

We spent the next hour cleaning and checking our weapons as best we could, using items from the kitchen. Nobody wanted a stoppage this morning. Slick drills, quick kills.

We decided to leave the bolt-action rifle in the trunk; Jack kept hold of the Ruger. I could tell he liked it. He kept pulling it out and inspecting it with a look of satisfaction.

I strapped the hunting knife to the side of my backpack for quick release. We had enough weapons for a precision strike. We would have to use speed and the inherent deception of our clothing to carry out a lightning raid. Extraction would be planned depending on the scenario we faced. I accepted that the odds were bleak.

———

At seven in the morning, we headed out below a clear blue sky. I drove back onto the expressway with a sense of foreboding and headed north. The next few hours would determine whether we would live or die. I wanted the former but suspected the latter.

Lea directed me to take Exit 9, and we merged onto Otter Creek Road toward South Monroe. Just before the road joined South Dixie Highway, I squeezed my foot against the brake.

A thick jumble of cars blocked our path, stretching as far as the eye could see. A jam like this seemed unlikely for a small city. Lea had a theory that Genesis Alliance might have started tidying up the immediate area around Monroe and used this place as a dumping ground.

We took the only option available and proceeded on foot. Making my way through the tangle of cars, I noticed a lack of corpses in the vehicles, which backed up Lea's idea.

I began to consider the location of the dead after detecting a strong smell of decomposition just as we arrived at the junction. A mechanical digger was parked next to a large pit in the opposite field. Ripped clothing hung from the teeth of its bucket. From our position, I could just about see the top of a pile of corpses.

Jack stared open-mouthed. Lea turned away and covered her face. Nothing surprised me anymore. I had already come to terms with the depths of depravity displayed by Genesis Alliance.

"Keep focused, Lea," I said. "We need to get our hands on some black clothing."

"This way," she said and headed north on South Dixie Highway.

She led us through an area of residential housing, wooden white frontages, standard fare, before office blocks and shops hugged either side of the road.

After ten minutes of walking through our strangely clean, quiet, and creepy surroundings, she turned right into a retail plaza.

Somebody had worked hard to whip this place into shape since Friday. It had the look of any other small pre-Activation city, but on closer inspection, violent evidence remained. Blood smeared areas of the sidewalk, and fragments of shattered glass gleamed on the road.

We stayed tight against the buildings as we proceeded to the entrance of a large clothing store. Mannequins casually posed in the windows in summer clothing. One had a sweater tied around its shoulders and pointed skyward. The type of place where I bought work clothes back home, not the kind of shop that stocked a shirt that was worthy of a big night out.

There wasn't a soul in sight; nevertheless, I consciously maintained a high level of vigilance. We were close to Ron's house, and people had cleaned this area in the last few days.

I pushed open the store's glass door and slipped inside. The shopping area seemed relatively intact. Clothing hung neatly from rails in size order, and folded sweaters were piled on a table for a half-price sale. The checkouts were splattered in blood.

Lea led us to the men's department, and we looked around for suitable outfits to fool Genesis Alliance. Jack and I found some well-fitting black cargo pants and turtleneck sweaters. I tucked the hunting knife into the belt and slung my rifle over my shoulder.

Jack slipped the Ruger into the front of his pants and admired himself in a full-length mirror. "How do I look?"

"Good enough to shoot."

Lea swished a changing room curtain to one side and strode out in her black outfit. "Are you guys ready?"

"Ready as we'll ever be," Jack said.

I admired her bravery. In her shoes, a weasel like Jerry would go back with his tail between his legs and leverage the relationship with Ron's niece. Lea was bigger than that.

Jack headed for the store entrance. He quickly moved to his left behind a shoe display.

I ran up to him and ducked behind the boxes. "See something?"

"There's a Rover outside."

"Facing the store? Have they seen us?"

Lea bumped up behind me. I felt her hot breath in my ear. "How did they find us?"

"I don't think they've seen us," Jack said.

I peered around the boxes for another look. Two men stood by the hood of a Rover and smoked cigarettes. Genesis Alliance—who else could it be?

"I'd really like that Range Rover," I said. "We could go straight to Ron's."

"We can't start shooting," Jack said.

"Why don't we trick them?" Lea said. "Remember Jerry saying he didn't know all of the other members, as anonymity helped protect the organization?"

"Wouldn't patrols in the local area know each other?" Jack said.

I took another look. "Lea, do you recognize them?"

She peered around the display. "One looks vaguely familiar. We should wait for them to leave."

"We can't wait here all day," Jack said. "In two hours that activation's going to hit."

I thought about ways to take them out. We didn't know local strength or if any others were in close proximity.

"I'll fool the two outside by saying I want to turn myself in," Lea said. "I'll tell them about Martina."

"You're giving yourself up to them?" I asked.

"I'll say I've decided to return to Genesis Alliance and draw them toward the doors."

"Bring them in," Jack said.

Lea was putting her body on the line for the group. All doubts about her allegiance fizzled away.

She composed herself with three deep breaths, moved in front of the door, and pressed her hands against the glass. "It's Lea. I've come back to see Ron."

She had balls of steel. I wouldn't let her down.

"They're right outside the fucking door," she said through pursed lips.

Jack and I both held our rifles like clubs. No shots to attract attention. Just a caveman-style beating.

Lea pushed open the door. "Did you hear me?"

"Ron said we might be getting some visitors," a male voice said. "Are you alone?"

"Yes, come in and search me."

"No, you come out here."

"And be searched in the middle of a parking lot?" Lea said. "I'll tell Ron you were pointing guns at my face. Come in where no one else will see."

"Fuck it, have it your way."

Lea took several paces back. They were coming.

Two large men appeared one behind the other. Jack and I moved immediately. I thrust the butt of my rifle at the first man's temple. He dodged to one side and the blow grazed his shoulder. I moved to strike again.

He hunched toward me and said through gritted teeth. "You motherfucker!"

We came together and punched furiously at close range. Neither of us had time to use our weapons. The same thing must have been happening with Jack. I could hear scuffling to my left. Where was Lea?

I managed to get a few heavy blows in but took equal punishment. I went for my knife and lost my balance. He smashed his fist into my ear, and a high-pitched tone whistled through my head.

I tried a kick to the groin and knee but couldn't connect. The strong arm of my assailant kept me at bay. I dropped my head, trying to avoid any more punches to the face, and forced him backward with my left arm.

I stopped swinging my right arm and forced my thumb into the corner of the man's left eye socket. He roared with pain and slammed into me. I staggered and fell to the ground. He dropped straight on my chest like an old school UFC fighter.

Lea appeared to the left of the man and swung the butt of her Beretta at his head. He avoided the blow and connected with a powerful uppercut to her chin. She screamed and skidded across the shiny store floor. The full weight of his heavy frame pinned my arms down. I turned my face to the left as he hooked me in the jaw.

Two large hands locked around my throat and started choking me. I frantically tried to wriggle my arms free but couldn't move them. In desperation, I bit the man's thigh. He snarled and tightened his grip. He raised my neck off the floor to get a better grip.

The last thing I remembered, a boot swung toward my attacker's face. My head hit the floor, and everything went black.

———

Pain coursed through my body as I opened my eyes. Voices sounded like they were underwater, and blurry figures sat over me. Two women leaned close to my face, shouting. A man was screaming in the background. After a few seconds, I came to my senses. The two women merged into one, and I recognized Lea.

"Thank God, you're not dead. Are you okay?" she asked.

My mouth felt dry. I swallowed and felt a stabbing pain around my Adam's apple. I could only just see out of my left eye, and my head throbbed. I sat up cautiously.

My attacker slumped on the floor to my left. I found out later that Jack had kicked him in the face, and Lea had repeatedly slammed the butt of an AR-15 into the side of his head until he lost consciousness.

Jack's opponent lay on his back screaming. His right arm was bent back in an unnatural inverted "V" shape, and blood streamed from his eyes.

"What happened to him?" I asked.

"I managed to knock him down and snap his elbow with my boot."

I winced and looked at the man again. Jack must have gouged his eyes too.

Jack stood above me and also had a swollen face. "Let's finish this."

I stood up and propped my arm against the wall to keep my balance. "Have you checked them for radios?"

"They're clean," Lea said. "We've got their ammo too."

She led me through the entrance, and I squinted in the bright sunshine as I looked around. I felt another wave of pain jolt through my head and paused for breath.

"I'll drive," Jack said.

"Don't be stupid," Lea said. "I'm the one that knows where we're going."

Jack cursed under his breath and clambered into the back of the Rover. I took the passenger seat. I found a full bottle of water in the cup holder. The grooves on the cap stung my fingers when I twisted it open. I took a couple of gulps, and poured the rest over my head to try to clear it.

I twisted the rearview mirror toward my face and checked my swollen eye. "That was a close-run thing."

"Couple of hours till the next activation," Jack said. "We've still got a shot."

We had no other realistic option. Running away would likely mean death. If we wanted any chance of a future, it was now or never. A deep surge of anger jolted through me.

"So you're in then, Lea?" I asked.

"Of course I am. Why wouldn't I be?"

"All the way in?" Jack said.

"All the way," Lea repeated.

"Straight to Ron's," I said.

"I hope you both realize this will probably be a one-way trip," Jack said.

"Genesis Alliance wants us dead, an activation is just around the corner, and they've killed our family and friends," I said. "I'd rather go down fighting than bow to these people."

Jack and I gave each other a knowing look. One we'd shared on the football pitch as kids, at the local pub when a bully tried to knock a woman about, and when we faced the harsh slopes of Mount Elbrus. A job had to be done.

Lea pulled out of the parking lot, headed toward our destiny. The next few minutes were filled with silent contemplation. I wondered how Ron managed to create such fear among his patsies. A monster like that would be unrepentant, I imagined, but I would probably feel the same way if I put a bullet between his eyes. He deserved nothing less for the part he'd played.

———

Lea breezed the Rover through the quiet streets of Monroe. I expected to run into a checkpoint at any minute and kept my rifle at the ready.

I thought about the tantalizing prospect of the men at the plaza being perimeter guards and that we had punched through Ron's ring of all-round defense.

Lea slowed along Conant Street, a residential area packed with detached, single-story white houses. I guessed this wasn't America's most affluent street, but compared to the working class areas of the UK, the people who lived here had it good. Or *did* have it good.

"We're coming up to Oak Street—this is it," Lea said. She dropped our speed and continued forward.

Two people, carrying rifles, stood at the end of Oak Street. I ducked into the passenger footwell, and Jack lay across the backseat. Lea slammed on the brakes.

We expected some form of resistance. It seemed unlikely that Ron would let anybody get within range of his house. The presence of the guards at the end of his street suggested that Ron was home.

"We can't stop here for too long," Jack said.

I checked my watch. Nearly ten o'clock. We had an hour, tops. "Wind the windows down and drive slowly toward the guards. When we get close, tell us which side of the vehicle they're on."

"Where do you want me to go after that?"

"Drive straight up in front of Ron's. Whatever happens after that, we're committed."

Lea paused for a moment. "What if you don't take the guards out?"

"We will," Jack said. "Just make sure you get close enough."

Lea pressed the accelerator. "They've seen us, but they're not moving."

It felt like Lea drove past the street. I put it down to my adrenaline slowing everything down.

She said, "They're both armed. Rifles by their sides. They're coming around to my window . . ."

"Stop talking," Jack said. "Let us know when they're a few yards away."

Lea's arms stiffened against the wheel. *"Now!"*

I sprang from the footwell and saw two guards a yard away from Lea's window. I aimed for the closest, a female, who opened her mouth and stepped back. I fired twice into her chest. She dropped to the ground. I heard Jack's rifle fire three times in quick succession.

I jumped back into my seat and continued to aim out the window. "Drive."

Lea sped away from the scene and swung the Toyota onto Oak Street. I didn't need to look back to know the result of our actions.

She screeched to a halt in a matter of seconds. "We're here. It's the one on the right with the picket fence and blue door."

"Out. Get out now," I said.

Lea flung her door open and scrambled out. I dived over her seat and jumped out of the same door. Jack already crouched beside Lea with his AR-15 ready.

I turned to look through the vehicle windows at Ron's house.

Jack nudged my shoulder and pointed left and right. Two black Range Rovers parked at the far ends of the street—about three hundred yards from us in either direction. This had started to feel like a suicide mission, but we had to roll the dice.

The only way we would get out of this alive would be to capture Ron and use him as leverage to escape. We had to move quickly as we were exposed on the street. If more Genesis Alliance showed up, they could quickly turn us into Swiss cheese.

"Ron needs to be taken alive. Are you ready to move?" I asked.

"Lea, what's the layout?" Jack said.

Another Rover came around the corner, blocking our escape.

"Fuck it," I said, "there's no time. Straight through the front door."

Ron's front door opened. An old man with silver hair, wearing a red-checked shirt and cream trousers, held up his hands. He looked as jovial and harmless as he did in Anthony's picture. But Jerry and Anthony had been sincerely afraid of him, so I had to keep up my guard. Anyone crazy enough to come up with this "save humanity" plan had to have a few screws loose.

"Is that Ron?" Jack asked.

"That's him," Lea said, sounding grim.

He glared over at us. "There's no need for all of this. Come in, and I'll fix you a drink."

I looked at Jack in confusion. He shook his head. "The guy's a psycho."

"Come on in," Ron said and beckoned us toward the house.

I looked at either end of the street; cut-off groups blocked our escape routes. I checked my watch. Fifty minutes before the next activation.

"It could be a trap," Jack said. "Why reveal yourself like that?"

"That's the way Ron is," Lea said. "He's a cool customer."

"Let's take up his invitation and capture him," I said.

"I'm game," Jack said. "What do you suggest?"

Weapons bristled from the open windows of the Rovers on either end of the street. If we ran, it would be a turkey shoot.

With time in limited supply and our lives hanging in the balance, I decided to take positive action. "If we find any raised weapons, we shoot first and ask questions later. The first chance we get to take Ron, we do it."

"After that?" Lea asked.

"We'll make him tell us how to stop the activation," I said.

"Let's go," Jack said.

Lea stood up and walked across the street toward Ron's front door. Jack and I followed behind.

As we walked up the drive, Ron appeared and gave us a sly look. "Leave your weapons outside. I'm sorry, but it's the house rules."

"Do you really expect us to do that?" I said.

Ron wafted a hand toward the south end of Oak Street. "Depends whether you want to take on machine guns I've just stationed at either end of the street."

I looked to my left and saw a squad of black-clothed men cautiously approaching.

"They'll take you too from that range," I said.

Ron sighed and put his hands on his hips. He turned to Lea. "Why didn't you tell these two gentlemen that I've never allowed any weapons in the house?"

Ron didn't seem threatening. A real-life wolf in sheep's clothing.

I tried to appear confident, but the swelling face and bruised jaw were probably telling as much as they were hiding. As I looked across at Lea, I noticed that the vehicles had closed in, and armed men were crouched around them. One had an LSAT ready to spray us with lead. We were surrounded at close range.

"What if we just kill you now?" Jack asked.

Ron scoffed. "What do you think happens after that? Put your guns down, and come on in."

He disappeared back into the house.

The goons tightened their circle around us. If we turned on them, it would take a huge slice of luck for us to get out of Monroe alive. With Ron out of the line of sight, they could fire at will.

"Let's do as Ron says," I said. "I can't see any other way out of it."

"Neither can I," Jack said. "You lead the way, Lea."

Lea placed her Beretta on the lawn and entered the house. In the front entrance, she took her shoes off and placed them on a faded brown rack.

We both laid down our rifles and followed.

"Ron also doesn't allow outdoor footwear in the house. He loves his carpet," she said.

This seemed absurd, but the situation we found ourselves in left us no option. I slipped off my boots and placed them inside. Jack took off his, and Lea led us into a large, open living area.

The décor had an old-fashioned feel. Around the immediate edges of the room were two brown leather recliners and a matching couch. In the center, a wooden table held four coasters on top. At the far end, an Art Deco–style table and chair set and a drinks cabinet. The lush cream carpet felt bouncy under my socks.

Big band music played softy in the background. This supposedly welcoming room felt more dangerous than the airport terminal.

"How do you boys take your coffee?" Ron called from another room.

Jack looked at me with a puzzled expression. I shrugged my shoulders.

"Please don't be fooled by him like I was," Lea whispered.

"He's not trying to fool us yet," Jack said. "He's offering us a drink."

"NATO standard," I called out.

"Excuse me," a shout came back. "Do you mean regular?"

"What does he mean, Lea?"

She shrugged. "Not sure. It's different wherever you go."

It didn't really matter. I had bigger things to worry about. "Regular's fine."

We stood around the coffee table. Lea's hands trembled. Through the sheer curtains, I could see figures moving outside. I walked over and pulled the material to one side. Our AR-15s and Lea's Beretta were gone. We still had the Ron hostage option.

Ron appeared from an entrance at the far end of the room, holding a tray with four mugs on it. "Don't just stand there. Have a seat."

Jack and I sat in the two recliners, and Lea sat on the couch. Ron put the tray on the wooden table and handed Jack a mug, then me. "Imagine if this were your last drink."

"What?" I said.

I couldn't believe this madman had just served me coffee with a death threat.

He passed Lea hers. "I know how you take it, sweetie."

He picked up the final mug, took a loud slurp, sat on the couch next to Lea, and put his hand on her thigh. "You caused me a couple of minor headaches, Lea. At least you're back now."

"Minor fucking headaches?" Lea replied with venom, brushing off his hand. "I think you've caused more than a couple of those in the last few days."

Ron shook his head. He turned to me and narrowed his eyes. "You two have caused me a major headache. You've left me little option."

Lea jumped up. "I want to see Martina."

Ron feigned a false smile for half a second. "All in good time, honey. Now sit back down."

Jack poured his full mug of coffee straight down onto the carpet in a circular motion.

Ron sighed and took a sip of his drink. "Drop the tough guy act. You're way out of your depth, son."

I couldn't believe the confidence of this man. He either knew how things would proceed or was totally insane.

"We're here to stop the second activation," I said, "although you've probably guessed that."

Ron clasped his hands together and leaned forward. "Now why would you want to do that?"

"Why do you think? To stop everyone who is left from killing each other."

"That's not the intention of the second activation, you fool," he said. "The next objective is to rebuild. You've been listening to that idiot Jerry Caisley. I know you were at his farm."

"It doesn't matter what he told us," I said.

Jack jumped to his feet. "We came off a plane and witnessed your handiwork. Stop bullshitting us."

Ron flashed his teeth and slowly raised a finger at Jack. "Sit down or be put down. The choice is yours."

Jack glanced at me. I said, "Do as he says, for now."

Ron stood and started pacing slowly around the room. After a moment, he turned to me and said, "When I buy my groceries, I pay a price. When I eat a donut, I pay another price. When I drink too much whiskey, I pay a price. Do you see where I'm going with this?"

"No, not really," I said.

"You've taken something from me. Members of my team. What price are you and your brother going to pay?"

"The square root of fuck all," Jack said.

Ron ran his hands through his hair and took a deep breath. He jabbed his finger inches from my face. "You should really keep that one on a lead."

"Stalling for time isn't going to work," Jack said. "We can do this the nice way or the nasty way. You know why we're here."

Ron ignored Jack and focused on me. "The second activation is designed to round up survivors for processing. Genesis Alliance is going to rebuild a better society than you could ever imagine."

"Do you expect us to believe that after what we've seen?" I said.

"The devices are multipurpose," he continued. "They will eventually be used as a sophisticated communication and control network throughout North America. The next activation will compel all survivors to head for a prison in Michigan. From there, we will process everyone and allocate jobs, titles, and resources in order to build again."

"Let me guess," I said. "If we want to know more, we have to speak with your boss?"

Ron's left eye twitched. "Both of you are on thin ice. I'd advise against second-guessing my overall reach."

"You're just another patsy," Jack said. "Just like those two clowns in Orange County and Hermitage."

Ron continued to ignore Jack. "Does your poodle have a name?"

"I'm Harry, and that's Jack," I said. "And you can't seriously expect either of us to buy your bullshit."

"Just hear me out. One of the reasons for the cluster deployment of the North American devices was so that we could handle this part in a phased approach. Activating in different areas at different times avoids the very issue you raise. There're also geographical distances to factor. Don't think we haven't considered every angle."

"We?" I said. "You don't run the show from a house that stinks of cigar smoke."

He stooped in front of my face. "Pay attention, Harry; it might just save your pitiful life. The effects won't subside from the next activation. They have to be locally neutralized. We'll do that once the person is safely under lock and key and ready to listen to reason."

I couldn't believe that he continued to try and push his plan, almost like he was trying to impress me. A real weapons-grade psychopath, considering he probably had an idea what we had been through.

"Why would anyone do what you say? You've probably killed all of their family and friends," Jack snapped.

"What choice do they have? I can offer survival and things they have probably never even dreamed of owning—an expensive car, a nice boat, whatever they want. All I expect in return is that they play a part in forming a comfortable new world for us all to live in."

"Great, a nice car to cruise the bloody mess you created," I said.

"And if they say no?" Jack asked.

Ron let out a deep breath and spun to face Jack. "They will form part of the manual labor force. I have taken into consideration that some people will not be open-minded enough to accept reality. They will be de-neutralized."

Lea jumped from the couch. "De-fucking-neutralized? You're completely mad. I don't know why I never saw it before."

His left eye twitched again, and he clenched his right fist. "Careful, Lea, we don't want Martina thinking you're a nasty bitch."

"Where is she? What have you done to her?" Lea shouted as she stepped toward him.

He took a couple of paces back. "Be very careful of your next move, lady. I don't have time for this."

Her eyes widened. I could see she wanted to attack. Ron would too. He didn't strike me as the stupid type—more like insane and confident.

Ron produced small handheld radio from his pocket and pressed it against his mouth. "Bravo eight, there's some trash to take out."

Two large, armed men walked into the room and aimed their rifles at us.

Ron pointed in my direction. "You've broken a house rule, Harry. I said no weapons. Hand it over."

He gestured to the hunting knife, hanging from my belt. I paused, reluctant to give away one of our last chances of freedom.

"Just do it, Harry. Do you really think you can get out of here with just a knife?"

A guard stepped forward and trained his rifle on my face. I didn't want to put Jack or Lea at risk by trying anything heroically stupid, as the odds were firmly against us. I slid the knife from my belt and held it handle first toward the man. He snatched it out of my hand and shuffled back.

"That's better," Ron said. He pointed at Lea. "Handcuff her. She's like a wild animal."

"No, you can't do this!" she yelled.

As she leaped up and tried to escape toward the back entrance of the room, one of the men grabbed Lea by the hair and threw her back onto the couch.

"Stop them, please. Jack! Harry! Stop them!" Lea cried, looking at Jack and then me.

Ron stood between her and our recliners. "Don't even think about making a move. No harm is going to come to her."

"You're a total nutter," I said.

He waved the two men to the front door. "She's okay here for now. Secure her and wait outside until I call for you."

Jack looked at me. I didn't know what to do, and it seemed he didn't either. I sat forward in my chair and felt completely helpless as one of the thugs slipped cuffs around Lea's wrists. They both left the room after twisting her back into a sitting position.

The only way any of us were getting out of this was to hear Ron out. But if he tried a similar thing on me, that's when I would make my last stand. I picked up my coffee cup and imagined swinging it into his temple.

"Do you think you're going to cuff us too?" Jack asked.

Ron shook his head. "No, not unless you make me." He sat back down on the couch and crossed his legs. "You're not Butch Cassidy and the Sundance Kid, so listen to me."

"It doesn't seem like we've much of an option," I said.

"I suppose that's true, but I do have options for you . . . if you want to hear them."

"Don't listen," Lea said.

He patted her on the shoulder. "One more word, missy, and you won't be seeing my lovely niece again."

We hadn't given away our freedom just yet. The rush to Monroe, coupled with a somewhat naïve belief that we could put a stop to all of this, had made us narrow-minded. We should have known that it wouldn't be a straightforward operation that we walked away from in triumph.

"Options?" I said.

"You've both done incredibly well to get here from New York. Although it's unfortunate that you've killed members of Genesis Alliance, you did it to survive. I understand that—"

Jack threw his coffee mug across the room. It smashed against the wall, showering the record player with broken pieces of pottery. "Why did you do it? Most of our family and friends are probably dead because of you."

Ron winced and reached for his radio. He stopped himself and took a deep breath. "All forms of effective resistance had to be taken out. That was part of the plan. Because of that, I effectively control North America. I run this local operation, and you better start remembering it."

"You've created a nightmare," I said. "What about the rest of the world? What about all the deaths?"

"That's not my problem," he said with flippancy that defied belief. "My job now is to pick up the broken pieces and provide the best lives we can for the remaining population."

"What about Northern England?" Jack said.

Ron snapped his head around and grimaced. "Who told you about Northern England?"

"Jerry did. Now answer my question."

"Trust me: That is not your immediate concern. Now, back to business. I need some strong players after losing part of my team. You're obviously a resourceful pair. You made it all the way here and brought Lea home—"

"Why would we join you?" I said.

"How long do you think your luck is going to hold out, Harry? Even if you made it out of here, and I'd rate your chances of that at around one percent, how long do you think you would survive? At best, you'd have a life as a laborer for Genesis Alliance. At worst . . . ?"

"At least we wouldn't be under your control. You can't be serious."

He had us backed into a corner. A situation that usually caused Jack to bite. He sat with his jaw clenched on the recliner next to me. I tensed, expecting him to fly for Ron at any moment.

Ron checked his watch and nodded to himself. "You haven't got long, so let me paint you a picture. You join my security team, and I make sure you live out the rest of your natural lives in relative safety. You've seen the world outside; it's a dangerous place."

"Don't listen to him. He's mad," Lea said.

Ron ignored Lea and cleared his throat. "Here's my alternative solution. I have you taken out and shot by the side of the road." He pointed at Jack. "Him first. You can watch, Harry, before we put a bullet in your brain."

"Your security team?" I asked. "You're completely crackers."

"You're starting to bore me," Ron said and checked his watch again. "I don't have time to give you any more details."

"What exactly do you want us to do?" Jack asked.

I expected Jack to assault Ron and felt slight relief that he didn't react. Our best chance would be to play this out until a decent opportunity arose.

"You're just the kind of guys I need to maintain order and orga-nize our resources. This is a one-time offer. You've seen the state of the country; the task ahead for Genesis Alliance is significant. There's going to be a long cleanup operation while the infrastructure is repaired or restarted. You can play a significant role in creating our new world. Are you in?"

"I want to talk to Jack in private," I said.

Ron stood and pointed his bony white finger at me. "I haven't made anyone else an offer like this. You can either be a part of history or be purged from it. The choice is yours. I'll give you two minutes. If you're with me, come to the kitchen. If you're not, leave my house."

He turned and walked out of the room.

I pulled back the sheer curtains and gazed out of the window. Armed men still surrounded the house.

"It looks like we've two options," I said. "We take him out and try to escape through the back of the house. Maybe find out where they carry out the activations and destroy the machine. The other option is to join him."

"I don't like him," Jack said, "but he's our best chance of getting out of here in one piece."

The emotional burden of the last week had weighed heavily on Jack. I'd witnessed it through his actions. Our battle from the airport to Monroe would count for nothing if we did anything stupid, and I felt glad he could think clearly about our choice.

"I agree," I said. "Because he's a megalomaniac, he probably won't consider betrayal over his grand vision. We stay alive, find out more about Genesis Alliance, and take it down from the inside."

"Guys, there has to be another way," Lea said.

I hauled her off the couch. "You want to see Martina, right?"

She frowned. "Yeah, but—"

"The only realistic way I can see us getting on top of this situation is if we do what he says. I don't want to watch Jack get executed outside. Do you?"

She gave me a look suggesting I had suddenly become the bad guy.

"Ron's not getting out of this scot-free," Jack said.

"I know, Jack," I said, "but what do we gain by going down in a blaze of glory?"

He shrugged his shoulders. "I'm just sayin', he needs to pay for what he's done."

"You're both going to be Ron's bitches?" Lea said.

"I don't want to spend the rest of my life as a brainwashed laborer or have our bodies dumped in that large pit this afternoon. Think about Martina," I said.

Lea bowed her head and shook it.

Jack bolted up from his recliner. "We're out of options. Let's go through and see him."

I grasped Lea's arm and led her toward the back room, conscious of our two-minute warning. "Just remember: Play his stupid game, and we'll have time for revenge. That should keep our minds focused."

I ushered her through the entrance, which led into a kitchen. Ron stood over what looked like a control panel. He spun to face me.

"You've made the smart decision," he said and pressed a button on the panel. "Stand down, guys."

Ron walked over to me and shook my hand. "Welcome to Genesis Alliance."

He stepped across to Jack, so I took the opportunity to have a closer look at the control panel. It looked like something designed in the 1970s, much like the décor of his house.

In my peripheral vision, I saw Jack's arm rise to meet Ron's handshake. As it carried on in an upward motion past the height of Ron's chest, I turned to look. He had his Ruger in his right hand.

I remembered him tucking it down the front of his pants in South Monroe.

Ron froze. His eyes widened.

Jack pulled the trigger.

ACKNOWLEDGMENTS

We would like to express our gratitude to the many people who saw us through this book:

Paul Lucas from Janklow & Nesbit, for his advice, support, and the fantastic job he did in finding us such a great publisher in 47North.

Emilie Marneur and Sana Chebaro from the Amazon UK team, who have guided us through every step and have been a pleasure to work with.

Jennifer Gaynor, our excellent structural editor.

Jill M. Pellarin, our equally as good copy editor.

Harry Dewulf, Monique Happy, and Amanda Shore, our indie editors who helped us create and smooth our initial drafts in 2013.

Mike Meredith, David Spell, and Jean Dunn for your beta reading and support.

Finally, and most importantly, our readers. We've had some great feedback, communication, and encouragement from you in the last twelve months. We wish we could mention you all, and we appreciate the time you have taken to read our book.

ABOUT THE AUTHORS

Darren Wearmouth was born in Yorkshire and spent six years in the British Army's Royal Signals Division before pursuing a career in corporate technology. After fifteen years working for telecommunications firms and a startup, he decided to follow his passion for writing. A sportsman, he loves watching and playing football, cricket, and golf. His other hobbies include reading, mountaineering, and socializing. He also has a hidden talent for Italian cooking. He currently resides in Manchester, England.

Marcus Wearmouth was born in Yorkshire and also spent six years in the British Army, serving in the Royal Electronic and Mechanical Engineers. He graduated from Northumbria University with a degree in surveying and now owns a consultancy specializing in subsidence. Marcus loves spending time with his two wonderful children, Andrew and George. He currently resides in Harrogate, England, and is secretly a very gifted bagpiper.